# STYX
# & STONED
## BY
## BOONE BRUX

For Patty Ann and Suzie Q.

Thanks for all your support and love.

1

# CHAPTER ONE

Las Vegas! All expenses paid!

Normally, a trip like that would be a dream come true for an overworked, widowed, mother of three. Here's the thing, though; situations rarely worked out as I imagined. And usually not in my favor. So, when my boss, Constantine, offered—well, not actually offered…more like handed me—the plane ticket to Vegas and told me in no uncertain terms I'd be attending the GRS annual convention, I was instantly suspicious.

GRS stands for Grim Reaper Services, of which I, Lisa Carron, am their newest grim reaper. And sadly, the least adept. I was getting better, but I'd been a reaper for less than a year and had nowhere near the skills my partner Nate possessed.

And don't get me started about Constantine. He's our crazy hot Alaskan leader, but I still hadn't decided if he

was human. Actually, I'm scared to be alone with him. Not
in a hockey-mask-psycho-killer way. More like, if I was
ever pressed up against his body, I wasn't sure I'd be able to
stop my hands from roving to his forbidden zones. I just
couldn't be trusted in a situation like that.

So here I was in sunny Las Vegas, seven kid-free
days, and none of it costing me a dime. I should have been
giddy, spinning around the baggage claim area like Maria in
The Sound of Music. But, like I said, circumstances were
never what they seemed. I couldn't shake the feeling that
this week had nothing to do with Lisa time and everything
to do with other people's agendas. Even so, I planned to
take advantage of the numerous luxuries the hotel spa had to
offer.

The airport's electronic doors slid open and the hot
desert air enveloped me. Exhaust clawed at my throat. I
gasped and squinted against the blinding Vegas sun. How
did people live in this heat? The better question might be,
why? Sixteen degrees and accumulating darkness—that's
what I'd left behind in Anchorage. Las Vegas was like anti-
Alaska.

I hauled my ancient, massive suitcase toward the line
of taxicabs, beads of sweat instantly forming across the
bridge of my nose and forehead. The material of my long-

sleeved T-shirt clung like a second skin, and the sun reflecting off the pavement, plus all the altitude changes, made my head throb. My flight had left Anchorage at midnight and I'd spent several hours wandering around the Seattle airport, waiting for the tram to start up so I could get to my concourse. Tired didn't describe my current condition.

Now I understood why people huddled like vampires inside the dark, cool casinos. Sit at a slot machine receiving free drinks, or venture into the blistering heat to stare at Hoover Dam. I know what my choice would be.

"Cab?" A valet waved me over and pointed at the first cab in the long line waiting at the curb. His tone was all business. "Right here."

I lopped toward him, but he'd already focused on the person behind me, and was moving to the next cab. I shoved my bag toward the cab driver. "The Venetian, please."

"Excellent." He grinned, his white teeth gleaming against his dark skin. "Please, get in and enjoy the air-conditioned comfort of my cab."

His thick Indian accent and invitation made him sound like a commercial for the cab company. While he manhandled my suitcase toward the trunk of the car, I climbed into the back seat. A sigh hissed from me when the cool air hit my skin. I tossed my jacket and purse next to me and leaned my head against the back of the seat. My eyes drifted closed. Several thumps vibrated against the back seat, sending a pang of embarrassment through me. No matter how many times I'd packed and unpacked to thin out what I'd need, I still ended up with far more clothes than I could possibly wear in a week.

I lifted my head and opened my eyes, squinting against the sun streaming through the front window. For the first time I noticed the older man sitting in the front passenger seat. "Oh, hello." He didn't respond. Maybe he didn't speak or understand English. Now committed to the acknowledgement, I repeated my greeting. "Hi."

His head snapped around, his eyes widening. "Are you talking to me?"

"Yes, I am." Mystery solved about not understanding English. I smiled. "You're smart to stay in the car. That heat is killer."

"Very funny," he said, glaring. Then he shifted to face me.

"Crap." The downside of being a grim reaper was that I was always on the job. The right side of the man's head wavered like one of those heat mirages on the road. "You're dead." I scowled at him. "Aren't you?"

"Yes, I am." His lips pursed for a second, looking dubious. "How can you see me?"

"Just one of the perks of my job." The trunk slammed, making me jump. Conversing with ghost tended to be off-putting to those who couldn't see them. I rushed on. "I'm a grim reaper. If you'd like to cross over, I can help you with that when I get to the hotel."

The cab door opened, and the driver slid in, cutting off my conversation with the spirit. "Venetian, you said?"

"Yes please..." My gaze cut from the rear-view mirror to the identification card fixed to the dash. "Rashid."

"Yes, very good."

"Cross over?" The spirit launched into a tirade as the cab pulled away. "And leave this bonehead to run my company into the ground? No thank you."

Family drama, so not what I needed right now. After a minute of trying to ignore the ranting specter, I realized the only way to shut him up was to talk over him. "Rashid, does it always get this hot in Vegas?"

"Oh, yes." The cabbie smiled into the rear-view mirror. "But you're in luck—it's not supposed to get above ninety this week."

"That's lucky?"

His white-toothed smile reflected back at me, his head nodding vigorously.

I groaned. "How can you stand it?"

"I'm from India." His gaze darted from the road to the mirror and then back again. "My parents moved us here when I was twelve and opened the taxi business. When my father passed away a year ago, I took over." His smile widened. "Las Vegas is my home now. I love it here, heat and all."

"And if you spent less time enjoying the sights and more time working—" the ghost grumbled.

Again, I cut the spirit off before he hurled himself into another lecture that only I'd be privy to. "I think it's wonderful you love where you live." Glancing at the ghost, I added, "I'm sorry about your father's passing."

"Thank you. It was a great loss for the family," Rashid said.

"Of course it was." His father straightened, jutting his chin upward and crossing his arms over his chest. "I held this family together. Obviously, the entire household is lost without my guidance."

"But…" Rashid caught my eye in the mirror again and grimaced. "To be honest, he was a miserable man."

"Miserable?" The spirit's head whipped toward his son.

I sunk deeper into the seat, bracing myself for the wave of anger I knew would hit me in a few seconds.

"If working eighty hours a week to put food on the table for my family made me miserable, then I'm guilty." Like a blast of Vegas heat, the ghost's resentment pounded me—yet another the neat side effects of being a grim reaper.

"He was never happy with anybody or anything," the cabbie continued.

"What was there to be happy about? You're all a bunch of boneheads. Never listened to anything I said."

"On and on he'd rail about how we didn't appreciate what he'd built for us," Rashid said.

"Yes, I'm getting that," I mumbled to myself.

"Because you didn't." His father waved his hands in the air. "I'd barely been dead a month before this one—" He jabbed a finger at his son. "—started taking Sundays off. No respect. No respect!"

"Call me optimistic, but I like to think he's happy and in a much better place now."

Instead of the sarcastic snort I wanted to make, I pressed my lips together and nodded, giving him my best empathetic expression. "I'm sure you're right."

"Lazy dogs, every one of them." The ghost glared out the front window. "Your mother and I should have never reproduced."

"I'm certain he's exactly where he wants to be," I replied. That wasn't a lie, just the comforting truth Rashid, and every other person who'd lost a loved one, wanted to hear.

"I loved my father and I miss him, but I don't miss his constant complaining."

"Ungrateful…" The spirit faded, taking his angry mojo with him.

That's one downside of being a grim reaper. People think the ability to see the dead is cool. What they don't realize is that the afterlife isn't all white light and feathers. Sometimes it's just a lot of cranky ghosts that have their ectoplasmic panties in a wad.

Laying my head against the back seat, I let my eyelids drift shut. The driver switched topics and began regaling me with Las Vegas trivia. The combination of the cool air and my exhaustion made concentrating on what he said impossible, and after a few seconds, I dozed off.

When the taxi pulled to a stop in front of the hotel, I snapped awake, sitting forward with a jolt. A young man in a gray suit yanked open the door. "Ma'am."

"Oh…yeah." I blinked a couple of times, my lids scraping across my eyeballs. Still trying to get my bearings, I scooped up my purse and jacket, and scooted out of the cab. "Thanks."

Either Las Vegas had denser gravity, or my exhaustion was making it difficult to move my legs. Though Rashid had parked under the hotel's covered entrance, out of the sun, it was still hot, and I was anxious to get to my room and crank up the AC.

"You made it." Nate's voice sounded behind me. "I was getting worried."

I pivoted to face my partner and couldn't help scowling a little. He'd arrived the day before and had time to rest. As usual, his sandy-brown hair lay perfectly tousled, looking carefree yet stylish. "Were you worried or irritated?"

"I've checked us in." He smirked, not answering my question, and then handed me a small envelope. "The room number is on the inside of the booklet."

"Great, but…" I glanced at him. "We're not rooming together—right?"

"You wish, Carron."

"You wish I wished, Cramer." Okay, it wasn't the best comeback, but I was tired and either needed alcohol and something covered in cheese, or a bath and twenty-four hours of comatose sleep.

The sound of my suitcase hitting the ground thunked behind the cab, followed by the rattle of its wheels running across the tiled drive. With a pearly white smile in place, Rashid wheeled the bag to me. Before I could fish money out of my purse, Nate handed him a stack of folded bills.

"Thank you, sir." Rashid's smile widened. "You're very generous."

"And thank you for a clean, air-conditioned ride." I said, hooking my hand around the handle of my suitcase. "And information about Las Vegas. Truly enlightening."

"My pleasure." Rashid gave a slight bow and pulled a business card out of his front shirt pocket. "Call me for all your taxi needs—except on Sunday."

Nice. My own personal driver. I had no intention of leaving the casino, but I'd learned long ago my plans and fate usually raced along different tracks, sometimes colliding. I accepted the card. "I certainly will."

"Here, let me get that." Nate took the suitcase from me and wheeled it into the hotel.

My eyes narrowed on his broad back. Something was up. He was being exceptionally considerate, and I didn't like it one bit. I strode into the hotel after him, my senses on high alert. Again, lovely cool air greeted me when I entered the lobby. A myriad of dings, rings, and bleeps filtered in from the casino. At the sound of their taunting call my energy rallied. Maybe a few rounds of slots would help me unwind before crashing.

Scanning the grand entrance, my gaze skated over the opulent décor and landed on the milling crowd. My steps slowed to a stop. "Whoa."

Nate turned to me. "What?"

"Is it just me or are there a ton of ghosts in here?" At least half the people were spirits, floating through the living, talking, and some looking rather lost. Alaska didn't have near this number of spirits. "Is this usual of Vegas?"

"Probably." Nate guided my suitcase toward the elevators. "Don't worry about it now. We need to get to the GRS meet-and-greet."

"No." I groaned, my shoulders slumping as I stomped after him. "I need a shower and sleep."

"Later." He pressed the up arrow. "Put your suitcase in your room and come back to the third floor." His attention zeroed on me. "Attendance is mandatory—especially yours."

A niggle of foreboding surfaced and the hair on the back of my neck stood on end. I cocked my head. "Why especially me?"

The elevator to our right dinged, settled, and the doors slid open. We shifted, staying out of the way to allow the car to empty, and then entered.

When the doors closed, Nate punched the three and twenty-six. Still not looking at me, he said, "There are some people you need to meet."

The elevator lurched and started upward. I gripped the handrail, breathing deeply. Normally, I avoided elevators whenever possible. My induction into reaperhood had involved a convenience store shooting, an angry ghost, and the elevator to Hell. Even though I accepted my fate as a reaper, sometimes I still had problems reconciling the whole other world concept, and elevators seemed to be my trigger.

I focused on Nate and ignored my roiling nerves. He had a way of talking around things and I'd learned direct questions got the best results. "What people?"

"Other GRS personnel."

"Can't I meet them tomorrow?" I watched for any sign that he was keeping something from me. His lips pressed together and for a second his nostrils flared before he schooled his expression again. Bingo. Flaring nostrils were always a dead giveaway. "What aren't you telling me?"

"Nothing." He scowled but didn't meet my eyes. Liar. The elevator hiccupped to a stop on the third floor and the doors glided open. Before exiting he looked at me. "Thirty minutes, Carron, right here."

"Yeah, yeah." I punched the close door button three times, causing Nate to hop over the threshold as the metal slabs slid shut. "Jerk," I said to the empty car.

The elevator spit me out on the twenty-sixth floor. With no small amount of effort, I wrestled my suitcase through the doors that kept trying to close on me, and down the carpeted hall. Finally, I found my room. After a couple of attempts with my keycard, the light flashed green, and I pushed the door open. At last, home away from home.

The room was gorgeous, decorated in shades of beige and gold, with a few accents of red artistically tossed about. The furnishings were a little over the top, but I wasn't about to complain.

First things first. I found the thermostat and cranked up the air. The motor kicked on. Nice. A sigh eased from me. Next, unpacking. Some people lived out of their

suitcases when they traveled. Not me. I needed to nest—
make the room my own.

I unzipped my suitcase and pulled out my cosmetic
bags—yes, I had two. Like my clothes, I hadn't been able to
pare down the contents, and I'd ended up dumping all my
girl supplies into my bags. Better safe than sorry. I strode
into the large bathroom and began unpacking my arsenal of
beauty paraphernalia. Makeup, perfume, and lotion lined the
sink like tiny soldiers, ready for any cosmetic mission.

I picked up the fancy soap provided by the hotel. A
list of organic products went into making the luxury bar:
oatmeal, avocado, olive oil. I didn't know whether to bathe
with it or eat it. I gathered all the products and tossed them
into my cosmetic bag, hoping tomorrow the maid would
replenish my supply. By the time I went back to Alaska, I'd
be fat with luxury hotel products. Did I mention I might
have hording tendencies?

Sounds from the hall drew my attention. Leaning my
head out of the bathroom, I listened. Someone was
talking—or loudly slurring—directly outside my room. I
inched forward and pressed my eye to the peephole. A head
full of blond curls swayed into view. I couldn't see if there
were more people with her, but no doubt the woman was
drunk and probably trying to find her room.

As quietly as possible, I folded the safety latch over the door. It was doubtful the drunken woman could get in, but I wasn't taking any chances. On and on she mumbled about finding her key, tottering back and forth. She was persistent, I'd give her that much.

How long was she going to stand there, fumbling and blocking my door? Eventually I'd have to leave. When I pressed my eye to the hole again, the woman looked up. For a split second her image wavered and then she chirped, "Beep, beep."

Before the information registered and I could jump back, the blonde stumbled through the solid door—and passed through me. An icy chill sliced to my bones. Doubling over, I spun to face the ghost.

"What the hell?" I glared at her and slowly uncoiled my body. "This is my room."

The blonde staggered, raising her translucent arms out to her sides. Her body swayed right and left until finding her balance. Then she straightened and slowly turned toward me, holding up her index finger. "I beg to differ with you, madam." She pointed a garish neon pink fingernail at her chest, stumbled back a few steps, and then righted herself. "This has been my room since New Year's Eve, 2000."

"Really?" Another icy shudder rippled through me. "You've been haunting this room for over fifteen years?"

She wobbled and glowered at me. "Haunting?"

Crap. I hated when ghosts didn't know they were dead. Informing them that they'd passed on was like telling people their loved one had died. Only in this case the loved one was her. "Yeah, I hate to be the bearer of bad news but..." I took a deep breath and plunged forward. "You're dead."

She stared at me for a few seconds and then burst out laughing. "I know I'm dead, silly." An instant later she sobered. "Wait. How can you see me?" She tilted her chin down and pinned me with a stare. "Are you dead, too?"

"No." I rubbed my arms, trying to scrub away the lingering effects of getting body-slammed by a spirit. "I'm a grim reaper."

"Cooool." The word leaked out of her like air escaping a balloon.

"Yeah, cool, but we have a problem." Not chancing more contact, I stepped into the bathroom doorway, dearly hoping she would leave. "I'm here for the next week. So, either you let me help you cross over, or you find somewhere else to hang for the next seven days." I gave her a placating smile. "Okay?"

"Yeah," she said, waving her finger at me. "That's not gonna happen." After an ungraceful pivot, she made an unsteady beeline for the bed—my bed, and flopped down on it, patting the comforter. "But…" She closed her eyes. "There's plenty of room for both of us." Again, her eyelids popped open. "Do you snore?"

"Not that I know of." I moved to the side of the bed, staring down at her. "Why are you drunk? Are you always wasted?" I'd never encountered an intoxicated spirit and had assumed everybody converted to a non-inebriated state when they passed away. "Were you drunk when you died?"

"Gin and tonics, no, and yes." Slowly, she rolled to her stomach and rested her head on her hands. "I've been at a party."

"A ghost party?"

"I'm not sure." She furrowed her brow. "I mean, there were ghosts, but also living people." Her confusion melted and a dreamy smile spread across her face. "It was in this guy's suite upstairs. He's amazing."

"Is he a ghost?" I'd never heard of the dead and living mingling at a party, but what did I know about the afterlife, except that there was one? "Cuz, maybe you could stay with him."

Her eyes drifted shut again. "I don't think Big C is dead."

"Big C?"

"Yeah, the hottie who threw the party."

I didn't even want to know why they called him Big C. A quiet snore resonated from the spirit. "Hey." I nudged the bed with my knee. "What's your name?"

"Tandy," she whispered before sinking back into a drunken snore.

"Great." I glared at her for a few seconds and then whirled and stomped to the bathroom. Why had I actually entertained the notion that this week might be relaxing? Or at the very least, that I'd have my own room? "It frickin' figures."

I finger-combed my short, platinum hair and then spritzed it with hairspray. After that I flicked a coat of mascara along my lashes, then brushed my teeth. Standing back, I assessed my reflection. With only thirty minutes to primp, this was as good as it got. I retrieved my purse and room key, tossing Tandy a final glare. Hopefully she'd be gone by the time I got back.

No way was I sharing my room with a spectral party girl for seven days. If that meant hunting down Big C and pawning Tandy off on him, then that's exactly what I'd do.

# CHAPTER TWO

Nate waited outside the third-floor elevator. "You'll need this." He held out my conference badge. "How's your room?"

"It's fantastic." I slipped the black lanyard over my head. "Except for the dead-drunk woman passed out on my bed."

"Dead-drunk?" His brows pinched together. "As in really wasted, or as in dead and drunk?"

"Both." I scanned the people milling about the outer lobby of the conference area. To my relief there were no ghosts loitering up here. "She's very drunk and very dead." My gaze refocused on him. "Her name is Tandy, and she died on New Year's Eve, 2000."

"Y2K death. There were a lot of them. People thinking the world was coming to an end." He smirked and shook his head. "I don't know why I'm surprised your room is haunted."

"I know, right?" I nodded, propping my fists on my hips. "Hopefully, I'll be able to convince her to move on without force." I lowered my arms. "She wasn't very cooperative but if I explain to her the benefits she might agree."

"You can be very convincing." He placed his hand on the small of my back and started forward, guiding me through the crowd. "We can deal with her later. Right now we have a meeting."

"What kind of meeting?" I jogged a couple of steps, trying to keep up with him. "I thought it was a simple GRS meet-and-greet."

"That's going on too, but we're meeting with upper management." Damn his long strides and my exhaustion—not a good combination. "There's a matter they'd like to discuss with us."

I pulled to a stop. Now I knew how my kids felt. "Am I in trouble?"

"No." He slowed and faced me, cocking a brow. "Not yet anyway."

Another thread of suspicion that this all-expense-paid-work-vacation had little to do with improving my customer service and reaping skills crept through me. He strode down the wide conference hall. I gritted my teeth and jogged to catch up with him again. After several turns, we stopped at a set of tall golden doors.

While I caught my breath, Nate rapped twice. A few seconds later, one of the doors opened and a tall redhead, decked out in a black leather skirt, a matching tank top, and black boots stood just inside the room. I didn't think she was a Venetian employee, and the instant her emerald eyes leveled on me, all doubt about her paranormal status vanished. No way could this woman be human.

I've never had a girl crush before but if I did, it would be on her.

"Nate." Her voice poured over me like melted chocolate. "Looking good—as usual."

"Mara." Nate leaned in and kissed her on each cheek. "I'd heard you would be here but didn't believe Constantine."

"In the flesh." She arched a delicate brow. "Trust me, nobody is more surprised than I am." She frowned. "Not that I had much choice." Her gaze skated from Nate to me and she smiled again. "You must be Lisa."

"Hi." I accepted her outstretched hand. Warm tingles ran across my skin where we touched. Oh yeah, I'd switch teams for her. She smirked, as if reading my mind. A blush rushed over my cheeks and I released her hand. "Sorry if we're late. I just got here."

"Not late at all." She closed the door and pointed toward a man with his back to us. "Tabris is still on the phone."

Nate leaned toward me. "Tabris is the head of GRS."

My eyes rounded. "Of all GRS? As in, the entire world?"

"Yep." He grinned. "But don't be nervous. He's a nice guy."

That was easy for him to say. No doubt I'd do something to embarrass myself before this meeting was over. I ran my palms down the front of my shirt, feeling completely underdressed in the elegant surroundings.

Heavy gold velvet draped the arching windows, and a gilded desk stretched six feet across at the front of the room. Even though we were in the Venetian, I didn't think the soaring pillars and giant stone lions flanking them were part of the hotels design. Potted orange trees and ferns littered the room, and several plush chairs and chaise lounges were strategically placed for conversation. The once standard conference room had been transformed into a scene out of the Palace of Versailles.

A man rose from a chair near the desk and walked toward us. Handsome didn't describe him. He was a mix of Thor and the angel Gabriel, all rolled into one beautiful blond package. Tan and rugged with eyes that glimmered like glacier ice. They drew me in and I swore I could fall into them. Then he smiled and my knees nearly buckled. Dimples were my Kryptonite.

My jaw grew slack. I know this because Nate reached over and pushed my mouth closed.

"Nate and Lisa, this is my partner, Cam," Mara said.

"Partner?" Nate's brows shot up. "You working for GRS is a huge surprise, but partners? How did that happen?"

"Divine intervention." Sarcasm dripped from Mara's words.

"More like divine interference." Cam held out his hand. "Nice to meet you both."

"Hi." I shoved my hand toward the blond god. "Lisa Carron. Really, really nice to meet you."

Cam taking my hand and staring into my eyes was the closest I'd come to Heaven. The blue of his irises swirled, holding my gaze, and his deep voice wrapped around me like a warm blanket. "It's really nice to meet you too, Lisa."

I think I sighed—or squealed. I'm not sure. At first touch my lips went numb and my mind blanked out. It was awesome. Only Nate's super-charged scowl made it possible for me to let go of Cam's hand.

"Please, sit." Mara gestured toward the chairs. "It looks like Tabris is done."

"Whoa." I inched toward the seat but couldn't take my eyes off Tabris. "What is with you people?" The thoughts racing through my mind tumbled out of my mouth. I dropped onto the brocade chair. "All of you are crazy gorgeous."

Nate rolled his eyes, his mouth pinching into a thin line. I ignored him. The man should be used to me Ms. Magooing my way through situations.

A white smile spread across Tabris's face. He stopped a few feet from me and clasped his hands behind his back. In the same way Cam was all blond and golden, Tabris looked as if he'd been dipped in copper and bronze. "Thank you, Lisa."

"You're welcome, but seriously," I said, my gaze cutting from the group back to Tabris. "You three aren't human." I hesitated. "Are you?"

"No." Tabris sat opposite me and rested his arm across the back of the chair. He gave a quick shake of his head. Every glistening copper strand of his shaggy cut waved like wheat in the breeze and then settled perfectly in place. "Mara, Cam and I are something other."

"Other?" His bronze skin seemed to glisten, and I swore his amber gaze sparkled under the room's golden light. "What does that mean?" I glanced to Mara. "Or is that a need-to-know thing?"

"Not really," Mara said. "It's just that very few people have the nerve to ask."

I'd always had an inflated curiosity, so dangling the carrot of otherworld knowledge in front of me was like slapping my behind and shouting giddy-up. "Can I try to guess or would that be rude?"

"Please." Tabris held his hands out toward me, obviously enjoying my curiosity. "Give it your best shot."

"Oh, good." Mara crossed her legs and rested her folded hands in her lap. "This should be interesting."

I didn't know if they'd actually tell me if I got it right, but I couldn't pass up the chance. So far my repertoire of experiences with paranormal beings consisted of ghosts, porters, guardian angels, vampires, and a werewolf. These three didn't seem to fall into any of those categories.

"Let's see…great hair, eerily amazing eyes, skin I'd kill for, confident. Tabris, you're the head of GRS, so you must have quite a bit of power and authority." I reclined, assessing each one of them. "Mara and Cam, you possess the same qualities, and seem to have a close working relationship with Tabris." After several seconds I said, "I've got to go with angels. But not guardian angels, something—" I searched for the right word. "Higher."

Tilting his head toward me, Tabris smiled. "Two-thirds correct."

"Which two?" I asked.

Cam held up his hand. "The Archangel of Tolerance."

"And I am the angel of self-determination, willpower, and free choice," Tabris said.

"Then…" I glanced at Mara. "You're not an angel?"

"No, quite the opposite." The corner of her mouth quirked upward. "Try again."

What was the opposite of an angel? The word hovered on my tongue but I couldn't reconcile this beautiful woman sitting amongst angels as a… "Demon?"

"Give this girl a prize," Mara said.

"You're a demon? But…" I pointed at the two men. "I thought angels and demons were enemies."

"Sometimes, but not always," Tabris said. "Like angels, there are different levels of demons with different purposes. We have a number of them working at GRS."

I shook my head. "You're joking."

"No joke." Cam rested his elbows on his knees and leaned forward. "You can't have the good without the bad." He flicked his head toward Mara. "We work in the checks and balances department, keeping good and evil in balance."

"I have a special skill set and knowledge base about the Underworld that comes in handy." She smirked. "Not to mention my connections."

"Seriously?" I couldn't wrap my head around the concept, and to be honest, sitting so close to Mara now kind of made me nervous. "So, you're a succubus?"

A bark of laughter burst from Cam, and Tabris discretely hid his smile behind his hand.

Heat flooded my face, and I grimaced. "Oh crap, did I just say something stupid?"

"Carron, you asking Mara if she's a succubus is like Mara asking you if you're a hooker," Nate said.

My hands flew to my mouth. "Oh my God, I'm so sorry." Perfect. It had taken me less than five minutes to insult someone who could probably possess my body and make me do horrible things, like scheduling a colonoscopy or volunteering to pick up dog poop in our local parks.

"Really, Mara, I'm so sorry."

"No worries." She smiled, but it was more wicked than understanding. "I've been called worse."

"Boy has she ever," Cam chimed in.

She turned her dark green gaze on him, and I'm almost certain tiny flames flickered in her eyes.

"I think I'd better stop playing twenty questions before I cause the Rapture." If I could have crawled inside the chair, I would have. Reclining against the seat cushion, I folded my arms across my body and looked at Tabris. "Anyhoo, carry on?"

"Very good." He inhaled and pressed his lips together for a second before saying, "We have a bit of a situation that needs to be dealt with as quickly and quietly as possible."

"What kind of situation?" Cam asked.

Tension rippled around the group, amping up my nerves. If these four seemed concerned about a situation, then I definitely should be worried. Hell, I hadn't figured out why I was there in the first place. All this seemed way above my pay grade.

"It's Charon," Tabris said.

The group instantly relaxed—except for me. I still had no idea what was going on. "Charon? As in the ferryman for the River Styx?"

"Yeah." Cam eased against the arm of the chair. "Every few hundred years he ventures to the surface, parties, and heads back to Styx."

Nate had told me this story when he first tried to recruit me. What Cam had left out was that Charon usually knocked up a couple of women while on shore leave, thus ensuring the continuation of our reaper-line. Charon was to the grim reapers what Adam was to humanity.

"He announced his retirement before leaving." Tabris stood and paced behind his chair. "Normally, we wouldn't be concerned, but it's been a month and he's made no move to return." He stopped and leveled a stare at the group. "Even though he hasn't officially signed off on his retirement, souls are beginning to pile up on the riverbank."

"What happens if he doesn't return?" I asked.

"When there's no more room on the shores, the spirits will start flowing onto the physical plane." He clasped his hands behind his back again and his jaw tightened for a few seconds before relaxing. "If the souls aren't transported within a certain amount of time they are rendered unclaimed."

Rendered unclaimed conjured images of war orphans, obsolete androids, and the Island of Misfit Toys, none of which were happy. "I take it that's bad?" I asked.

"Very. Being unclaimed means a soul is up for grabs," Mara said. "By whoever can claim it first—angel or a demon." The corner of her red lip curled downward. "Trust me. I've seen this first hand, and it's not pretty."

A chill that had nothing to do with being cold wove its way up my spine.

"So—" Nate's hands lifted in question, his eyes boring into Tabris. "What do you need from us?"

Tabris reclaimed his chair. "Convince Charon to return to work."

"Convince him?" My eyes rounded at his request. "Why not just order him back to work?"

"I wish it was that easy." Tabris tapped his index fingers together with a steady, slightly nervous, beat. "There are a lot of nuances in the afterlife, one of them being that even though GRS monitors and manages soul transportation on the River Styx, Charon is more like an independent contractor because of his deity status. We own the ferry but not the boat captain."

"So get another boat captain," I chimed in, thinking the answer was obvious.

"Nobody else is qualified." Tabris's amber gaze held mine. "Not yet, anyway. The easiest solution is to convince Charon to return to work."

"How are we supposed to do that?" Nate asked.

"Carefully." Tabris shook his head "There are a lot of obstacles to overcome." His gaze settled on me again, making me flinch. "The first one involves you."

I tried to look away but couldn't. I was able to work up a solid glower, though. "Me? What have I got to do with this?"

"Nothing directly," Tabris said. "Indirectly, everything."

Some of my defensiveness melted. "Meaning?"

"Your porter is Hal Lee Lewya, correct?"

"Yes." My porter may have looked like a drag queen circus master with his shiny pantsuits and array of hats, but he was dangerous and unpredictable. We had an understanding—I'd bring him souls, and he'd transport them to where they needed to go. If something went wrong with the reap, we'd handle it. I didn't tell on him when he broke the rules, and he didn't drag me to the ninth circle of Hell. It worked for us. "Why?"

"Because…" Tabris stood and paced again. "As of yesterday, Charon's ability to move freely between the physical plane and Styx expired. If we're able to convince him to go back to work, Hal is the only one who can transport him."

Cam groaned and rubbed his face with his hand.

Mara gave a humorless laugh. "Good luck with that."

My gaze darted between Cam and Mara. "Pretend I have no idea what's going on," I said. "First off, why is Hal the only one who can transport Charon?"

"Because Charon is a mystical being, and it takes an equally powerful being to transport him back." she said, drumming her fingers on the arm of the chair. "Hal is the only porter who is his match."

"I know Hal is stubborn." Boy did I. The guy rarely made my reaps easy. The better I got, the craftier he became about transporting my souls. "But, if you tell him he has to do it then he will—right?"

A heavy sigh heaved from Tabris. "Again, no."

"Hal and Charon hate each other." Nate shook his head. "Big time."

"That's why we need you, Lisa." Tabris edge toward me, stopping a foot away. He towered above, his copper gaze swirling like a tiny galaxy of stars, compelling me to do as he asked. "Convince Hal to transport Charon."

Compulsions were a sensation I was very accustomed to, and I immediately recognized Tabris's attempt. Every time I turned around Hal was trying to make me do his bidding. Out of instinct, I clutched the raven pendant hanging around my neck. It was my connection to Fletcher, my raven familiar, and my shield against Hal's compulsions. Though Tabris's pull lessened slightly, it didn't vanish completely. In Alaska, Fletcher usually found a way to be around when I needed him. Now he was thousands of miles away. That's probably why the power of my pendant was weak. Good information if I'd end up dealing with Hal.

"Slow your roll." I stood and walked a few yards away, trying to break his influence. "What makes you think Hal will do what I ask?"

"He seems to genuinely like you." Tabris paused and nodded. "That is no small accomplishment, Lisa."

"Really?" My gaze narrowed on our fearless leader. I didn't care if he was the big GRS boss, my gut told me he was keeping something from me and I wanted to know what. "Why is Hal liking me something special?"

"You know how he is." He attempted one of his dazzling smiles, but the effect fell short. "In general Hal hates everybody. Even my bosses were surprised with how easily you two took to each other."

"Obviously our definitions of 'easily' are very different. I've got the bruises and nightmares to prove it." Again, I folded my arms over my chest. "If your superiors are so surprised with Hal and me, why did they pair us up in the first place?"

"As reapers go, you were the best option." His smile widened. "Your partnership could have gone either way and we credit you for its success."

My mouth sagged open, and I turned to glare at Nate. "Did you and Constantine know about this?" I held up my hand, stopping him from answering. "Of course you did. That's why you freaked out when you learned he was my porter."

"Partly," Nate said, "but mostly because I knew Hal got assigned very specific reapers—ones who were skilled." He grimaced. "I didn't even think you'd make it through the physical testing."

"Thanks, partner." Nate's skepticism about my reaper skills had never been a secret but hearing him admit it still sucked. "I feel like one of those piglets at the zoo they wrapped in a tiger skin and set in the mother tiger's cage. Will she adopt them, or will she eat them?" I raised my fist to the ceiling. "Hooray, she adopted them." I refocused on Tabris. "If I get Hal to agree—and that is a gigantic flippin' if, which will probably require a lot of promises I don't want to make—" I inhaled. "Who's going to convince Charon?"

"You four will work as a team to locate and persuade him he's needed back at work." The way Tabris stated this brooked no argument. "None of us have a choice in the matter. If we don't get the ferry moving again, the ethereal shit is going to hit the fan."

"Is that why the GRS Convention was pushed up a week?" Nate asked.

Nodding, Tabris said, "Yes, we're almost certain he's here. Personally, I don't think it's a coincidence."

"Meaning?" Cam sat forward, his gaze riveted on Tabris.

"Meaning, I think Charon purposely chose Vegas because the convention would be here." A sigh huffed from him and his shoulders sagged a fraction. "But I have no idea why. Maybe after you talk to him, we'll have a better idea about his true motives.

The group fell silent for a minute, the tension humming between us.

"What's he living on?" When they all stared at me with the same confused expression, I clarified. "For money?"

"Ah." Tabris nodded. "The gold he's collected for millennia from his tolls."

"So, basically a bottomless supply." I rubbed my hands up and down my thighs, trying to cull my nerves. "I was hoping he might run out of money, but that didn't seem likely—at least no time soon."

"No chance of that," Cam said, standing. "The gold is bottomless. Before the dead can pass through the arch to Styx, they pay the toll."

"Exactly. Until he officially retires, he'll continue collecting," Tabris added.

"Just like Disney World," Mara said. "So even if Charon isn't ferrying, he's still getting paid."

"Gee, how do I get that job?" I laughed.

Mara cocked her head. "You said Charon was the only one qualified, but I know the river. Why not let me ferry souls until we get Charon back on board?"

"That's generous, Mara, but you can't." Tabris's gaze darted to me, held a few seconds, and then cut back to the demon. "Only a handful of people are capable of commanding the ferry, but none of them are available right now."

"Then time is of the essence," Nate stood and pointed to the group. "Our first challenge will be finding Charon. Do you have any idea where he is?"

"He's been moving around, so locating him won't be easy." Tabris strode to the gold desk and plucked a slip of paper off the top. "Here is a list of places we know he's already been." He handed it to Mara. "Maybe take a quick look at those hotels, but my gut tells me he's moved on."

Cam leaned in and scanned the paper. "The Venetian isn't listed." He straightened. "Let's scope out the casino here tonight and if we don't find him, we can regroup tomorrow, come up with a plan, maybe divide and conquer."

"I'm a hundred percent in." At that second my stomach released a loud, protesting growl. "But I need to eat first. The only thing I've had since yesterday were two tiny pretzel packs and diet soda."

"Eating. Great idea." Mara clapped her hands together and rubbed. "I'm starving too."

"You're always starving," Cam said.

She shrugged. "It's the secret to keeping my curves."

"Me, too," I said. "Except my curves look nothing like yours."

"Your curves are perfect, Lisa." She locked her arm through mine and looked over her shoulder. "Coming, boys?"

I liked her. A lot. Anyone whose appreciation for food matched mine was okay in my book—even if she could probably burn my soul to cinders with just a touch. Yeah, Mara was definitely friend material.

# CHAPTER THREE

The list of Italian options stretched along the giant menu, but my eyes zeroed in on my favorite dish. "I'll have the four-cheese fettuccini with chicken and a side salad with ranch." I handed the waiter my menu. "Plus a big glass of the house merlot."

Nate's brows lifted. "Is that all?"

"Oh, and garlic bread," I added.

"Sounds good." Mara held out her menu. "I'll have the same."

I nodded my approval. "I'm sensing a real connection here, Mara."

"Scarier words were never spoken." Nate turned to the waiter. "I'll have the halibut and rice pilaf."

"I'll have the halibut, too." Cam handed off his menu. "Thank you." After the waiter left, he eased back against the chair. "So, is it just me or does this whole

Charon-Hal situation seem like a disaster waiting to happen?"

"Definitely," Mara agreed. "It will be a miracle if we can even locate Charon, and if we do, there's no way he'll agree to let Hal transport him. Or vice versa."

"What's up with Hal and Charon?" I leaned forward and laid my arms on the table. "Why do those two hate each other so much?"

"That's a long story, Lisa." Cam peered at me over his water glass and sipped. I waited, enjoying the way he said my name and the few seconds I got to stare into his mesmerizing eyes under the guise of listening. He swallowed. "They didn't always hate each other."

"Were they friends?" Even though I asked, I couldn't imagine Hal being friends with anybody.

"More than that," Mara interjected. "Brothers."

My mouth dropped open and then snapped shut as I wrestled with the information. "Brothers? As in the same parents?"

"Yes, they're the offspring of Nyx and Erebus," Nate said. "Nyx is the primordial deity of night and shadows. She's beautiful, but extremely powerful and ruthless."

"Erebus," Cam continued, "is also one of the first primordial deities of darkness—and Nyx's brother."

I scrunched up my face. "That's disgusting."

"I know, right?" Mara said. "A whole lot of weird stuff went on back then. Anyway, that's how Charon and Hal came to be."

"Hal's real name is Thanatos," Nate said.

"Wait." After becoming a reaper I'd researched all I could about superstitions of death and remembered seeing that name. "Wasn't Thanatos the original Death?" All three of them nodded. "Then I'm confused. Why is Charon the ferryman?" I asked.

"In the beginning Thanatos ran the ferry and was the only grim reaper." Shifting, Mara crossed her legs and folded her hands in her lap. "That was thousands of years ago. Times were simpler, fewer people. Being a reaper was less corporate and more…hands-on. In those days Thanatos personally retrieved and transported the souls."

The waiter arrived with our drinks, stopping Mara's explanation. Under the table, I tapped my foot, mentally hurrying the waiter along.

"Your salads will be out in a few minutes," he said.

"Great." My mouth stretched into a smile I didn't feel. Once he was gone, I swung back to Mara. "And?"

"One day the soul of an old man came due, but when Thanatos arrived to take him, his daughter, Katrina, didn't have any gold to ensure safe passage across the river Styx. Instead, she offered herself as payment to Death." Mara paused and took a deep sip of wine. "Mmmm, that's good." She set her glass down. "Where was I?"

"She offered herself," I said, glancing at Cam and Nate, who appeared equally enthralled by her story even though they probably knew it.

"Right." Mara leaned back again, settling into her tale. "So Thanatos accepted, because even though he encountered hundreds of people every day, they were dead. He was lonely and Katrina was filled with life."

An ache pushed against my chest. This wasn't some ancient fable Mara was retelling. This was Hal, my porter, the crazy transvestite-looking guy who scared the hell out of me. Though I didn't know how the story ended, I knew it wasn't good. Hal and his brother hated each other and he no longer ferried the dead. Nor did I believe Katrina was part of his life. Though Hal and I had never braided each other's hair and gossiped about the people we once loved, I got the distinct impression he was a loner.

"Did he take her to Styx?" I asked.

"Oh, yes." Mara nodded but didn't smile. "And they fell in love." She inhaled, then slowly let out the breath. "But the thing about the Underworld and the banks of the River Styx is that they're for the dead. The living can't survive there."

A sinking feeling pushed down on me. "What happened? Did she die?"

"That would have been a blessing," Cam said, frowning. His eyes were so full of sorrow it made my entire being ache. "She wasted away, her soul fading until there was nothing left but an empty shell—neither dead nor alive."

"But still Thanatos couldn't let her go." Despite her steady voice, Mara's eyes softened. "He loved her too much."

"That is so sad." My words came out as a whisper. "Poor Hal."

"Katrina being in the Underworld offset the natural balance of things," Cam said. "And finally, Nyx had to step in and handle the situation."

"What did she do?" I absently sipped the merlot, my attention riveted on the angel.

"At that point Katrina was more dead than alive, so Nyx did what Thanatos couldn't and reaped her, sending her on to Hades," Cam said. "In his mother's eyes, Thanatos had done the unthinkable. Because she couldn't trust him to do his job, Nyx replaced him as the ferryman with his brother, Charon."

"I don't know what other punishments she inflicted on Thanatos, but I heard they were brutal." Mara sighed. "Charon had always been in competition with his brothers and took every opportunity to rub Thanatos's nose in his failure."

"Sounds like a real jerk." An uncharacteristic wave of protectiveness toward Hal surged through me. My mission was to get Charon back to Styx. I just hoped I didn't throat-punch him first. "No wonder Hal wouldn't want to transport him."

"That is some seriously messed up family dynamics," Cam said.

"Yeah, and we have the pleasure of tip-toeing around it." I drained my glass and held it up. "I'll be needing another one of these."

Our meals arrived and even after listening to Hal's tragic history, I managed to enjoy my delicious fettuccini. Not only did I savor every bite, I cleaned my plate and still had room for chocolate mousse.

After dinner, the four of us strolled out of the restaurant and rode the escalator down to the casino level. Bells from the slot machines increased in volume the closer we got to the lower level, sparking the dull ache in my head again. What I really wanted was to go to bed, but knew Nate wasn't going to let me off so easily. "Where to now?"

"Let's split up." Mara stepped off the rolling steps. "Lisa and I will go this way." She pointed to the left. "Cam and Nate circle around to the right. Be sure the check the high stakes rooms."

Nate looked as if he wanted to argue but said nothing. I appreciated his protective nature—or maybe he wasn't convinced we'd stay on task.

I smiled, enjoying his struggle over not being lead dog. "Great. Let's meet back here once we've made the rounds."

"Sounds like a plan," Cam said.

Not waiting for my partner's approval, I turned and strolled with Mara along the gleaming inlaid walkway. Ornately patterned carpet stretched throughout the casino and massive crystal chandeliers, taller than the walls in my house, hung over the gaming table area. Nearly everything was gold and reflected off the chandeliers' prisms. I scanned the area, my gaze sweeping over the people. Suddenly, I realized I wouldn't know Charon if I saw him. "What does Charon look like?"

"Dark hair, dark eyes, but he can take on any form he wants." She lifted onto her tiptoes, straining to see into the center tables. "It's better to look for a man surrounded by a group of women or a fawning entourage. Charon is very vain and loves his admirers."

"I keep imagining him decked out with thick gold chains and a lot of chest hair."

An exaggerated shudder rippled through Mara. "Don't say that too loudly. It might give him ideas."

We wandered in and out of the gaming areas but saw no sign of the ferryman. By Las Vegas standards it was still fairly early, but the people were starting to filter into the casino. One thing I did notice was and an inordinate amount of men ogling Mara, but either she didn't notice or didn't care.

"So," I said, attempting casual conversation, "again, I want to apologize for that succubus comment."

She gave an absent wave. "Really, don't worry about it. I get that all the time."

"Is that because people don't understand demons?" I was dying to know more about Mara and her world, but at this point I wasn't sure which questions were politically correct and which were taboo. "I mean…you're the first one I've ever met."

"Are you asking if demons are misunderstood?" She gave a noncommittal shrug. "Sort of, but in a lot of ways people are wise to be afraid of us."

Goosebumps skittered across my skin. "I'll be honest, when someone says demons, I think of the Exorcist."

"Oh, my God!" Mara halted, her cool demeanor tightening into a full-on grimace and cringy spasm. "Scariest movie ever!" She held up her hands as if warding off evil and shuddered. "Scared the hell out of me, and that is saying something."

"I don't feel like such a wuss now that I know the movie scares actual demons." I mimicked Mara's shudder. "And I'm not proud of this, but I don't know if I would have stayed in the house after finding my kid floating three feet above her bed, looking and speaking like that." It was my turn to hold up hands in defense. "Just sayin'."

"I would have left a trail of fire behind me," Mara added. "Anyway, those demons do exist, but they're usually bound to the lower realms of Hell because they're so hard to control."

I crossed my arms over my chest, trying to ward off the creepy chill running up my spine. "What do you mean…usually?"

She shrugged. "Well, nothing is a hundred percent certain."

"Great, there goes my peaceful night's sleep."

"Don't worry." She placed her hand on my shoulder, sending a wave of warmth through me and extinguishing the icy fear. "You've got friends in high places." Her hand slipped away, and she smiled. "And now low."

"A year ago I would have never believed I'd be friends with a demon." I nodded. "That's pretty cool."

"Damn right it is." Pursing her lips, Mara scanned the casino area again, and then sighed. "Come on, we'd better finish looking for Charon or I'll never hear the end of it from Cam."

"Our bossy partners—yet another thing in common," I added.

Mara nodded. "Isn't that the truth?"

"Geez, there' are a lot of spirits around here." We veered to the side, avoiding a group of old lady ghosts. All of them sported blue T-shirts, Bermuda shorts, and fanny packs, and I had to wonder if they'd died all at once on one of those elder's trips, or if they'd made a pact to meet here after they'd passed. "Why hasn't somebody reaped these people?"

"I was wondering the same thing," Mara said. "There seems to be a lot more spirits than usual, but that's not our problem right now."

"Right." It wasn't like I had an overwhelming urge to reap the loitering ghosts. Being an overachiever wasn't really my style. Though I could multi-task the crap out of homework, making dinner, and holding a conversation with one of my kids, when it came to reaping I took it one assignment at a time.

We wove our way in and out of the table area, along the back walls near the giant slots and through the bars, but saw no sign of Charon.

When we finally made it back to the meeting point, Nate and Cam were already waiting. "See anything?" Cam asked.

"No." I rubbed my temple, trying to relieve the dull, irritating headache. "Relatively speaking, it's pretty quiet down here."

"We didn't find him either." Nate shoved his hands in his front pockets. "What now?"

A yawn pushed against my lips and I was helpless to prevent it from slipping out. Covering my mouth, I stopped fighting it. "Sorry."

"You poor thing. You must be exhausted." Mara turned to the men. "I don't think we're going to have much luck here tonight. Why don't we let Lisa get some sleep?"

"Good idea." Cam's smile was filled with understanding and patience. It became clear why he was the Archangel of Tolerance. "We'll put feelers out tomorrow at the conference. Maybe someone knows where the best party is."

"Thanks, guys." Relief washed through me. I'd gotten my second wind before dinner but the big cheesy meal put the kibosh on any delusions of rallying. "I promise, after eight hours of sleep—maybe ten—I'll be a new woman."

"I'm going to hold you to that," Nate said. Before my annoyance flared, he added a wink, silencing my retort. "Go on. Get some sleep."

"See you in the morning." I gave a quick wave and headed up the escalator.

The others made no move to follow me and I suspected they were still going to search for Charon. I mentally cheered them on but was grateful I didn't have to

participate. A hot shower, three ibuprofen, and a soft bed—
the perfect combination to end the evening.

The elevator at the far end opened, and I stepped in,
punching twenty-six. As the doors slid shut, the silver tip of
a walking stick jutted through the crack, stopping the doors
from closing. A hand slipped in and pushed the elevator
open again. Instinctively, I moved back to the corner,
making way for more occupants.

A handsome man decked out in black glided into the
elevator. Though not overly muscular, his presence filled
the car. My gaze darted to him and then back to the wall.
There was something vaguely familiar about him, but I
couldn't put my finger on it.

"Thank you for waiting," he said. A black goatee
framed his white smile and his dark eyes tracked up and
down my body before turning to the number pad and
pressing the thirty-seventh floor. "Can't stand waiting if I
don't have to."

"Yeah." I nodded. "Me too." Thirty-seventh? I could
have sworn the floors above the doors had been twenty-six
through thirty-six. Then again, I was tired and had probably
read it wrong. From his elegant appearance, no doubt he
was a high roller and probably stayed in one of the luxury

suites the hotel saved for its rich guests. "Been lucky at the tables?"

"Very." He turned toward me, giving me another assessing stare. "I love Vegas. Home away from home." With a casual toss of his head, he flipped his hair back into place. Except for the single strip of gray that framed his face, his hair was completely black. Same with his goatee. A thin band of gray ran down his chin but the rest of his beard was the color of coal. "How about you?"

"I haven't had the chance to try my luck yet." My shoulders lifted with a tiny shrug. "Maybe tomorrow." The elevator dinged and a second later the doors slid open. As I strode out, I said, "Good night."

"Good night…Lisa."

At the sound of my name, I spun toward the elevator. He touched his walking stick to his temple and bent in a shallow bow seconds before the doors pinched closed. How had he known my name? Conspiracy theories raced through my mind. I'd never seen the man before. When I turned back toward the hall, I caught a glimpse of myself in the mirror.

"Idiot." I still wore my lanyard and convention badge. "Of course, that's how he knew my name."

Even as I pulled the cord over my head, I couldn't shake the feeling that something had been off about my contact with him. Too tired to contemplate the twists and turns this trip insisted on taking, I headed to my room. Hopefully, Tandy had found other digs. If she hadn't, I just might have to reap her ass.

# CHAPTER FOUR

"Tandy?" When she didn't answer I let out the breath I'd
been holding. "Hallelujah."

Though bolting the door wouldn't keep out the
paranormal, it would stave off the drunks and housekeeping.
Before prepping for bed, I gave my mother a quick call. My
daughter, Bronte, had been acting weird for the past several
months, ever since she had been in a car accident. Maybe it
was normal teenage stuff, but I wanted to keep a close eye
on her just in case.

The only person more lovingly invasive than me was
my mother. When I found out I had to come to Vegas, she
had been the only one I felt comfortable leaving the kids
with, which shocked the hell out of me. Normally, I leave
them with my friend Vella, but I didn't need a fun-loving
sitter—I needed diligence. My mother and I rarely agreed

on how to parent, but I knew she'd be a dog on a bone if she caught the scent of anything fishy going on with the kids.

"Your father took the children to the movie and should be home any minute."

"Really?" My father had never taken me to a movie—ever. "Whose idea was that?"

"His," my mother said. "Some science fiction flick he's wanted to see. I can't stand those shows, and they all seemed really excited to see it."

"Well, that's nice," I said, trying to not let jealousy lace my words. "And how is Bronte?"

"She's great. Almost like she's turned a corner with everything."

Her announcement about my daughter's state of mind sounded slightly boasting, as if staying with my parents had been the magic ingredient to turn Bronte around. I gritted my teeth and inhaled, forcing myself not to read anything into my mother's words. "That's great, Mom. It's nice to not have to worry while I'm gone."

"How is your trip going?"

"Good." This was always the tricky part. My parents didn't know about me being a reaper. Keeping that fact from her had sharpened my avoidance skills to a fine point.

"Classes start tomorrow," I said. "They should be interesting."

"Well, don't work too hard and be sure to relax. You deserve it."

"Thanks. I will." I feigned a yawn which morphed into a real one. "Listen, I'm exhausted, so I think I'll hop in the shower and then hit the hay."

"I'll tell the kids you called," she said.

"Thanks for taking care of them. I really appreciate it. I love you."

"Love you, too."

After hanging up, I headed for the shower. Hopefully, there wasn't a limit on how much hot water I could use. The sprays pummeled my body, easing the tension of the day and turning my muscles to noodles. Oh yeah, I was going to sleep good tonight.

\*\*\*

The alarm erupted at seven o'clock the next morning. I jerked awake, rolled over, and fumbled for the off button. Once I'd silenced the timer's annoying shriek I clicked on my lamp, flopped to my back again, and nearly jumped out of my skin.

Tandy floated a foot above the bed, her translucent image curled in a fetal position. Damn it. I'd really hoped

she'd shack up with Big C—or anybody else but me.
Nothing woke a person up fast like finding a ghost hovering
over their bed. Her body drifted toward me and I pressed
into the mattress. I filled my lungs with as much air as I
could and then blew. Like a balloon, she glided in the
opposite direction and off the other side of the bed.

"Oops."

Completely awake now, I tossed back the covers,
grabbed my clothes for the day, and locked myself in the
bathroom. My hair stuck out in all directions from falling
asleep with it wet. Luckily, my style was short and spiky.
With a little help from some styling gel and hairspray, I
tamed the platinum mess to an acceptable level.

The rest of my routine, including getting dressed,
took another ten minutes. Low maintenance—I'd never
change. When I stepped out of the bathroom, I stopped.
Tandy hovered near the ceiling vent and I was momentarily
torn. Did I pull her out of the path of the blasting air
conditioner and tuck her in, or let her float around the room?
After a second, I grabbed my purse and badge. She'd be
fine.

On my way downstairs, Nate texted me the name of
the restaurant where he was having breakfast. He'd claimed
a table in the corner and was already set up with coffee.

"Morning." I slid onto the bench and tossed my purse beside me.

He glanced up and smiled. "Morning. Sleep well?"

"Like the dead, and apparently with the dead." I waved at the waitress, indicating I wanted coffee. "How about you?"

"Not bad. We decided to check a few of the smaller casinos on Fremont Street."

"Any sign of Charon?" I pushed my silverware aside to make room for my caffeine fix.

"No, but we really didn't think there would be." Nate rubbed his hand over his chin. "He's fat with gold right now and I suspect he's at one of the top hotels." He paused, allowing the waitress to set me up with coffee and refill his cup. After she left, he continued. "We'll start checking those after the conference classes."

"Classes?" The creamer pitcher halted halfway to my cup. "We're actually going?"

"Sure." He picked up a folder and handed it to me. "Here's your conference information. There are tons of classes. Go to the ones that interest you. The only thing that's mandatory is the business luncheon today."

GRS was printed in bold black letters across the folder, but no other defining description had been added.

Probably in case a non-GRS person got a hold of it. I pulled out the schedule. "Dealing With the Difficult Client. Your Porter, Friend or Foe?" I looked at Nate. "Seriously?"

"You'd be surprised how good some of these workshops are." He reached across the table and pointed to the nine o'clock class. "This one is great for newbies."

"Is Following the Rules Really That Important?" A sniff of indignation snorted from me. "Did Constantine make you point that one out?"

Sure, at times I was a bit of a rule-breaker, but only when I knew—well, was fairly certain—my actions wouldn't upset the balance of nature. And most of the time I had been right. Mostly. With a porter like Hal sometimes it was necessary to bend the letter of the law a bit.

"Actually, no." He folded his arms and rested them on the table. "Constantine didn't think you'd go to any of the classes once you found out about our mission with Charon."

"He knows me so well." I straightened, envisioning the biggest Bloody Mary they made, and some morning gambling. Instantly, my mood brightened. "So, I don't have to go?"

"I didn't say that." Nate scowled at me. It was an expression I knew all too well. "Even though we can't force you…" He hesitated, pinning me with a fatherly stare of disapproval. "You definitely could use the extra training."

I rolled my eyes. It wasn't a mature reaction, but I didn't care. It felt right. "Why do you always make it your mission to suck every drop of fun out of my day?"

"Probably because we have very different meanings of the word fun." He leaned back, allowing the waitress to set down a plate of dry toast and a bowl of fruit.

"That's for sure. For instance you actually know how to use Pi, while I'm good at eating pie." I finished pouring cream in my coffee and then stirred it in. "You find volcanology fascinating, whereas I always wanted to be a Vulcan." I squinted at him. "Similar, but different. Mine are fun. Yours are a snooze fest."

"Would you like to order something?" The waitress held her pad at the ready.

"Yes, please." I held my hands out and made a gesture with my fingers that was supposed to indicate rolling a tortilla, but probably in no way looked like that. "Do you have anything like a breakfast burrito?"

"We've got the Southwestern Burrito Deluxe."

I clapped. "Perfect. I'll have that."

"It's really good." Her eyes brightened. "Sausage, bacon, or ham?" She scrunched up her face. "Though why

anybody would put ham in a breakfast burrito is beyond
me."

"That is a crime against breakfast wraps
everywhere," I said. "Sausage, no green peppers, extra
onions and cheese, and can I get extra salsa and sour cream
on the side?"

"You got it." After scooping up the menu, she spun
and strode to the kitchen window, immediately attaching my
order to the rotator.

"I thought you'd still be full from last night's
dinner." Nate asked.

"Hello, have we met?" His ability to indirectly insult
me with a simple statement was a true skill. Impertinent, but
not outright offensive. "This body is a super reaping
machine. It requires constant fuel in the form of white carbs,
alcohol, and cheese."

"One day you're going to drop from a heart attack."

"When I do, you can reap me and get a new partner."
I gave him a tight smile. "One who gets as excited about
daily fiber as you do."

That drew a smile from him. "Mara can really put
away the food too."

"I love that about her." I sipped my coffee and then set the cup back down. "I wish I could eat anything I wanted and look like her."

"She doesn't always look like that." Nate bit into his toast and slowly chewed. "Her beauty comes at a high price."

"You mean being a demon?"

He nodded. "I don't know a lot about Mara, but I heard she was offered a job at GRS because she saved Cam's life. But like I said, I don't know any details."

"I would sacrifice myself for that man, too." I tried my best not to sigh, but a tiny whisper of one slipped out. "Lucky demon."

Nate swallowed hard, staring at me for a couple of seconds, and then took another determined bite of toast. Jealous? If he was, it was because he wanted Mara as a partner, not because I found Cam heavenly.

A few minutes later the waitress arrived and set a platter in front of me. It had to be the world's biggest breakfast burrito, reaching end to end on the oval plate. I smiled at her, true happiness filling me. "Thank you so much."

"Enjoy."

"You can't eat all that," Nate said.

"Is that a challenge?"

He harrumphed. "No, because if I say yes, you will and then crash in a food coma."

"But I'd be so happy." I shrugged and dug into my meal.

We ate in relative silence, both of us sifting through the offered classes and planning our day. Maybe I'd go, or maybe I'd end up at the penny slots off in some corner. Who was I kidding? As much as I wanted to bail, I wouldn't. Somehow Constantine would know and harangue me about it.

After eating, we headed to the Expo and Convention center. Even though I'd decided to make an appearance at the class on following the rules, I didn't want Nate to know I'd caved. He'd give me a smug smile that made me want to slap the cute off him.

"I'm going to hit the bathroom first." I inched toward the escalator. "So…I guess I'll see you at lunch?"

"All right," Nate said, while scanning his conference sheet. Then he looked up. "Text me. Maybe we can hook up with Mara and Cam at the luncheon."

"Sounds good." At least if the luncheon speaker was boring I could sit and stare at Cam. "Later."

With that, I pivoted and took a dizzying amount of escalators to the fifth floor of the convention area. The place was massive and surprisingly the GRS Expo took up a lot of the event space. Reapers had flown in for the convention from all over the world. Whether to attend classes and network, or as backup help if things started to go sour with this Charon situation, I didn't know.

This was my first convention of any kind. Until now I hadn't given my job much thought beyond earning enough to support my three kids and not getting killed or severely injured in the process. Maybe I needed to expand my outlook on being a reaper. It wasn't as if I'd be quitting anytime soon—or ever.

For some reason they'd hidden the Is Following the Rules Really That Important class on the upper floor in the last section of the conference rooms. It didn't appear any other workshops were being held up there, so I had to wonder if they'd chosen the location for the benefit of the new reapers, or because we were a rowdy group of rule-breakers and needed to be kept separate.

There were still fifteen minutes until the class started, so I ducked into the bathroom at the far end of the corridor to get rid of the four cups of coffee I'd managed to drink at breakfast. After doing my business, I exited the stall and moved to the sink to wash my hands. When I glanced in the mirror a reflection of a woman flickered in and out near the last stall.

At first, I didn't say anything, waiting to see if the ghost would show. I'm still fuzzy on how the whole ectoplasmic dimension worked, so most of the time I just went with the flow and didn't try to over-analyze the situation.

I waved my hand in front of the paper towel dispenser, my attention riveted on the spot. When the paper towels spit out, the spirit appeared again, translucent but clearly defined. The woman appeared to be around sixty, with salt-and-pepper hair, a kind face, and wearing a black smock and pants.

Slowly, I turned, not wanting to spook her—no pun intended. She seemed slightly confused, her gaze circling the bathroom as if trying to get her bearing. Finally, her eyes leveled on me. "Where am I?"

"The Sands Expo and Convention Center, fifth floor, end bathroom." I like to keep my explanations short and to the point. A lot of times a spirit can't handle too much info at once. I dried my hands and tossed the wadded towel in the trash. "What's your name?"

"Estelle Banner." She shook her head. "But I'm dead."

My eyes widened, surprised she realized this. Good, dealing with her might be easier than I'd anticipated. Still, I had to wonder who had fallen down on the job and not reaped her. "That's right."

"Then why am I back in this bathroom?" Her voice rasped out, as if she'd been a chain smoker. "One minute I was waiting in line to board the ferry and the next thing I knew, poof, here I am."

"Wait." I leaned my butt against the sink and braced my hands on the counter. "You'd already been reaped?"

"Yeah, by a sweet little Mexican gal named Anita."

"Do you happen to know how long ago that was?" If Estelle had gone through the reaping process, how the hell did she get back here? Only one answer came to mind, and I didn't like it. "When did you pass?"

She shrugged. "I have no idea, but it felt like I'd been waiting in that line for an eternity. When I first got to the river there was a small crowd. Then people just kept coming, and that ferry didn't move. We were squeezed together tighter than a virgin's thighs, standing room only."

"Oh, crap." Tabris had said that when the banks of the river got too full the spirits would flow onto the physical plane. It looked like that was starting sooner than he expected. "Well, nothing to worry about. I'll get this sorted out." I attempted a confident smile I didn't feel. "But it may take a little time."

"No problem." She sauntered—well, more like drifted with a sashay—to the mirror, assessing her reflection. "I like it here. Nice and quiet."

"Is this where you died?" A bathroom was a weird place to haunt. I figured there had to be a reason. "Is that why you returned?"

"Naw." She picked at her perpetually ratted hairdo. "I used to work here, housekeeping. This is where I'd come on my breaks to have a smoke." She turned to look at me and leaned her hip on the counter. "Nobody ever used this bathroom except for the employees. Kind of our secret sanctuary."

"That's nice, I guess." People had to find their happy places where they could. However, discovering Estelle here did not make me happy. After class I'd go see Tabris, or maybe I'd pawn the job off on Nate. He loved brown-nosing the superiors. "I need to take care of a few things, but I'll check on you later with an update on your situation."

"Don't worry about me." She pulled a pack of spectral smokes out of her pocket. "I'll be here, enjoying my cigarettes and the quiet. Just like old times."

"Great, see you soon."

She gave a nonchalant wave. Even though I'd quit smoking a while ago, the smell of cigarettes still tempted me—even if it was from a ghost. That revelation came from the spirit of an old lady who had haunted the McDonald's Playland near my house. Avoiding all contact with temptation was best. I already had too many bad habits— Alcohol—Carbs—Kitten videos. No need adding one I'd already kicked.

As I exited the bathroom I nearly collided with Mara. "Hey, what are you doing up here?"

"Probably the same thing as you." She grimaced. "To get a lecture on following the rules."

"Right, I forgot you're new to GRS, too." Yet another thing we had in common.

"Yeah, let's say that's why I've been ordered here." She inhaled, as if readying herself for battle. "I'd rather sit through one of Cam's lectures on tolerance."

"I debated not coming, but didn't want to listen to Nate lecture me." I heaved a long-suffering sigh. "Shall we do this?"

She nodded.

The classroom was located at the end of the hall. Only five rows of chairs had been assembled and three in the front row had already been claimed by two women and a man.

"I feel like we're going to after school detention." When we entered, they turned and stared at us like three wary owls. I ignored them and edged into the back row. "How's this?"

"Fine." Mara scowled at the other students. "I'd hoped there would be more people so we could sneak out after it started."

"I like the way you think." Dropping my purse on the floor, I lowered to the metal folding chair. "Not with this crowd, though."

After giving us the once-over, the three attendees turned their attention back to their laptops, and the array of binders and colored pens spread across their legs and neighboring chairs.

Leaning toward Mara, I whispered, "I feel like a slacker. Maybe I should have brought a highlighter set or something."

A snort of laughter shot from her, but she quickly sobered and straightened. I followed her gaze. A man sidled toward us, his shoulders and hips rolling in opposite directions as he ambled. I think it was his attempt at a macho cowboy walk, which ended up looking like he suffered from a bad rash in his nether region. Instantly, my skeeve alert erupted.

"Ladies." He stopped at the end of our row, leering at us. "The name is Jimmy." His mustache wriggled under his nose, looking like a giant caterpillar when he smiled. "And lucky for you—" He grabbed the folding chair in front of me and flipped it around, hiking his booted foot onto the metal seat which positioned his junk at eye-level. "—I'll be your instructor today."

Before I could stop myself, my gaze zeroed in on his crotch. Sweet Jesus, that couldn't be all Jimmy. Realizing I was staring, I jerked my head toward Mara, giving her a wide-eyed stare.

She, however, didn't appear to be as mortified as me. Her stare hovered on his privates, the corners of her mouth twitching in a smile. I don't think it was in appreciation as much as amusement. After an uncomfortable length of time—and I mean uncomfortable for me because both Jimmy and Mara seemed unfazed—her eyes cut to his face. "Wow, our instructor, lucky us."

"I know, right?" he said. "Been with GRS for twenty years. Ten in the field, ten teaching this class." He winked at us. "Don't be intimidated, though." His attempt at being suave came off sounding like bad porn dialogue. "I'll be gentle with you."

"Ten years—that's a long time." A soft pout formed on Mara's full, red lips. "What happened? Injured in the line of duty? Is that why you're teaching?"

"Oh, I've been hurt plenty of times, nearly died twice." He settled his arm across his bent leg. "But that's not why I teach."

"Did you get in trouble for breaking the rules?" I interjected. "And now you're forced to teach this class? Is being stuck on the fifth floor, way back here—away from all the fun—part of your punishment?"

"I teach," he blurted before regaining his cool, "because it's my calling." He focused on Mara, his mouth curving into a smarmy grin. "Shaping fresh minds…" His gaze descended to her boobs and back up. "…and bodies for GRS is an honor, and I'm good at it."

"Well, I can't wait to get started," Mara said. "When will that be, exactly?"

"I like to see an eager pupil." He held out two sheets of paper and shook his head, flipping his yellow-blond hair off his forehead. "You lovely ladies will need my class handout."

We each accepted a paper, and I dearly hoped this would put an end to his flirtatious shenanigans. No such luck. I attempted a Jedi mind trick. These are not the girls you want to flirt with. But when he continued to linger—and ogle—I realized I still didn't possess that awesome power.

"Well, thanks for this." Mara waved the paper. "Can't wait to soak up all your knowledge."

"A lot of people say that," he said, nodding. I think the smile he flashed was meant to be sexy, but it made him look like he was trying to fart. "I'll be around after class if you have any questions." Neither of us replied. For my part it was because I'd thrown up in my mouth a bit. "Or I'll be around tonight." He winked at Mara. "I put my personal info on the front of the handout."

"I'll keep that in mind," Mara said.

"I bet you will." He winked again, and I had the overwhelming desire to poke his offending eye out and throw it against the wall. "All right…" He straightened and strode to the front of the room. "Rules. What are they and who needs to follow them?"

Mara leaned toward me, keeping her voice low. "I see why they stuck this class back here."

"Seriously." I cringed. "What the hell was that?"

"I'm not sure, but I think we just got Jimmied."

"Well, he needs to keep his Jimmy to himself," I whispered.

"I wonder if he calls his junk 'little Jimmy.'" Mara's eyes narrowed. "Baby, Jimmy wants to show you some love."

I pinched my lips together, repressing a laugh, and then said, "When I'm alone I touch my Jimmy."

"Besides a noun, I think Jimmy can be both a verb or adjective." Mara held up her finger, as if giving a lecture. "For example: he Jimmied his new sports car. Or, why don't you go Jimmy yourself?"

"If he Jimmies me one more time, I'm going to flip out." My mind reeled with possibilities. "He really Jimmied up that test."

Before Mara could add to our collection, the instructor interrupted, cutting off our Jimmyisms. "Do you ladies have a question or a comment?"

We straightened.

"Busted," I whispered.

"Sorry, no—" Mara paused. "Jimmy."

I manage a solid two seconds before I burst out laughing. "Sorry." I made the universal sign for locking my lips and throwing away the key. "Please...continue."

Jimmy's vibe switched from suave to suspicious. Under his constant watch, there was no chance to slip out. During the next two excruciating hours, Jimmy not only explained more than a hundred rules but also shared his personal experiences. Each incident had been life or death, and he'd always come out a hero. By the end of the lecture I'd concluded that the class was some kind of cruel initiation newbies were subjected to.

If necessity is the mother of invention, then endless boredom is the mother of revenge plots. The two-hour loss of my life, listening to Jimmy relive his glory days, was Nate's fault, and I blamed him fully. He'd played me, knowing I'd come to the class even though I didn't want to. Revenge was a dish best served cold, preferably while eating chips and salsa, and drinking a big-ass margarita. Cheers, Nate.

# CHAPTER FIVE

At eleven o'clock, Jimmy finally released us. To be honest, I hadn't learned anything new. The bottom line was, don't break the rules, or else I might start a chain reaction of biblical proportions. Got it. If it meant not ever having to attend Jimmy's class again, I'd never step out of line—well, I'd try really hard not to.

"The thought of sitting through another class makes me want to light somebody's hair on fire." A determined expression set squarely on Mara's face. "What do you say to a little gambling and a Bloody Mary?"

"Yes, please!" Pressing my hands together in a prayer position, I gave her my best puppy eyes. "But can we stick to the penny slots? It's all I can afford to lose."

"Who said anything about losing?" She patted my hands. "First penny slots, then maybe I'll tempt you with something a little more dangerous."

"I'm a chicken when it comes to money." I lowered my hand. "Especially when I don't have it."

"All right," she said, continuing down the corridor.

Her "all right" sounded anything but compliant to my wants. The one thing I couldn't forget about Mara, no matter how much I liked her, was her demon status. If I were smart, I wouldn't trust her with the smallest things. Then again, rarely did I heed my own advice.

It took a few minutes of wandering around, feeling the vibes of the machines, before we settled on two slots. Unicorns flashed on mine, and ladybugs and butterflies danced across Mara's.

"Drinks?"

I started and turned to see the casino waitress smiling behind me. Usually I burned through several dollars before catching the attention of a waitress. "Bloody Mary for me, please."

"Make that two," Mara added.

The waitress jotted down our order, smiled again, and said, "I'll be right back."

I plopped onto my seat and shoved a five-dollar bill into the lit slot. "Come to mama."

Mara fed in a dollar, hit the max bet, and won a thousand pennies. She smiled. "I like this machine."

"Yeah." Beginners luck, probably. I pushed my button and lost twenty-five cents. Undaunted, I slapped the max bet button again and lost another quarter. "Damn it." For a second time, butterflies and ladybugs danced across Mara's machine, music blaring. Then came the endless ding of coins being deposited to her credits. I swallowed my jealousy, but my voice involuntarily raised an octave when I said, "That's fantastic."

"I've never played penny slots before," she said, smiling at the dancing bugs. "It's fun."

"Tons of fun." I hit the spin button and lost. I glanced around. "Where's that waitress?"

Mara smiled at me. "Any luck?"

"No." I lowered my bet to fifteen cents and spun, this time winning back six. Instantly my mood lifted. "This is how they get you—take, take, win, and then lose twice as much."

"Have you ever played the dollar slots?"

A snort of laughter huffed from me. "No way."

The waitress arrived in record time and delivered two gigantic Bloody Mary's, a bevy of vegetables and olives shoved into the glass. After accepting the drinks, we each laid a dollar on her tray. "Good luck, ladies."

"I've been wanting one of these since I got here." I took a long sip. The chilled, spicy juice flowed over my tongue and down my throat. "That is so good."

Mara drank, her eyes growing wide, and then nodded. "That should wash away the bad taste Jimmy left."

Holding my drink, I pressed my max bet again. No win.

"So…" The bells on Mara's machine dinged. She waited until the credits finished adding and continued. "Tell me about yourself. Are you married?"

"Widowed." I watched the center unicorns line up and stretch into a single unicorn, sparkly lights dancing around the row. "I won." Happiness blossomed inside me as two hundred credits beeped onto my machine. "I officially love this game again." I looked at Mara. "What was I saying?"

"You're widowed?"

"Oh, right." I refocused on the unicorn and pressed the button again. "Jeff died about a year and a half ago."

"I'm so sorry." Mara took a tiny sip, and then asked, "You didn't have to…reap him, did you?"

"God, no." Since I'd just lost half my winnings within ten seconds of getting them, I swiveled in my chair.

"I became a reaper after Jeff died—actually because Jeff died."

Mara's hand rested on the spin button, but she didn't push it. "How so?"

"I was the next one on the list. When he died, I popped onto GRS's radar." That memory still made my stomach knot. "And get this." I pulled two speared olives out of the glass. "I had no idea Jeff had been a reaper." Using my teeth, I slid the green ovals off and chewed. "There are still a lot of unanswered questions about things, but I've been trying to focus on the kids and getting us back on our feet."

"No idea?" She mirrored my action, tapping the sword on the side of the glass. "That must have been a shock."

"A little bit," I said around the food, and then swallowed. "My introduction to grim reapers consisted of Nate locking me in a mini-mart bathroom with him and one really pissed off ghost and then calling his porter." I shuddered. "He's super creepy."

"That's crazy." Even though Mara attempted empathy, she couldn't contain her laughter. "Sorry, it's not funny, but—it is."

"The sad part is that it's so typical of my life."

"Well, you passed all of GRS's tests, so that proves you've got the makings of a grim reaper." She cleared her throat. "I know Nate reaps violent criminals. Who do you reap?"

I stared at her for a few seconds before turning back to my machine and slamming the max bet button. "I don't want to talk about it."

"Why not?" My response sparked Mara's interest even more, and when I didn't answer, she verbally prodded me. "Come on, tell me. I promise I won't laugh."

"Yes you will." I hit spin and lost.

"No I won't. Come on, Lisa, tell me."

She wouldn't give up. I knew this. Accepting defeat, I swiveled back to her. "Stupid people."

Her brow furrowed, and she shook her head. "What?"

"I reap people who have died in stupid ways." I'll give her credit; Mara didn't laugh—right away—but the corners of her mouth twitched.

"Give me an example of somebody you'd reap."

"Gator wrestlers. Idiots who jump over bomb fires. One time I reaped a guy who rode across thin ice on a snowmobile while wearing a pumpkin on his head. There's no end to the variety of reaps I might be subjected to." I stared at her for a few seconds and then said, "Now you can laugh."

"I'm not going to laugh." Though she wasn't able to contain all of her amusement, and let only a small chuckle escape, her reaction wasn't completely humiliating. "Okay, maybe a little, sorry. But that's really Jimmied."

"Jimmied to the max." I shrugged and pushed my spin button with a lot less vigor. "I'm used to it."

"Listen," she said, "the type of clients you reap has no bearing on the caliber of reaper you are." She tapped a red fingernail on the metal ledge her drink rested on. "For being so new at this, you've already gotten Tabris's attention. That's saying something."

I looked at her. "Only because Hal is my porter."

"I know." She held out her hands in question. "And what's up with that? Why do you have a minor deity as your porter?"

"Because, Mara, it's part of the cosmic joke that is my life."

"I don't think so." She waved her finger at me. "You're special. They know it." She pointed toward the ceiling, but I figured she meant higher up than the Venetian management. "Nate knows it, and..." She pointed at me again. "Hal knows it."

"Well, I wish somebody would tell me." I hit the spin button, effectively draining my credits to zero. "I could use a little specialness about now."

"Come on." Mara cashed out, snagged her credit ticket from the machine. "Let's go over here."

"Where?" I stood and took another drink.

"Do you trust me?"

No, but I wasn't about to tell a demon that. "Of course."

She glanced over her shoulder and smirked, as if she knew I was lying. Facing forward again, she wove her way through the machines, across the casino, and then stopped at a Blazing Sevens machine. "Max bet this one."

"It's a dollar slot." I shook my head. "Three dollars a pop. Do you know how long I can play the pennies for that?"

"Have faith." She draped her arm across the top. "And stick a twenty in."

I eyed the machine, trying to sense its vibe, but felt nothing. After a few seconds I sighed and dug in my purse. Dollars were stored in the front pocket for easy access. Twenties I had to dig for. I pulled out the bill and ran it through my fingers, trying to flatten it. "One time, that's it."

"That's all you'll need." She plucked the money from me and fed it to the slot machine. The credits dinged, the number twenty lighting up. "Max bet."

"Three dollars a spin?" I cringed, my hand refusing to hit the button. I could have bought souvenirs for all three kids with those twenty dollars. "This is nuts."

"Do it."

Again, I exhaled, accepting the loss of my money and spun. No win. Not even two for a cherry. "See."

"Keep betting." Mara didn't look at the payout window, but instead stared at me, smiling.

I pressed it again, this time winning two dollars. Mara's fingers began to drum on the top, near the light. I hit the max bet button. The wheels spun an overly long time and when Mara stopped drumming, the slots clicked into place.

"Oh, my God, I just won a hundred dollars." I reached to cash out, but Mara covered the button.

"Try again."

"Are you kidding? I've never won this much. I could totally get the kids actual gifts instead of a key chain or lame T-shirts."

"How about great gifts for them, for yourself, and extra to pay next month's bills?"

"Right." I laughed, but when she continued to stare at me, my smile melted, and my gaze narrowed. "Are you controlling the game?"

"How in the world would I do that?" She grinned so innocently I knew she was lying.

Being a demon probably had a lot of perks. Causing a slot machine to pay off seemed like a simple feat for a minion of the Underworld. But should I let her? Wouldn't it be cheating? Guilt over being dishonest lasted about two seconds. I slapped the spin button. The three windows spun round and round while Mara drummed her fingers against the machine. When she stopped, the sevens lined up, paying out sixteen hundred dollars.

My mouth dropped open, and I sat frozen, staring at the amount ratcheting up on my credits. When it finished, Mara pressed the attendant button. "Now you can cash out."

I looked at her, slowly composing myself and whispered, "Thank you."

"For what?" She shrugged. "It was your money."

"Yeah, but…"

She nodded, holding my gaze, "But nothing. You played the slots like a million other people and got lucky."

I shoved the straw in my mouth and drank. Aa much better option than talking and chancing someone overhearing me. While we waited for the attendant, we sipped our drinks. Mara appeared calm and not a bit guilty. I, on the other hand, felt like every security camera watched me, assessing my every move.

Finally, the assistant arrived. After another ten minutes, we were on our way to the luncheon, my purse sixteen-hundred dollars heavier. Once in the hallway leading to the convention center, I said, "Thanks."

Mara was silent for a second and then replied. "You're welcome."

We never spoke about the gambling again, both of us having sat through Jimmy's extensive lecture about no personal gain from situations. Finding out whether a demon nudging a slot machine in her favor fell into that category wasn't something I wanted consider too deeply. And even though the money I won wouldn't pay an entire month of bills, it certainly wouldn't hurt, so I wasn't complaining.

Remembering Nate wanted me to text him, I pulled out my phone. A few seconds later, it vibrated with his reply. "They're near the front of the banquet room on the left side, toward the kitchen."

"Let's not tell the boys we've been gambling for the last hour." Mara flipped a swath of auburn hair over her shoulder. "I like to keep Cam guessing about what I've been up to as much as possible."

"Roger that."

We passed through the double doors at the front of the banquet room. The room was relatively empty, the last classes before the luncheon not having released yet, which meant Nate would guess I hadn't gone. Cam stood and waved us over to the table they'd commandeered. It sat two rows back on the very end. Probably to get a good view of the speaker.

I claimed the seat beside Nate and Mara sat next to Cam. Six seats were still empty, and I didn't know if Tabris or anybody else would be joining us.

"So," Nate said, "what did you two do this morning?"

Mara cocked her head and sneered. "What did we do? We got Jimmied, Nate. That's what we did."

"Jimmied?" Cam cleared his throat, obviously trying to repress his smile. "Would that be the infamous Jimmy from the following the rules for newbies class?"

"The same." Mara dug into the breadbasket and pulled out a roll. "As if you didn't know."

"It wasn't that bad, was it?" Nate asked, his mouth stretching into a smile.

"Yes, it was that bad, Nate." I glared at him. "No woman should ever be subjected to Jimmy." I followed Mara's lead and chose a fat onion roll. "Now I need to shower again." I bit into the bread, more out of irritation than hunger, and chewed. "You set me up and I will get you back."

Nate held up his hands in defense. "All I did was tell you about the class."

"Total manipulation." I jabbed my roll at him. "You knew I'd take the bait if you threw in that Constantine didn't believe I'd go."

"It's not my fault you have a need to prove yourself."

I glared at him. "Gee, I wonder why?"

When I first became a reaper, Nate took every opportunity to let me know he didn't think I'd make it. Over the past months I'd proven I could do the job. Unfortunately, my successes had been littered with just as many screw-ups. What did he expect? Most of the time I was reaping idiots. I never knew whether they'd cooperate and transfer without any trouble, or if I'd end up chasing them through the Alaskan wilderness.

Deciding I didn't want the conversation to continue in the same vein, I switched topics. "Hey, I was in one of the bathrooms on the fifth floor and I met a ghost."

"Did you reap her?" Nate asked.

"No, she'd already been reaped."

His quasi-interest ratcheted, and his eyes cut to me. "Already been reaped?"

I nodded.

"Then why was she in the bathroom?"

"I think the better question is how," Cam said.

"Exactly." The thought of spirits seeping onto our physical plane made the bread turn sour in my stomach. I set the roll on a small white saucer. "She said she'd been waiting in line for the ferry, it started getting crowded, and then poof, she was in the bathroom."

"That's not good." Mara folded her arms over her chest and crossed her legs, settling against the chair. "I think Tabris is off on his timeline, and spirits are already crossing back over."

"I agree," I said. "It sounded like Estelle, the ghost in the bathroom, got squeezed out. From what she said, she wasn't doing anything but standing in line."

A spirit passed through the kitchen door, gliding through the tables, and out of the banquet room.

"Maybe all these ghosts loitering about isn't so natural for Vegas," I said.

"You might be right." Nate stood. "We need to tell Tabris. Maybe he has an emergency plan."

"If he doesn't," Cam said, "I think we can count on putting in some overtime."

I watched Nate stride out of the room, the sinking weight of responsibility pushing against my shoulders. I'd been in Las Vegas less than twenty-four hours and already I was embroiled in an epic crisis. I picked up my roll and shoved the rest in my mouth. It just frickin' figured.

# CHAPTER SIX

The luncheon started on time with no indication of trouble. GRS employees chatted with their tablemates, seemingly clueless about the banks of the River Styx backing up like faulty plumbing. Speakers droned on about the mission of GRS, our role in the great corporation, blah, blah, blah. I fidgeted in my seat, unable to concentrate on anything they said. The longer I sat, the more anxious I became.

Dozens of questions popped into my mind. Which spirits were spilling back to the physical plane? Violent criminals, grandmothers, children? Was there any kind of filter for those who were freed? When the other reapers caught wind of the problem, they still wouldn't be able to reap. There was no room on the banks. Maybe, by some miracle, we'd coax Charon back to Styx before things got out of control, but…what if we didn't?

"Ms. Carron?" A thin Asian man leaned next to my ear. "Mr. Tabris would like you and Ms. Mara to join him in his office after the luncheon."

I turned my head, looking into the black gaze of Tabris's assistant. He hadn't asked if we would go, and I wasn't about to tell a high-powered angel, and my big boss, no. I nodded. "Of course."

The man straightened and strode back to Tabris, delivering the message.

Hoping Nate had a better handle on the situation than I did, I turned to him "Why do you think he only wants to talk to Mara and me?"

Nate watched Tabris for a few seconds before replying. "I don't know." His expression relaxed, and he smiled. The action was forced, not making me feel any better about the upcoming meeting. "It's probably nothing, maybe just an update on Hal."

Even as he offered an explanation, I could tell Nate didn't believe it—neither did I. Whereas my stomach was a jumble of nerves, Mara appeared cool and collected, as always. I'd only known her for a day, but doubted there was much that flustered the demon. I wished some of her coolness would rub off on me.

When all the speakers were finished, and the attendees began filing out of the banquet hall, Mara and I followed the flow. For once the slow-moving crowd didn't bother me. Something about being summoned didn't sit well. I hoped Tabris was going to simply update us on what he wanted, or the situation, but the fact that Cam and Nate hadn't been ordered to come made me uneasy.

"Is it just me, or is this weird?" I asked.

Mara glanced at me. "Weird is a relative term when it comes to the ethereal administration." We skirted a group of GRS employees, chatting about the inspirational messages at the luncheon. "Totally clueless," she mumbled.

"Blissfully ignorant," I added. "Must be nice."

Several corridors and turns later we stopped in front of the set of golden doors. Mara raised her hand, preparing to knock. "Ready?"

No, but that wasn't an option. "Yep."

She rapped and the door instantly opened. Tabris's assistant ushered us into the room, sealing the door behind us, and then left through another door located behind one of the pillars. In the semi-circle of overstuffed chairs and settees sat eight people. Immediately, I could tell they weren't reapers. An air of authority surrounded the group, as if they had the right to openly assess Mara and I as we edged into the room. The urge to grab her hand like a scared child made my fingers twitch, but I repressed the impulse, not wanting to look like a wuss.

The hair on the back of my neck prickled, which usually meant trouble or the presence of supernatural beings. I figured it was fairly safe to assume this was some kind of ethereal council. I just hoped Mara, and I weren't getting voted off the island.

I glanced at her. As usual, she was the vision of cool, but I did notice her spine stiffened slightly when she first saw the collected group. She must have recognized them for what they were, which meant once again, I was the least informed. Typical.

When we stopped in front of the gathered group, Mara bent in a low bow, lasting a good five seconds. Not knowing who these people were, but figuring better safe than sorry, I mirrored the demon's action. When she rose, so did I. Still the people didn't speak, which I found very rude. Maybe that's because I have a tendency to over talk in awkward situations. Fill the silence—that's usually my modus operandi.

A door to the right slammed, jerking my attention away from the unwavering stares. "Oh, good," Tabris said, striding toward us. "You're here."

"Sorry if we kept you waiting," I said, not meaning it. The less time we had to spend with this group, the better. "We had to fight the luncheon crowd."

"You're right on time." He stopped beside me. "Lisa and Mara, I'd like to introduce you to the GRS board of directors." Pointing to two women and two men sitting to the right, he said, "These are Heaven's members." Then he indicated the group to the left, also two women and two men. "And Hell's members."

"Really?" My eyes widened. I couldn't help it. Every time I blinked, somebody hit me with new information a low-ranking reaper shouldn't be privy to. I shook my head. "I never knew there were so many representatives from—" Even though Tabris had just described them as Hell's members, I couldn't force the H-word out. Like an idiot, I simply pointed to the floor.

That drew a smile from an elegant-looking man on Heaven's side of the grouping. "I'm sure you've heard the phrase, 'there would be no good without evil.'"

I nodded.

"This is one of those circumstances. We work together for the greater good."

"Wow, that is so not what I was raised to believe," I blurted.

"Hollywood," Tabris said. "The truth is boring and wouldn't put butts in the seats, so they embellish the situation."

"You're probably right, but…" I contemplated the stories I'd grown up believing. "I think the real reason people cling to the good and evil battle is because they need a clearly defined villain, hero, and solid guidelines to live by."

"I couldn't have said it better." Tabris indicated two empty seats at the end of the half circle and then pulled up a chair for himself. He sat and smiled at me. "Please, sit."

As I took my seat, I chanced another look at the gathered group. There wasn't a single thing that distinguished Heaven's reps from Hell's. No horns or halos. No pitchforks or harps. Even one of Hell's reps was dressed all in white, totally blowing my perception of Hell's minions out of the water.

"So…" I shifted in my seat. "Have we done something wrong?"

"Not at all." Tabris gestured toward the group. "As you know, the situation with Charon is escalating. Already the spirits are filtering back, which means the riverbanks are full, and no more spirits can be delivered."

"The longer those souls remain undelivered, the greater the chance of being claimed by rogue demons," said a young woman from Heaven's side. "Balance between good and evil will be lost, which could set events in motion that we won't be able to recover from."

"That's why we need to take preemptive action," Tabris said.

"What kind of preemptive action?" Mara asked, echoing my own question.

"We—" he swooped his hand around the circle, "— need your help."

My gaze skated to the silent group. All sixteen eyes were leveled on me, and I suddenly knew what a deer in the headlights felt like.

"Of course, we'll help any way we can." I managed a half-smile, which none of the group returned, and then faced Tabris. Keeping my train of thought was a lot easier if I focused on him. "But shouldn't Nate and Cam be here, too? Personally speaking, Nate is a lot better at this kind of thing than I am."

"No," said the woman dressed in white. "Right now, you are the only one who can help us keep this contained." Even though she spoke softly, her silvery-blue gaze speared me. This was a woman who didn't take crap from anybody or hear the word no very often—if ever. "We also have need of Mara and her knowledge about the River Styx."

We looked at each other, Mara's signature eyebrow arching in a silent WTH.

"What we are asking of you is a little unorthodox," Tabris said. "But desperate times call for thinking outside the box."

"What is it you want me to do?" A thousand possibilities popped into my head—none of which I liked. "This doesn't involve seducing Charon, or traveling into the bowels of Hell, does it?"

"Nothing like that, Lisa." He gave a disingenuous chuckle that raised my first row of defenses. With deliberately slow movements, Tabris folded his hands in his lap and swiveled in his seat, giving me his full attention. A lazy smile coupled with the slight tilt of his head was his attempt at reassurance through body language. Warning sirens went off in my head. Whatever bomb he was about to drop, I knew I wasn't going to like it.

He inhaled, and I braced myself. "We need you to ferry the dead."

His words bounced right off my head, refusing to sink in. "Come again?"

"Charon has made no move to return, and someone needs to start ferrying the dead across the river." The deep voice of the large black man, one of Hell's reps, cut through the room. He placed his ankle across his knee and draped his arm across the back of the brocade chair. "At this time, you are the only person capable of running the ferry."

"Me?" He'd said that like I was the obvious choice, which was ridiculous. A doughnut eating contest, I'm in. A sci-fi movie marathon, again, I'm your girl. But ferrying the dead, not so much. "I've never driven a boat in my life. I mean, there was that one time I took a day cruise on Prince William Sound, but I didn't drive the boat." I pressed my hand to my stomach. "I get seasick."

"None of that matters," a white-haired woman from Hell's team stated. "And Mara will help you navigate the waters."

"We are both happy to do our part," Mara said, "but with all due respect, asking something like this from us raises a lot of questions. At the very least, I think we deserve to have them answered."

Go, Mara.

"I understand." Tabris's smile was placating, but from the tight press of his lips and the touch of coldness in his eyes, I could see he was running out of patience. "We

don't mean to appear callus. It's just that the situation is
rather dire and getting worse by the minute." He held out his
hand toward Mara. "Please, ask your questions."

"Styx is treacherous for souls. Many are lost, even
when Charon is ferrying. Why would you put the fate of
thousands of souls in our hands?"

Okay, so my concern had been about why they'd
asked me to ferry, not about losing souls. Treacherous river?
That sounded horrifying. A wave of nausea to rolled
through my stomach. Talk about pressure.

"Yeah, that's a good question to start with," I said,
trying to sound unrattled.

"At this point we have no other choice." Tabris
swiveled a few inches more to directly face me. "There are
things about you, Lisa, that make you the only reaper for
this job. I'm not at liberty to discuss that right now, but let
me reassure you, you're quite capable of doing this." Next
he turned to Mara. "You offered to ferry when we first
talked because you know the route and dangers. Lisa will
need your help."

"The most important thing right now is to keep as
many souls safe," said the woman in white. "And we need
to do it as quickly and quietly as possible."

I flinched. "You mean not tell Nate or Cam?"

"I mean," she tilted her head toward me, "telling no one."

"We're supposed to help in the search for Charon and convincing him to return." I wiggled a finger between Mara and me. "How do you suggest we explain our absence?"

"You won't have to." Tabris shifted, addressing the group again. "When you pass through the gates to the shores of Styx, time stops. You will return at nearly the same moment you left. Nobody will ever know you departed."

"Seriously?" I asked. Man, the things I could do with the ability to stop time. Exercise, read the stack of books next to my bed, learn to play the guitar, while still maintaining my schedule as maid, chauffeur, and chef. "They'll never miss us? Never know?"

"The only way would be if somebody saw you leave or arrive, or if you tell them," Tabris said. "Which I highly suggest you don't."

"Yeah, of course." I gave Mara a questioning glance. She shrugged, obviously as clueless about the situation as me. "So, just how do we get to the River Styx?"

For the first time since I'd met Tabris, the angel appeared wary. He gave me a tight, humorless smile. "Hal."

"No." The word popped out of my mouth before the wisdom of contradicting the board's order registered. "I mean," I said, backpedaling, "I thought he hated Charon. Why would he agree to help?"

"Perhaps he won't," Tabris's gaze darted to the far corner of the room for several seconds and then back to me. "But, it would be best for everybody if he willingly agreed."

I looked at the corner. At first I didn't see anything but a shadow. As I turned back to Tabris, a movement caught in my peripheral vision, but when I glanced in that direction again, all I saw was the dark empty corner.

"Okay, I guess I'll trust you on that." I didn't. Even though these people were from higher echelons, I doubted Hal would cower to their demands. "So what do we do now?"

"I think you should check out the situation for yourself." Tabris stood. "Why don't you call Hal?"

This was all happening so fast. Slowly I rose, unsure my legs would hold me. "Now?"

"No time like the present," he said. "First, can you shut off your phones? Multidimensional travel can be hard on electronics."

"All right." I fumbled with the power button and dropped my phone into my purse, slinging it across my body. "But I'm just calling him, right?"

"Yes, just summoning," Tabris said, gesturing to where he wanted me to stand.

I eyed him, a thread of wariness winding its way through me. Mara joined me, and the rest of the group rose, filing out to the open area of the room. Everybody watched, waiting for me to summon my porter.

I cleared my throat. "Hal." Nothing happened, which was normal for him. "Hal Lee Lewya."

A thin, pink light flashed near one of the stone lions. I shifted, focusing on the expanding strip. It stretched into a long line and then expanded, forming a door. The glow dimmed, and the elevator opened. In his usual style, Hal stood squarely in the center of the car, decked out in royal blue satin pants and shirt, a gray velvet brocade duster, and black motorcycle boots. His yellow gaze peered at me over the top of tiny silver oval sunglasses. He looked less like a transvestite circus master, and more like a rapper. Instead of donning one of his many vibrant hats, today Hal wore his hair down, hanging in glossy black waves over his shoulder. Jealousy poked at me. I'd kill for hair like that. So unfair.

"Lisa." His deep voice filled the room, and his gaze remained riveted on me, ignoring the others. "Not your usual summons, I see."

"Hey, Hal." I clasped my hands behind my back and shifted to my other foot. "How's it going?"

He continued to stare at me, but didn't reply.

"So much for small talk." I released a deep breath and plunged forward. "We need your help."

Hal's gaze flickered to the group and then back to me. After several seconds, he said, "No."

I glanced behind me, but nobody moved to back me up. It was becoming clear that dealing with ethereal upper management wasn't much different than in the real world. Toss me into the lake to see if I'd sink or swim. So, this was all on me.

I glared at Hal. "You don't even know what I was going to ask you."

"You need transportation to Styx so you can ferry the dead." A sneer curled the corner of his mouth. "Because my brother is being an idiot—again."

"Uh, okay, so you do know." The fact that Hal already knew amped up the anxiety racing through my body. One because of the precarious situation with the souls, but also, how the hell did he know these things? Could Hal somehow spy on me—like when I was in the shower, or executing my killer dance moves when I was home alone? "Why won't you help?"

His yellow gaze skated slowly over the room, the sneer fixed on his mouth. "I didn't make this mess." He sniffed. "Let my brother take responsibility for his actions for once."

"Yeah, yeah, I get that," I said, holding up my finger. "The problem is; he isn't taking responsibility. Actually, we can't find him. Now the dead are spilling back into the physical world."

He shrugged. "Still not my problem."

It was clear Hal had dug his heels in over this issue. The conflict with Charon ran deep, and it appeared he had a long, unforgiving memory. I ran through the list of things I could possibly bribe him with.

"If you help, Hal…" I swallowed hard. The things I did for this job and humanity. "I'll let you take me for a ride around Hell."

Hal's last reaper had ventured a little too close, and Hal had snatched him up for a spin around several circles of Satan's playground. Currently the guy resided as a permanent resident in the psych ward at one of Anchorage's behavioral centers. No way did I want to end up a drooling nutcase but taking me for a ride in his elevator was the one thing he constantly tried to talk me into. Either he wanted to see if I was made of stronger stuff than my predecessor, or Hal was just a sick bastard.

My offer drew an evil grin from him. Hal smiling is off-putting at the best of times. Today his expression held an extra measure of wickedness. "Tempting, but still no."

Finally, Tabris chimed in. "I don't think you understand the severity of the situation."

"I understand completely." Hal's fingers skimmed down the edge of his duster to a metal cylinder at his waist, hanging from a chain belt. "If you truly understood the situation, you wouldn't have asked for my help."

"There are times when we must put our differences aside and act for the greater good." One of Hell's representatives stepped forward. He reminded me of Nate's porter, Pick. Dressed in a crisp suit and tie, his shoes sparkling under the golden lights, he looked like an attorney for the mob. "This is one of those times. Duty dictates you help."

"I'm not much of a team player," Hal growled.

Silence blanketed the room. Nobody moved, the tension ratcheting. As the only mortal human there, I figured I had the most to lose if some kind of supernatural rumble broke out. I understood Hal's position. Mara and I hadn't been given a choice in the matter either, and we didn't have the turbulent history that he had with Charon. Still, I was willing to do my part.

"So, you're going to be a dick about this?" I asked.

Mara's eyes rounded and she gave me a quick look. Tabris coughed and then cleared his throat.

"Yes, Lisa." Hal grinned. "I'm going to be a dick."

I crossed my arms and hit him with my best glower. "Jerk."

"All your name-calling and pouting will not change my mind," Hal said. "So, if we're finished—"

"We are not finished." The voice of a woman ricocheted around the room, seemingly echoing off every wall at once.

A lot of things happened at once. The smug expression melted from my porter's face. The group of powerful supernatural beings flinched in unison, turning toward the corner of the room. And I tried to look everywhere at once, as usual, having no idea what was going on.

Careening my neck, I peered in the direction everybody else was looking. The shadow in the corner of the room churned, condensing to form a woman. Ebony hair danced around her shoulders and settled along her arms. Sooty smoke swirled over her hips and down her legs, dissipating to leave her clothed in one killer gown. She glided across the room, her coal-black eyes riveted on Hal.

The most movement I was willing to risk was a glance at the other occupants. The head of every board member bent in a slight bow, their eyes fixed on the floor. I glanced at Tabris, and then Mara. They were doing the same thing. I never claimed to be a genius, but if angels and demons were cowering at the sight of this woman, I probably should too.

I bowed my head low, making it clear I was the submissive dog in the group. In the face of supernatural power, I found pride to be a useless commodity. Survival instinct on the other hand—priceless.

A set of gorgeous ebony sandals stepped into my view. My curious nature warred with my desire to remain alive, but survival won out over peeking. It didn't matter, though. Cold fingers gently grasped my chin and lifted my head. We were the same height, but where I was platinum and blue-eyed, this woman was the incarnate of darkness.

My gaze locked with hers. It was fathomless, but not cold. Neither dead and emotionless, nor full of life. The longer I stared, the deeper I fell. Creation, dark space, vast intelligence, and knowledge I struggled to comprehend. She was the beginning, a part of the greater whole. Her name slipped from my lips in a whisper. "Nyx."

Her head tilted, and she smiled. Love and approval poured through me, and I had to blink back the tears suddenly burning behind my eyes. Emotions surged, nearly swamping me, and I barely managed to maintain my composure.

Her gazed roamed my face for a few more seconds and then lowered her hand. She turned to Hal, who still stood silently glaring at his mother.

"She is your reaper?" Nyx asked.

He hesitated, and then defiantly lifted his chin. "She is."

Nyx nodded, looking back at me, her eyes tracking down my body. "I approve. She is a good match for you." As quickly as she'd drawn me in, she turned, dismissing me. "You will take her to Styx."

Hal remained silent, not agreeing or disagreeing with her.

"I know your grievances, Thanatos," Nyx continued. At the sound of his real name, Hal bristled. "I admit, I usually do not meddle in these affairs, but as you and Charon are my sons, I feel compelled to intervene. This situation cannot continue, and you've left me no choice but to exert my authority. You will do as you're told." Again she cocked her head and leveled her black eyes on him. "And you will not harm her."

"Wait, what?" My head jerked toward Hal. Had he been considering that? It wasn't my fault they were making me ferry souls. Why blame me? His teeth pulled into a feral snarl. I took a step back. Whatever that reaction meant, I was pretty sure I wouldn't like it.

"This will happen—now." Nyx pivoted and waved Mara and me toward the elevator. "You will take Lisa and Mara to Styx so they can first assess how dire the situation is. You—" She paused, driving her point home. "—will wait outside the gate until they return. You will not accompany them." Taking each one of our hands, she walked us to within a yard of the elevator and stopped. "They are under my protection. Is that clear, Thanatos?"

With a mocking bow, he bent low. "Crystal clear, Mother."

She released our hands and gestured toward the elevator.

No, no, no, no. My body refused to move. Self-preservation demanded I get in the elevator, but paralyzing fear rendered me immobile. Crazy how strong terror can be.

Here I was, in a room full of beings that could probably think me out of existence, but what terrified me most was getting in an elevator with Hal.

Thank God for Mara. She grasped my hand and pulled me forward. With tiny steps, we closed the short distance. Bile crept up my throat, and I was sure that's where it would stay. Hal's eyes boring into me didn't help. Mara entered first and then turned and tugged me forward. Forcing my right foot to step across the elevator threshold was one of the toughest things I've ever done. The hardest? Taking that second step.

# CHAPTER SEVEN

When Nate first laid out the ground rules after I became a reaper, never let your porter touch you was a biggie. I took that to mean that Hal wasn't the only porter with a perilous streak. But nevertheless, here I was, standing less than three feet from one of the most dangerous porters—the original Death—intent on taking a ride to the netherworld in his elevator, and all without my partner's knowledge. Yeah, that sounded exactly like something I'd do.

I crammed my body into the corner, placing Mara between Hal and me. She was a demon, and frankly, a more logical choice for a buffer. The door slid shut, sealing the three of us inside. Though the elevator was more spacious than I had originally thought, it still wasn't big enough in my opinion.

None of us spoke. When the elevator started to move it hitched upward slightly, and I braced myself for a drop.

Instead, my body pressed to the right, as if we were moving sideways. I glanced at Hal, chancing the first dialogue. "We're not moving down?"

"No." He leaned against the opposite wall, his arms held wide, and his hands resting on the gold handrail, he continued his silent stare.

"Oh." Brilliant comeback. I glanced at the ceiling, the floor, and after five seconds, I'd looked at everything there was to see. Nervousness triggered my need to fill the silence. "I expected we'd descend."

Hal heaved a long-suffering sigh, as if replying to a question I should already know the answer to was a huge burden. "Up, down, sideways…it's relative to where the souls are dropped."

"So the River Styx is a sideways trip?" I asked, goading him to speak.

"It depends where I'm at when I start the journey." He peered at me over his glasses. "If I am in Hell, then the elevator would travel upward."

"Once you leave the physical world," Mara added, "Time and dimensions shift. Astral planes have different rules of physics. It's impossible to know them all."

I nodded, understanding the basics of what she said. My eyes cut to Hal. Thankfully he wasn't staring at me anymore. I relaxed a little, feeling more confident that he wasn't going to go against his mom's command, and that we'd actually make it to Styx in one piece. I pushed for more information. "What about the river? You said it's treacherous and a lot of souls were lost. How so?"

This time Hal spoke. "Styx isn't just a river. It's an entity, tempting and toying with the souls. If the soul submits to the desires of the water it will be dragged under, unable to reach its final destination."

"That's horrible." Pressure pushed against my chest. I'd be responsible for all these souls. The magnitude of my situation weighed down on me. "Is that what they call Purgatory?"

"No, there are many phases of Purgatory," Hal said, slowly opening up with information. "Currently, standing on the banks waiting for the ferry is Purgatory for millions of souls."

"Millions?" The number shocked me. I'd imagined several thousand, but millions? How the hell was I going to transport that many souls? Maybe they squished together or folded up for convenient storage. "Just how big is the ferry?"

"Big," Mara and Hal said in unison.

"Man, this is so unfair." I crossed my arms over my chest and slumped against the wall. "Stupid Charon."

"To say the least," Hal mumbled.

A thousand questions tumbled through my mind, but I wasn't sure I could handle more enlightenment about my responsibility. "You should have music playing. Something soothing."

The Girl from Ipanema flared from speakers in the ceiling. My mother listened to the song when I was little. Even though I didn't know the words, it was impossible not to shimmy a little to the catchy beat. Mara gave me a sideways glance and then shook her head.

After what felt like two or three minutes, who knew since time stopped or didn't exist down here, Hal said, "We've arrived."

"I'm going to leave this here." I dragged my purse strap over my head, dropping it in the corner. Butterflies fluttered and dipped in my stomach. What would we find when the elevator door opened? Mara and I inched toward the front. "Okay." I nodded at Hal. "Ready."

"Holy shit," Mara whispered.

When he'd said millions of people, he hadn't exaggerated. The spirits spread out before us, a sea of bobbing heads, filling every available spot. Still, from inside the elevator the place was eerily quiet. Maybe once they arrived here, spirits couldn't communicate with the living. Whatever the reason, it sent a tingle up my neck, resulting in a shudder.

My mouth dropped open and my feet wouldn't move, this time preferring to remain inside. The once horrifying elevator now seemed by far the safest place. Clouds rolled above us, churning with a dozen shades of pink and gray. Though there was no actual sun, periodically rays of light streamed through the turbulent clouds, but were quickly swallowed up again.

"I'm going to kill him." I looked at Mara. "When we find Charon, I'm going to literally tear him to pieces."

"I'll help." Mara stepped out of the elevator first. "Okay, all we have to do is check out the ferry, and then get out of here."

"Hal, you're going to wait, right?" I jabbed my finger at the ground. "Not bail on us?"

"That's tempting, but no, I will not leave." His lip curled in a tiny sneer. "I have no wish to face my mother's wrath—again."

Mommy issues worked for me if it kept our getaway car—or elevator—close by. "Okay." I exited and stopped next to Mara, inhaling. "What's that smell?"

Lifting her chin, she sniffed. "Smells like a little bit of a lot of things. Fire, brimstone, salty air."

"And flowers." I blew out my breath. "Too weird. I'm having information overload."

"Ready?" Mara asked.

"No, but I don't think anybody cares? Let's do this as quickly as possible, and then go drink heavily."

"I'm so there."

The elevator perched on a ledge above the river, overlooking the expanse of the banks and surrounding area. It was one of the few spaces not occupied by a body. We picked our way over the uneven ground and descended slick, moss-covered steps that had been cut into the side of the rock face.

Once at the bottom, I braced against the jostling crush of the crowd I knew I'd have to endure and stepped off the last stair onto a brick path. To my surprise the crowd flowed around, and even through us. Just like on the physical plane, the spirits sliced me with icy chills.

"Well, that's convenient," I said, glancing at Mara.

She vigorously rubbed her arms. "Convenient but freezing."

"Welcome to my world." I pushed forward, gritting my teeth against each spirit that passed through me. "They don't seem to see us."

The souls made no indication they knew we were there, with not even a glance in our direction. Walking among them, I could now hear low, murmuring voices, as if I were listening from underwater, but I couldn't make out actual words. If the spirits didn't know we were there, getting them onto the ferry might prove to be problematic.

We stopped a few yards before the massive arch spanning the brick roadway. To the right sat a shallow golden bowl about five feet across, heaped with gold coins. I flicked my head toward the treasure. "Charon's pension."

"A never-ending income stream." She shook her head, still rubbing her arms. "Must be nice."

"Yeah, and we're doing the work for him." I pointed at the arch. "Look, you can just make out the ferry."

Standing on her tiptoes, Mara craned her neck. "I wonder how many souls we can take in one trip."

"I guess we'll find out when we run our first ferry trip. I'm just hoping we don't lose anybody." The thought twisted my gut into knots. "Or crash."

"We'll do fine," Mara said unconvincingly.

Stone columns soared and arched fifty feet above our heads, the opening as wide as a six-lane freeway. The structure's grandeur was fitting considering it ranked right up there with the pearly gates or the gates of Hell—not that I'd seen either, thank God.

When I took a step forward to pass under the arch, an electrical charge raced over my skin, making my toes and fingers tingle. I gasped as the intensity increased.

"Is this normal?" I attempted to turn my head and look at Mara, but my entire body remained immobilized.

"I don't know." Her voice held a hint of panic, which in turn made me freak out a little.

Before I could launch into a full-on anxiety attack, the electrical sparks skittered outward to the tips of my fingers, feet, and head, creating a two-foot circle around my entire body. A high-pitched buzzing replaced the tingles, and I was able to move again. I looked at Mara, and when she took a step toward me the electrical circle burst, sending a shock-wave out in all directions, blowing her off her feet.

Unable to stand, I dropped to my knees. Pain shot through my legs, but I ignored it and crawled across the brick path to Mara. "Are you hurt?"

She slowly sat up, pushing her mass of red hair out of her face. "I don't think so." Resting her arm on her bent knee, she rubbed the back of her head. "What the hell was that?"

"Sorry," Hal called from the ledge. "I forgot to tell you about the arch." He grinned, and I knew he hadn't forgotten at all. "No living can pass unless authorized. You'll be fine now—able to move freely in and out."

I waved a hand, acknowledging that I heard him. When he turned and reentered the elevator, my wave curled into the bird. "Jackass."

"Oh, he thoroughly enjoyed that." Mara struggled to her feet. "Even left his box to watch."

"Since he's the one who broke that rule in the first place, he's probably the reason they have that damn arch," I growled.

"No doubt."

My legs felt like I'd climbed a hundred flights of stairs and a groan seeped from me when I stood. "I'm only thirty-five, but I still think I'm too old for this shit."

"I'm six thousand," Mara said. "I'm definitely too old."

"You're six thousand years old?"

"Give or take a century." She started down the path.

"It's so unfair," I mumbled, following her.

When we passed under the arch a loud gong rang, followed by several clicking sounds, like a ticking clock. Without warning, the bowl of gold tipped, dumping its contents. The coins rattled and clanked, reminding me of the good old days in Vegas when the slot machines paid out in real money. A minute later, the bowl tipped back and settled into place.

"I think Charon just got paid." Mara propped her fists against her hips. "I'll help you kick his ass when we find him."

"Deal." I smiled, happy to have a partner in crime.

The whole electrical vetting process must have changed our physical presence. Though spirits still passed through us, they no longer felt like blades of ice. It was a welcome relief, especially since I was having serious concerns about freezing to death before we delivered a single soul. The other change was that the souls could see us now and seemed to recognizing us as figures of authority. Plus, it was as if someone had tuned the radio to a clear station. The low murmurs crystalized to understandable conversations. I cringed against the sudden noise increase.

The spirits watched us pass, some attempting to follow us to the shore, but the crowding made it difficult for them to move much beyond where they were.

After passing through the last layer of spirits at the edge of the river, the ferry came into view.

"Whoa," I said, trying to take everything in. "That is something you don't see every day."

"You can say that again." Mara took a step toward the water. "I've never been this close before."

"I doubt many people have."

The ferry was like nothing I'd ever seen—or could have conjured up on my best creative day. It sat on top of the water, as if hovering. Two giant pontoons measuring at least a fifty yards in length stretched underneath the body of the ferry. Made of wood, an intricate pattern had been carved into each float, and where the pontoon curled upward at the front, figures sprouted from the wood. On the right an angel rose from the tip, its wings curling above his head, and its right hand extended. On the left a demon stretched upward out of the wood, its left arm outstretched as if reaching for someone.

To me, the ferry looked like an ancient catamaran. The glass dome of the hull bowed over the top of the floats and wide worn steps descended into the belly of the vessel. I assumed that's where the spirits sat, though there was quite a bit of room on the deck. Toward the front another set of carved stairs wound upward to what was probably the helm, and from where I'd steer the ferry. The only thing that didn't look mystical and ancient were the numerous strings of party lights hanging along the outside of the hull. Charon's personal touch, no doubt.

"Excuse me?"

I turned to see the spirit of a middle-aged woman shouldering her way to the front of the line. "Yes?"

"Do you work here?" she asked.

A ray of light broke through the cloud and glinted off the numerous sequins decorating her jade green running suit, blinding me. It seemed even in death women of a certain age gravitated to this apparel. My mom had three such warm-up suits—or cruise-wear, as I called them. Every time she wore one, her thighs made a shush—shush—shush sound that could be heard a mile away. One time I told her she needed to slow her power walk down, or she'd burst into flames from the friction. She didn't think it was funny.

I shielded my eyes with my hand and glanced at Mara, silently asking her what I should say to the spirit. She shrugged, which was no help at all, so I pasted on a smile. "Yes."

"Finally." The woman reached behind her and pulled a short, round man to her side. "My husband and I have been waiting forever. Wasn't this cruise supposed to leave days ago?"

"Cruise?"

Her frosty pink lips puckered, and she waved a translucent brochure at me. "Yes, we bought first-class tickets for the Eternal Sunshine cruise."

"Me, too." The spirit of a man, who looked like he was straight out of Hell's Angels, stepped forward, towering over me. "I don't like waiting."

I backed up a few feet, but the crowd flowed forward, all talking at once. "My colleague and I are here to assess the situation." I held up my hands, trying to quiet the spirits. "If you'll give me your attention for a minute, I'll explain."

The mob fell silent. Not a peep, cough, or shuffle emanated from the multitude. Even the water seemed to stop lapping at the shore.

I swallowed hard and flashed the best cruise director smile I could muster. "I want to thank you for your patience during this inconvenient time." I lowered my hands. "But good news, the ferry will start running later tonight."

The crowd exploded with cheers.

Mara held up her hands, again silencing the spirits. "First we need to do a routine check on the ferry to make sure everything is operational. Once we report back to our superiors, they should give us the green light to start transporting."

Again, the spirits burst into celebratory whoops. Not wanting to stay and answer a million questions—literally— we climbed onto the wooden dock and briskly walked along the ferry, putting distance between us and the throng of spirits. In the middle of the boat hung a ladder. For some reason I'd expected stairs or a gangway—something less piraty.

After scaling the narrow rungs, I hoisted my leg over the ledge and hefted the rest of my body onto the deck. Mara followed, clearing the side of the ferry with little effort. At its most basic, the boat appeared to be a mystical, ancient vessel. Carved railings depicted scenes of death, resurrection, and tormented souls. Square frosted panes of glass created the dome over the hull. When light broke through the clouds, each piece glimmered like mother-of-pearl.

"It's beautiful." I bent and examined a scene that looked like it was straight out of Dante's Inferno. "Kind of."

"Yeah, I hear death-retro is back in style. Let's check out the captain's box."

"Good idea." On our trek to the front of the ferry, I ran my hand along the cord hanging from the hull. "The party lights are a nice touch."

"I wonder what other personal touches Charon added."

We climbed the stairs to the helm. Level with the angel and demon curling up from the tip of the pontoon, the captain's box sat directly between them at the front of the ferry. The space was bigger than I'd expected. Though the steering wheel dominated the forward section, the rest of the helm had been decked out like a man cave. A leather couch and chair were shoved in the corner behind a coffee table. At the end of the couch an entertainment cabinet housed a stack of electronics, CDs, tapes, and albums. More party lights crisscrossed overhead, creating the impression of a ceiling, and a bar cart sat against the far side wall.

"Is that a kegorator?" I said, pointing to a mid-size refrigerator with the tap handle embedded in the front of the door.

"I hope so." Mara plucked a plastic cup from a stack on the bar cart and yanked on the handle. Golden liquid and white foam spilled into her cup. "Sweet!" Mara said, in a high, sing-song voice. She handed me the full glass and poured one for herself. "This will make things so much better."

"It certainly can't hurt." I sat down in the leather chair and propped my feet on the coffee table. The beer was icy cold and perfect. "Oh, my God, that's nice."

A happy growl vibrated from Mara. She licked her lips, giving an extra smack for good measure, and took a seat on the couch, also putting up her feet. "Ya know, this might actually be fun." When I scowled at her, she continued. "I mean it. Our first trip might be a little rough. We have to figure out the obstacles, things we shouldn't do, but this could be our me time."

"You mean like pedicures and journaling?"

"Okay." She grimaced and shrugged. "If that's your thing. I'll probably just read."

"And since Nate and Cam aren't here, there's nobody to boss us around." I chugged a few gulps and wiped my mouth with the back of my hand. "You're a diabolical genius."

"You have no idea," she said, before downing her beer.

# CHAPTER EIGHT

True to his word, Hal was still waiting for us when we returned from checking out the ferry. "Did you ladies have a nice time?"

"We had a really good time, thank you very much." I marched into the elevator. "Or should I say, no thanks to you."

That drew a full white-toothed smile from him.

Before entering the car, Mara stopped next to the porter and speared him with her most intimidating demon glare—flames included. All that gained her was a deep chuckle. Thrusting her chin in the air and huffing with disdain, she strode into the elevator, pivoted, and crossed her arms over her chest, continuing to glower at him.

"It wouldn't have mattered if I told you or not," he said, stepping inside and closing the doors. "You had to be vetted before you could enter."

"Yes, but you got a little too much joy out of watching us get blown off our feet." I mirrored Mara's stance, leveling the stare I used on my kids when they were being difficult. "Not cool."

Another grunt of laughter rumbled from him and the elevator lurched sideways, starting its trek back to the physical world. The smile still playing across Hal's mouth challenged my ability to keep quiet. It had been centuries, if not millennia, since he'd been to the river, and I was certain Hal was more than a little curious about what we'd found. But I'd be damned if I'd give him an inkling of insight. Obviously, Mara felt the same way, and we rode in silence the entire trip back.

The lack of conversation didn't seem to bother him one bit and when the door slid open, depositing us in the bathroom on the fifth floor of the Expo Center, he simply bowed and then disappeared.

"Say, that's pretty handy," Estelle said. The ghost perched on the edge of the sink, smoking a cigarette. "Then again, I guess grim reapers got to travel fast, like Santa Claus."

"Something like that," I said. "Estelle, this is my friend Mara. She's helping me with the overpopulation problem."

The ghost took a long drag on her cigarette and then blew out, sending a cloud of spectral smoke at me. "How's that going?"

"Uhh, it's going." I inhaled, savoring the smell, and then released my breath. "We should start seeing some progress tonight."

"Well, we'll just wait here until you give us the heave-ho."

"Us?" I looked around but didn't see any other spirits.

"A couple of my high school buddies popped in." She took another puff. "They're checking out the casino. Never been to Vegas before."

"Lucky them. Okay, I'll keep you posted on things." I walked to the door and rested my hand on the handle. "You need anything?"

"Nope." Estelle patted the pack of cigarettes in her pocket. "I'm good."

"It was nice meeting you, Estelle," Mara said.

"A pleasure."

We exited the bathroom onto an empty hall. "If what Tabris said is true, it should still be around one o'clock." I pressed my hand to my stomach. "I'm starving."

"Me, too." Mara locked her arm through mine. "Let's grab a bite and then go shopping."

"Shopping for what?" My reserve savings had been eaten up fixing our old heater. "I've got about a hundred dollars total."

"Wrong." Mara pulled me to a stop. "You won sixteen hundred dollars about…" She held up her bare wrist, as if looking at the time. "An hour and a half ago."

I'd completely forgotten about the money. Our Blazing Sevens adventure seemed like it happened days ago. Maybe it had. Since time didn't exist outside the physical plane, we could have been at the river for a month.

"That's right." I squeezed her arm. "Thanks to you." A contented sigh flowed from me. "Still, I can't spend too much. So, what are we shopping for?"

"It's just my opinion," Mara said, "but if we're going to ferry souls, we each need killer outfits."

Fashion wasn't my strong suit. "What did you have in mind?"

"For me, I'm thinking of something in red leather, pants, boots, maybe a corset vest."

"If anybody could pull off that outfit, it's you, Mara." I laid a hand against my chest. "I, on the other hand, have no desire to jam all this lusciousness into anything designed to make me sweat or cut off circulation to valuable parts of my body."

"Of course not." She released her hold on my arm. "Comfort first, always. We'll find your style and you'll love it."

I doubted that but thought it best not to contradict her. We chowed a couple of burgers at the fast food place in the food court and then headed to the Grand Canal shops. Expensive stores were housed in a facade reminiscent of Venice. In the center meandered a blue river, complete with costumed gondoliers, who worked large paddles attached to black gondolas. I'd probably never get to Italy, but it was fun and easy to imagine I actually was there.

Surprisingly, I found the perfect outfit in the first store we went into. I stepped out of the dressing room and held my arms out, doing a full turn. "How do I look?"

"Fantastic." Mara circled me, stopping to run her hand down the black-on-black skull print skinny jeans. "I should get a pair of these."

I lifted the hem of my black long-sleeved T-shirt and hooked my thumb inside the waistband. "They've got some stretch." I dropped the shirt and squatted. "I could even wear these—" Catching the eye of the sales attendant, I changed reaping to, "—to work."

"And the boots?" Mara pointed to my feet. "Comfy?"

"So comfy." I did a jumping jack. "And I love the wedge heel. Sexy and sensible."

Mara turned to the hovering attendant. "Do you have a jacket? Something that tapers in at the waist and is longer? Nothing boxy."

"Let me check." The sales clerk bounced out of the dressing area and returned less than a minute later. "How about this?"

"Love, love, love," Mara said, taking the black and gray pinstriped sweater duster from her. "It's so classy."

The fit was perfect, and I had to admit, I looked amazing. "This works."

"You look hot. If I were a lesbian, I'd totally go for you," Mara said.

"I am a lesbian," the clerk chimed in, "and ditto to what she said."

"How can I not buy this outfit after praise like that?" I fingered the price tag and choked. "Three hundred dollars for the sweater? Holy crap." Finding each price tag, I quickly tallied the total. "Seven hundred and fifty dollars."

"Don't forget the boots," said the clerk. "They're three-fifty."

My mouth dropped open. The most I'd ever paid for any item of clothing was two hundred dollars for snow boots. Those, at least, had been useful. This was purely for fun.

"We'll take it," Mara said, reaching over and pushing my mouth closed.

"Excellent." The clerk held the dressing room door open. "I'll package everything and ring you up when you're ready."

"Hold on, I need to think about this." I stepped away from the clerk in case she had any crazy notions of helping me undress. "I can't spend that kind of money on myself." Even though we were in a high-end store, I hadn't realized just how high-end. "I've got bills to pay and a thousand dollars goes a long way."

"We'll be out in a minute," Mara said to the clerk, dismissing her. When alone, she turned to me. "There's more where that came from."

"What? Money?"

"Yes." She grabbed me by the shoulders and spun me toward the dressing room. "So please, do something nice for yourself and buy this outfit."

"I don't feel right about cheating the slots again, Mara." I hooked my fingers on the door and peered over the top at her. "Not because I'm holier than thou, but because it will catch up with me. Somehow, karma will pay me back."

"Fine." She shooed me with her fingers. "We'll ask Tabris to cover it. After all, we're working for GRS. The least they can do is buy us adequate clothing for the job."

"Do you think they will?" I kicked off the fabulous boots and peeled the skull pants to my ankles. The outfit really was perfect. "What if they don't?"

"I guarantee they will."

Mara's promise lacked conviction. A moral dilemma raged inside me. I knew I could buy the clothes and somebody would reimburse me. The question was who— GRS or Mara? If Mara, then where would she get the money? My guess was from a slot machine. The answer had come full circle, back to cheating the casino. I weighed the difference between me personally doing the gambling versus accepting money and not asking questions. My moral compass rocked back and forth, refusing to point true.

I gathered the clothes, hugging them for a second, and then held them out the door. "I'm going to Hell."

"Some of us have already been there." She gathered the clothes. "At least you're in good company."

Instead of the red leather corset Mara had wanted, she chose a more subdued ensemble, limiting the red leather to the pants. She paired them with a flowy black tunic that would have looked like a lampshade on me, and black-spiked-heeled-ankle boots. Tonight, we would both be sexy and sensible.

After hitting a couple of stores for accessories, we went to our rooms to get ready for the evening. I pulled out my keycard and froze mid-swipe. Music filtered from inside my room. Elvis? I shoved the card in the lock and pushed open the door.

Tandy bounced up and down on the bed, dancing in circles. Five ghostly Elvis impersonators stood around the bed, performing iconic pelvic thrusts and hip moves, while belting out Hound Dog.

I dropped my purse and bags on the floor next to the bathroom and edged into the room. "What's going on?"

"Hey, Lisa." Tandy spun, bounced, and pivoted again. "Meet my new friends. Elvis's, my roommate Lisa."

The closest Elvis moved toward me, shaking his hips. His white jumpsuit stretched tight across his belly, working overtime to keep him contained. He lifted my hand and bent to kiss my knuckles. A chill rippled up my arm. "Nice to meet you, pretty lady."

"Hi." I tugged my hand free. Unfortunately, it seemed the no-chill zone was limited to the riverbank. "New friends?" No doubt these guys were more regurgitated souls. "How long have you men been back?"

Tandy stopped bouncing. "They popped into Big C's suite about three hours ago and we decided to bring the party down here."

"Great." I would have protested, but what was the point? Convincing Tandy to vacate the room had proven fruitless so far. I doubted she'd change her mind. If the party still raged when we got back from ferrying souls, then I'd put my foot down. I slipped behind a young, skinny Elvis and opened the dresser drawer, pulling out fresh undies and my black bra. "I'm going to take a shower." Making sure not to touch any of the spirits, I eased out and backed to the bathroom. "I don't care if you stay but this—" I pointed to the bathroom. "—is a no ghost zone. Got it?"

The group started singing again and Tandy shot me two thumbs-up before breaking into hip swivels. I'd have to trust that they'd keep their word and let me shower in peace. I grabbed my purse and bags, hauling them into the bathroom with me, and locked the door. Not that locks would keep them out, but it made me feel better.

After showering, I took extra time applying my rarely used makeup. I attempted a balance between natural and whore paint and think I nailed it. Before doing my hair,

I dressed. Thankfully, the clothes looked just as good in the bathroom as they had in the store. Another few minutes on my hair and I was ready. I unlocked the door and strode into the room, hoping to get Tandy's opinion, but the ghosts were gone. Dang, the one time I wanted to show off a little and there was no one to model for.

"I look good." The doors of the closet were full-length mirrors and gave me a view of the entire scope of my outfit. It had been a long time since I'd felt anything close to sexy. I wondered what Nate would think about my look. Would he even notice? "Who cares? I like it."

I pulled my phone out of my purse and turned it on. Text notifications pinged one after the other, all from Nate. I scrolled through. The last message he'd sent said we were to meet in the lobby in fifteen minutes.

The rest of the messages were varying degrees of "Where are you?" and "Where have you been?"

"How about a 'please' or 'can you be ready?'" I mumbled.

I replied with, "On my way" and dropped the phone back in my purse. Another message dinged, but I ignored it. As I closed the door, my phone dinged again. For crying out loud, the man needed to learn patience. I strolled to the elevator, choosing not to reply.

At the tenth floor, my phone erupted in my purse, the theme song from The Addams Family blaring. I fumbled inside and pulled it out. It was Nate. The elevator settled, and the doors slid open. He stood with his back to me, the phone pressed to his ear.

I marched over to him and stopped. "What?"

He jerked around and clicked off his phone. "I've been texting you all day. Why didn't you answer?"

"Because you're not the boss of me, nor are you my husband or father." I propped my hand on my hip. "Besides, I did answer. I just texted you that I was on my way down."

"Yeah, five hours after I first messaged you." He threaded his fingers through his hair and gave me his familiar scowl. "I was concerned something had happened."

"Like what? I was off gambling instead of learning ten ways to deal with a difficult client?"

His frown deepened. "No, about what Tabris wanted."

Crap, I'd forgotten the last time Nate had seen me was just before our meeting with the GRS board of directors and Tabris. I took for granted Nate usually knew more about any given situation than I did. Him being in the dark about me ferrying the souls hadn't registered. Plus, Mara and I had already put in a full day, but to him the night was still early.

Time ran together and keeping straight the physical plane hours and time spent at the ferry might be more complicated than I originally thought.

"Oh, Tabris, right." Luckily, Mara and I had come up with an explanation while shopping. "He wanted to get things settled with Hal."

"Did you?"

"Yes." I fidgeted with the strap of my purse. "The GRS board of directors were there to make sure he complied."

Nate eyed me. I could tell his keen powers of deduction smelled a lie, or more like a half-truth. "Hal agreed? Just like that?"

If I said yes, he'd know I was lying or keeping something from him. "Not exactly." I glanced around, making sure we weren't overheard. "Nyx was there."

Though only for a few seconds, I'd rendered Nate Cramer speechless. His eyes rounded to the size of Chucky Cheese tokens, narrowed, and then widened again. "What did she... How... You actually saw her?"

"And held her hand." I regretted the comment immediately. There was a thin line between sounding believable and revealing too much. "She forced Hal into agreeing and made him promise not to hurt me."

Again, Nate didn't speak, taking in the information. "Wow, Carron, that's…" He shook his head. "I'm not sure what that is."

"Tell me about it." Some of the tension eased from my shoulder. As a person Nate could be a bit of a dickwad, but as a partner he was solid. It felt good, and right, to tell him as much as I could about our meeting. "I will say, I'm pretty sure Hal will keep his word. Nyx is one scary lady."

"That's what I've heard." He reached out and gently gripped my shoulder, his gaze locking with mine. "Are you sure you're all right? Nothing else happened?"

Whenever Nate showed genuine concern, it knocked me off balance. Sarcasm and bantering were much easier to deal with. I mustered my most reassuring smile. "I'm fine. The whole meeting took about fifteen minutes."

His hand slid from me. "Then what did you do?"

I held out my arms and performed my dressing room turn. "Mara and I went shopping. Do you like?"

His eyes tracked down my body, lingered on my breasts a few seconds longer than was polite, then widened when he realized the pattern on my pants were skulls, dipped to my feet, and jumped back to my face. "It very reaperesque." He gave a single nod. "You clean up real nice, Carron."

"I told her the same thing," Mara said, sauntering toward us, her spiked heels clicking against the polished floor. "Worth every penny."

She'd created an intricate twist with her hair that was pinned high at the back of her head, leaving the ends to form a messy, but stylish spray of shiny red strands. Her makeup was sultry but not slutty. The woman—demon—was physical perfection, and I had to wonder if this human body was her original form. I'd already insulted her with my succubus question. No way was I asking if she had a tail and horns.

"You look beautiful, too," I said. "Love those pants—on you."

"Hey, guys," Cam said, stopping next to Nate.

Wow, he was hot. It was probably blasphemy to entertain naughty notions about him, but I couldn't help it. He was everything I'd imagine an archangel to be, golden and gorgeous. I bet he was smooth and muscular all over. No back hair. He probably never farted or scratched his junk. At least not in public, or in my fantasy, around me. I smiled—and maybe gave a dreamy sigh—because Mara arched a questioning, and rather sarcastic brow at me.

"Is it just me," Cam continued, "or are there a lot more spirits now than there was this afternoon?"

We all turned and surveyed the casino. They were everywhere, meandering along the walkway, playing the slots, even a couple sitting on the edge of a chandelier.

"Whoa, that's a lot of ghosts." I pointed to a group of people walking behind the strolling ghosts. "Reapers."

"I wonder if they're going to try to reap them," Mara said.

"They might get them in the elevator." Nate shook his head. "But they'll pop right back up here."

"We need to find Charon." Cam placed his hand against Nate and my back, as if rallying the troops. Tingles and warmth spread across my skin where he touched. I could have stood like that all night. "As quickly as possible."

"Yeah, we do." I smiled up at him.

Nate reached across Cam and grabbed my wrist. "Lisa and I will check out the high roller area." He tugged me to his side. "It's better if we act like couples. Two beautiful women might draw too much unwanted attention."

My irritation at being led around like a dog vanished with his compliment. He might have been right, but seriously, like Cam and Mara together wouldn't draw too much attention. I rolled my eyes and pulled my arm out of his grasp. "I've got my phone. Text me if you find anything."

"Sounds good," Cam said.

Mara gave me a pointed stare and a knowing smile before following Cam. On this trip I had two partners: Nate for reaping and Mara for the covert operations—and shopping. We wound our way through the casino, heading toward the high-stakes table. Twice, ghosts suddenly appeared in our path, at first confused by their surroundings, and then floated away.

"We need to find Charon." Nate reached for my hand again and guided me around the spirit. "I doubt Vegas is the only city getting an influx of ghosts."

"For sure." My answer made me sound like a valley girl, but his need to keep touching me made it difficult to concentrate. By nature, he was a protector, but it wasn't like I hadn't had my share of encounters with the supernatural. Sometimes it seemed he still didn't think I could do the job. "Let's head over there." Again, I pulled my hand from his and moved in front of him. "There's a crowd at that far table."

Cheers exploded from the group as we approached the roulette wheel. I instantly recognized the man with the pile of chips in front of him. He'd been in the elevator with me on the first day I arrived. Several living humans flanked the guy, and even more spirits crowded around, floating in and out of the table. One particular ghost I knew very well.

"Tandy." I pointed at her. "The bouncing blond spirit." That seemed to be her natural waking state. The girl never stood still. "She's the one sharing my room."

Nate's eyes widened. "Wow, she's got really big—"

I glared at him.

"Energy."

I harrumphed. Energy my ass. "I've seen that guy before. He was on the elevator with me the first time I went to my room. He called me Lisa, but I thought it was because I was wearing my name badge."

"Could be a coincidence, but my gut is telling me we found our man." Nate pulled out his phone and texted Cam. "They'll be able to tell us if that's Charon."

The group around the roulette table cheered again. Tandy threw her translucent arms around the guy. "You're the luckiest man I know, Big C."

"Big C?" I made the connection instantly and looked at Nate. "I can't believe it took me so long."

"What?"

"Tandy told me about this high-roller, staying in the penthouse suite. She called him Big C."

"C, short for Charon," Nate said, putting the pieces together.

"Right. It didn't register until I saw the two of them together."

Mara and Cam pulled up next to us. "Oh yeah," Mara said. "That's Charon."

"Definitely," Cam confirmed. He lowered his voice. "So, how should we approach this?"

"We could politely ask him to have a word with us, present our demands, and negotiate with him," Nate said.

"Or better," Mara chimed in, "I could threaten an eternity of torment in the fiery pits of Hell."

My head snapped to face her, my brows lifting as high as they could go. "Can you actually do that?"

"No." She gave me a satisfied smile. "But I'd be willing to try."

"Lisa!" My name cut through the din. Tandy continued to bounce and wave. "Look, it's my friend Lisa,"

All eyes turned toward us, including Charon's. His gaze skated over the four of us and a slow smile stretched his mouth. "Ah, the pretty lady from the elevator." He continued to stare at us and said, "Scoot over and make room for my new friends. Lisa—" He patted the chair next to him. "—you sit here."

"Or," I whispered, "We could do it like that."

"Be careful," Nate said in a soft voice. His concern would've been endearing, but then he added, "Don't blow it."

I glared at him. "One of these days..." Nate gave me a tiny shove forward before I could finish my threat.

"Come on." Tandy held onto the back of the chair. "Right here, Lisa."

I circumvented the table and pulled the chair a few inches toward me, not wanting to rub thighs with Charon. Mara, Nate, and Cam moved to the far end of the table, watching us.

"Do you gamble, Lisa?" Charon asked.

"Sometimes, when I'm in the mood." I was willing to bet Charon's friendly demeanor was pure show, and that he knew exactly why we were there. "But I rarely win."

"You never know." He smiled but still didn't look at me. Instead he placed numerous stacks of chips on different numbered squares. "Maybe your luck will change tonight."

"I highly doubt that."

The dealer made his announcements for final bets and then flicked the ball into the wheel. The ball circled a kagillion times before dropping into red thirty-six. I'd never played roulette before, but from the explosion of cheers, and the heaping stack of chips the dealer shoved at Charon, I figured he'd won.

He scooped the piles toward him and then plucked several from the stack and tossed them to the dealer.

"Thank you, sir," the dealer said, dropping the tip into a pile.

"I'll be back." Charon stood. "But right now I need a drink." He looked at me. "Why don't you and your friends join me?"

I stood and smiled. "We'd love to."

A young woman dressed in the casino uniform moved forward. "We'll hold your winnings at the cashier cage, Mr. Charon."

"Thank you, Amanda." He turned to Tandy. "Sweetheart, why don't you get the suite ready for tonight's party?"

"Okay, Big C." She leaned in and kissed him on the cheek. A second before she evaporated, he smacked her on the rear end, making her squeal with delight.

"You do know Tandy has a major crush on you." I sent a pointed stare at the three and flicked my head for them to follow, begging them to follow. They squeezed through the living and dead, finally falling in behind us. "Right?"

"She's sweet," Charon said. "Likes to do things for me."

"I bet." That drew a chuckle from Charon, but he didn't reply. "So…" I tugged nervously at the edges of my sweater. "Do you actually win, or do you give the roulette wheel a helpful nudge?" The question was my attempt at facilitating dialogue, a term our family counselor used when the kids and I were in therapy. I thought it had a nice ring to it. "I promise I won't tell."

"Let's just say I lose sometimes." He drew a gold coin from his pocket and flipped it in the air, then caught it. "But I win a lot more."

I'd seen a whole mess of those coins earlier that day at the arch leading into the River Styx. If I'd had any doubts, this was our man, I didn't now. "Aren't you afraid of karma? Like cheat and you will be cheated?"

"I believe we make our own fates, Lisa."

Karma usually found me, and she wasn't all that friendly. I went out of my way to never walk under a ladder and occasionally threw salt over my shoulder—just in case there was any truth to superstition. However, Charon had been around a long time, and probably had a firm grasp on the rules and nuances of the paranormal world. Like each entity's responsibility, or which deities never to seat next to each other at a dinner party because an eon ago one of them turned into a salamander and slept with the other's mother.

A behemoth of a man stood at the entrance of the lounge. When he saw Charon, he unhitched the red velvet barrier, allowing us to pass. Getting used to this kind of treatment would have been easy. Once inside, a super-model grade hostess showed us to a seating area near the back, and then disappeared.

"Please, sit." Charon claimed an oversized leather chair at the end, forcing the four of us to sit on a curved sectional, facing him. When we were settled, he crossed his legs and eased his arm across the back of the chair. "Now, let's talk about why I'm never going back to Styx, shall we?"

# CHAPTER NINE

Charon's announcement that he'd never return to the ferry caught me off guard, and from the glances exchanged between the others, they were just as surprised.

"You can't mean that," I said.

His humorless smile wavered between determined and angry. "I've never meant anything more in my life."

"You've seen what's happening," Nate said. He waved his hand in the direction of the casino. "Already the spirits are spilling back to the physical plane."

"Fun, isn't it?" His smile morphed to extremely satisfied status. "I bet Tabris is having an angelic cow right about now." He shrugged. "But, it's not my problem. I'm retired."

"Are you?" I asked. "Tabris said you haven't officially signed off on that."

Charon shrugged. "A minor detail. I'll get around to it. Really though—" He held up his hands. "What's the hurry? It's not like there's anybody who can ferry?"

My gaze cut to Mara, and hers to me. Then she tilted her head and smiled at him. "So, what's your plan—live at the casinos and party it up?"

"For a while." He gave a nonchalant shrug. "Then I think I'll travel. Maybe buy one of those RVs and hit the road. I've always wanted to visit Hershey, Pennsylvania. I heard it smells like chocolate."

I recognized the glint in his eye. Bronte, my fifteen-year-old daughter, got that same look when she was trying to get a rise out of me. He was bluffing, and I was pretty sure he'd pulled Hershey, Pennsylvania and the RV trip out of his butt. I doubted Charon harbored any desire to see any historical sites in America. Having three kids made me an expert on sniffing out shenanigans and lies. Charon put on a good show, but I knew ulterior motives when I heard them.

"I've never been to Pennsylvania," I said. "But, I did get to meet someone exciting today." I pointed at him. "Your mother."

"That's funny." Charon's smile faltered. "I highly doubt you'd meet my mother—and live to tell about it."

"Hmm, I could have sworn it was her." I tapped my chin and narrowed my gaze. "Beautiful, dark, all smoke and ash with a touch of terrifying?"

"That definitely describes her." The strained smile remained fixed, but he straightened, uncrossing his legs and signaling to the waitress. "So, tell me, if you really met dear old Mom, what did you talk about?"

"Thanatos." I used Hal's real name in case he didn't know about his brother's stage name. "Nyx insisted he transport you back to Styx."

Three waiters placed a bucket of ice and champagne, a bowl of strawberries, and a tray of glasses on the center table. Charon pulled the bottle from the ice and poured himself a glass, downing it in one gulp. Fixing his eyes on me, he stabbed me with a humorless smile. "And did my brother agree?" Before I could answer, Charon waved a dismissive hand. "Of course, he did. Whenever my mother snaps her fingers, he jumps."

More mommy issues with a big dash of sibling rivalry. The more Charon talked, the more I understood him. Though I hadn't puzzled out his motivation for quitting, I did think I'd be able to get the story out of him with the right kind of persuasion.

"You don't jump at your mother's command?" I asked.

"I was wondering the same thing." Mara gave an exaggerated grimace. "I met Nyx, too. She's seriously intimidating."

"You met Nyx?" Cam asked. "Why didn't you tell me?"

"I forgot." The look she gave her partner screamed 'Not the time, Cam'. She turned back to Charon. "You were saying?"

"Nyx and I have an…" He hesitated, flipping the gold coin between his fingers. "Understanding."

"What kind of understanding?" I asked as nonchalantly as possible. To hide my interest, I grabbed a glass from the tray and held it toward Mara, silently asking. She nodded vigorously. "An understanding like you do your job, she'll stay out of your business understanding?" I poured a glass and handed it to her, and then handed another glass to Cam. "Or a *you're not speaking to each other* understanding?" I sat back, giving Nate one of the two glasses I held and turned my attention to Charon. "If I'm not being too nosy."

"Let's just say she owes me a big favor." Charon filled his glass and reclined. "So, if you were hoping she'd be able to order me back to the ferry, you're going to be disappointed."

That was exactly what I'd thought would happen. From the way Nyx had ordered Hal, around and he hadn't even peeped in protest, I'd figured she'd put her dark deity mom thing down and Charon would jump, too. What kind of favor could Nyx possibly owe her son? The only thing I could think of was Charon taking over running the ferry.

I took a big gulp of champagne and swallowed. Bubbles rushed up my nose, causing my left eye to squeeze shut against the burn.

"That's too bad." Cam set his glass on the table and gave Charon a sad, but tolerant, smile. "With the riverbanks full, spirits are appearing back here, this problem has gotten the attention from top levels, and they're not happy."

Instead of the information intimidating Charon, the comment seemed to please him. This time his smile was genuine, and his attitude eased back to indifferent and in control. "Let them scramble for a solution. They won't find one. Do you know why?" We shook our heads in unison. "Because I am the only one qualified to ferry the dead."

"What about Thanatos?" Mara asked.

"I guarantee that idiot will never be allowed to set foot in Styx, let alone claim the ferry again."

My gaze darted to Mara again and then back to Charon. He was wrong on two accounts. He wasn't the only one qualified to ferry the dead—somehow, I'd made the grade. And it was true Hal wasn't allowed past the arch, but today he'd stood on the grounds of Styx. Though we'd been sworn to secrecy about our task of ferrying the dead, my gut also told me to keep any information, no matter how big or seemingly insignificant, quiet. There might come a time when letting him know would come in handy, but for now I wanted to play my cards close to my chest.

"What about your other siblings?" Cam asked. "Wouldn't they be able to run the ferry?"

"Ker, possibly, but he's too violent. He destroys first and asks questions later. If they haven't offered him the job yet, they won't—wisely so. The guy has issues." He held up his fingers, effectively rattling off his slew of brothers' and sisters' names, and the reasons why they couldn't be the ferryman. "And lastly, Hypnos. He's such a bore. Puts everybody to sleep—literally. He'd have the entire ferry in a coma before it ever arrived. Not only could the souls not get to their appointed destination, they couldn't reincarnate." He fisted his hand. "So, you see? There's nobody but me."

I did see, and his reasoning was solid. But I didn't think we were beaten yet. My mom radar continued to ping loudly. I'd bet my new boots that this had nothing to do with him truly wanting to retire.

"Well, I guess you're holding all the cards." Setting my glass on the table, I looked at Cam, Mara, and Nate. "We tried." The three stared at me, and by their identical furrowed brows, were equally confused about why I'd given up so easily. I turned back to Charon. "So, what's this I hear about a party?"

"Yes, my party. You've got to come." He unfolded from the seat and produced a keycard. "Thirty-seventh floor, leave your morals and inhibitions at the door."

"I thought the hotel only had thirty-six floors," Nate said.

"Does it?" Charon held the card out to me. "Eight o'clock."

I took the keycard, not wanting to miss my chance to work some child or reverse psychology on him. "We'll be there."

"Until then." He skirted the table. "Please stay and relax. Order anything you want—on me. I can afford it."

He laughed at his joke, which wasn't really a joke at all, because the guy was loaded. Nor was it all that funny. As he strode to the exit, Charon hummed and twirled the walking stick he carried, the silver tip glinting under the low lighting. It was the departure of a man who believed he had everybody over a barrel. Maybe he did. Maybe I was naively optimistic that we'd be able to fix this situation.

"That was rather unproductive," Mara said.

"If what he says is true, he's holding all the cards." Nate stopped the passing waitress. "Could we get a couple of menus, please?" When she was gone, he leaned forward, resting his arms across his thighs. "There's got to be some way to convince him to go back."

"I can't believe they didn't plan for this." Cam gestured toward Mara. "We've been around a long time. There's always a contingency plan."

"Always," Mara said, nodding her head. "But so far the higher-ups have chosen not to grace us with their infinite wisdom on the matter." She drained her glass. "I need more of this."

"Here's my two cents, for what it's worth." I smiled and held up a finger. "I think we should go to the party." I lifted a second finger. "Butter him up and try to get on his good side." Already this was turning into a long night. "Something tells me we're not getting the whole story from him."

"Is that your reaper intuition at work?" Mara asked.

"I've got three kids. I know bull crap when I hear it."

Mara looked at Nate and Cam. "Do you boys have a better plan?"

Cam shook his head. "I've got nothing."

"Me, either." Nate rubbed his hands over his face and released a growly sigh. "This is so frustrating."

"We have to keep the faith that this will all work out." Mara picked up a menu. "But first I'm going to order a bunch of expensive food and drinks. I know it won't put a dent in Charon's wallet, but I'll feel a lot better trying."

After several rounds of lobster dip, stuffed mushrooms, and nachos with the works for me, we waddled out of the lounge and headed to the elevator. We had to wait a few minutes before snagging the empty elevator we needed, the one with twenty-six through thirty-six on the gold panel.

"There's no thirty-seventh floor." Nate turned to me. "Where's the keycard?"

I pulled it out of my back pocket and handed it to him. When he shoved it in the slot, another lit button appeared on the panel. All of us bent and stared at it, as if that would make something happen. I reached out and jabbed the button. The elevator lurched to life and when it stopped a minute later, the doors opened onto the expansive foyer.

We stepped out, but none of us moved forward.

"I'm pretty sure this isn't one of the hotel's luxury suites," Nate said.

"Or even its penthouse suite," Mara added.

I glanced up and gasped. The domed glass ceiling revealed the night sky, but instead of twinkling stars, spiral galaxies, distant suns, and billowing clouds of colorful space dust churned and rotated across the blackness of space. It looked like a picture the Hubble Spacecraft sent back to earth.

"I don't think we're in Kansas anymore," I muttered.

A loud trumpeting echoed through the foyer seconds before a full-sized elephant stomped across the entrance of the suite. The four of us stood riveted, watching as the animal disappeared behind a gold column.

"Please tell me you guys just saw an elephant," I said. If they hadn't, I seriously needed psychiatric help and heavy medication.

"Yep," Nate said, resting his hand on my shoulder. "And it was wearing a yellow and black tutu."

"Okay, good." I inhaled. "You don't think he's got other wild animals roaming around in there…" I swallowed hard. "Do you?"

"Let's hope not." Mara stepped behind Cam, gripping his upper arms. "But just in case, you go first."

"This job keeps getting better and better," Nate muttered.

We crept forward but stopped at the entrance and poked our heads out. For my part, if this was a designated elephant crossing, I wanted to stop, look, and listen before charging into the room. With no pachyderms in sight, we inched forward.

My mind knew I was in the Venetian hotel, but my eyes could have sworn we'd been transported to a sultan's palace. Gleaming, white marble floors stretched down arched corridors—corridors that physically couldn't fit at the top of a hotel. White stone pillars soared upward and disappeared into the cosmic ceiling.

"This is a lot bigger than my room," I said. "However, I did get a nice bar of soap."

Mara's laugh came out as a snort.

"It sounds like the party is this direction." Cam pointed toward the arched hall to the left. "I hear music."

We skirted a peacock that had wandered into our path and followed the music. The din increased, the sound of voices blending with the heavy beat of techno dance music. At the end of the walkway stretched a massive room.

Already dozens of corporeal people and even more ghosts were there, mixing and mingling, as if the living and the dead socializing was the most natural thing in the world. A section of the room had been claimed as a dance floor. Bodies, both solid and translucent, bobbed up and down to the beat.

I flicked my head toward the dancers. "Well, that's something you don't see every day."

"I think just about everything here we wouldn't ever see," Nate said. "Let's find Charon and start schmoosing."

The male servants were tall and thin, their skin the deepest black. Each one wore a short white skirt held in place with a wide gold belt and carried trays loaded with drinks and food. I snagged a small square of chocolate from one of the trays and popped it in my mouth.

"Oh, my giddy aunt, that's good." I jogged after the server and commandeered three more pieces. Then walked back. "Best chocolate ever."

Nate gave me a look of irritation, but I ignored him. I never pass up good chocolate. We waded into the room, passing various entertainers, a fire-breather, belly dancers dressed like genies, jugglers, acrobats, and a guy with a monkey wearing a tutu. Though when the guy took the monkey onto the dance floor, I figured he was probably a guest and not an entertainer after all. Exotic birds perched on orange trees, and several deer pranced around the space, their hooves clacking on the marble. And I knew somewhere lurked a gigantic, hat-wearing elephant.

"There. Charon." Mara pointed to the far wall. "Surrounded by his admirers, as usual."

Dressed in purple and black velvet lounge pants and what looked like a black pirate shirt, he reclined on a gold velvet beanbag chair. To his left sprawled a scantily clad, well-endowed brunette, and between his legs stood a three-foot-tall hookah pipe. He took a long draw on the metal tip. Smoke billowed inside the green glass belly of the pipe and then circled around his head when he slowly exhaled. His glassy gaze traveled over us and a lazy grin spread across his face.

"My friends, you made it." He motioned to a group of large square cushions and beanbags. "Come, sit."

Not knowing how long we'd be there, I opted for one of the huge beanbags, so I'd be comfortable. Nate dropped beside me, nudging me over. I glared at him. "There are other cushions you could sit on."

"No, this is good," he said, laying his arm across the back behind my head. "Cozy."

I scooted over a couple of inches. "Weirdo."

Cam sat next to Mara, and she gave him the same irritated glare, but he didn't move. If I didn't know better, I'd say our partners had made a secret pact not to let Mara and I out of their sight. I guess I couldn't blame them. They liked being in charge, and the fact that they hadn't been invited to the meeting with Tabris had probably dented their egos.

I sniffed. Whatever was in the pipe smelled like cloves and burning leaves. The smoke settled around us, heavy and thick, at first making me dizzy, and then just gave me a headache. This is one of the reasons I never smoked pot in high school. While everybody else was feeling groovy, I fell asleep, nursing a headache. Back then it was a bummer. Tonight though, I was happy for the headache. It kept me focused on our goal.

The loud music made it difficult to talk and as the night wore on, the more stoned and inebriated Charon became. I couldn't imagine spending eternity doing this. What a waste.

"Let's dance." Nate stood and pulled me to my feet before I could protest. He dragged me against his body and put his mouth next to my ear. "When we come back, sit next to Charon and see if you can make progress with him."

My heartbeat quickened, and I found it difficult to focus on what Nate was saying. I couldn't help it. I always turned into a complete girl when a guy held me like that, even if just for show. Nate's gentle grip on my arms made me feel safe, as if he had everything under control. His intimate whisper brushed against my ear and sent in pleasant tingles down my neck. The way my body pressed against his made me want to lean in even more, which was ridiculous, because he was Nate, the partner who more often than not thought I was a doofus.

"Okay," my agreement rasped from me.

I let him lead me to the dance floor and pulled my hand from his. The music pounded, the bass louder than the rest of the melody. People and ghosts flailed about, and one blond head in particular bounced up and down to the beat. Tandy had been a party girl in life and was still rocking it in the afterlife.

It had been a long time since I'd danced anywhere besides alone in my living room, and I had to mentally command my feet to move. Nate shuffled from side to side, keeping his steps contained to a three-foot area. Eventually, Mara and Cam joined us, but both seemed to actually be enjoying dancing. Mara's hips swayed, and she did that sexy move women with confidence do, swooping their hands up and under her hair, and then locked her arms over her head. Cam reached and pulled Mara to him. She touched her forehead to his and lowered her arms over his head and neck before backing up.

I knew flirting when I saw it, and sparks were definitely flying between the angel and demon. I'd never asked Mara about her and Cam, figuring their relationship was a lot like Nate's and mine. From the way Cam was watching her move, there was more to their story. Or maybe they were just high from whatever was in the hookah pipe.

The song ended. Pretending to be tipsy, I stumbled toward Charon, and dropped onto the beanbag next to him. When he looked at me, I gave him a dreamy smile. "Hi."

"Leeeeeeesa, my reaper." He snorted at his own joke. "Are you enjoying my party?"

I gave him my best eyes-closed, bobble-headed nod, complete with a dopey grin. "I'm having the best time." Then I sobered. "But you really need to hire somebody to follow that elephant around with a pooper-scooper."

It took about five seconds for my suggestion to register. Then Charon burst out laughing, his head falling back to rest against the chair. "A big pooper-scooper." His arm slid down the swell of gold velvet, and he patted me hard on the back several times. "I like you, Lis."

"I like you too, Char." I propped my elbow on the beanbag and rested my cheek against my hand. "Can I call you Char? We're friends now, right?" I slurred my words a little. "Actually, we're family. Sure, it's like eleventy-million times removed, but we're still related." I poked him in the chest. "I should call you Grandpa."

"You can call me Char, but not Grandpa." His brow pinched together. "That makes me sound old."

"Okay, only Char." I smiled at him.

His eyes peered somewhere around my forehead area before drifting downward to waver on my face. It took a second before he focused on my eyes and then smiled. "Did I tell you I like you?"

"You did," I said, nodding once.

"You're not like the other reapers. You're fun."

"You're fun, too." I tapped him on the chest again and then let my hand splay across it. "And I understand."

He squinted at me. "What do you understand?"

"Why you want to retire." I toyed with the lace dangling from the neck of his shirt. "Same thing day after day. Up and down the same river. It probably got boring."

"No." He waved a finger back and forth. "The job was good. I was my own boss, great pay, but I got no respect from anybody." Turning his hand, he pointed to himself. "I was the one who saved the day when Thanatos screwed up, but did anybody say 'Thanks, Charon. We appreciate you stepping in?' No, they didn't."

"That really sucks." Even though I had a job to do I actually understood how he felt. Being a mother had a lot of the same qualities. Always putting out fires, saving the day, doing the icky stuff nobody wanted to do, and getting little to no thanks. I nodded, my fingers patting his chest. "You deserve some kudos." If I could get him talking, maybe he'd let something slip we could use. "Well, let me be the first. Thank you, Charon, for taking over the ferry and fixing a bad situation."

"You're welcome." He grinned but his gaze veered to the side of my head and then back. "Thanks for saying so. You're the only one who has so far." He held up his hands and shrugged. "Is a little appreciation too much to ask?"

"No."

"Is an atta-boy too difficult to manage every century or so?"

I shook my head. "Absolutely not."

"That's all I want." He shrugged again. "A little respect."

"You know what I say, Char?" I leaned in. "Fuck'em." Sometime the F-bomb is the only word that will do. This was one of those times. I waved my free arm in a big arc. "Fuck 'em all."

"Yeah." He imitated me, nearly smacking me in the face when his arc swung wide. "They don't deserve me."

"Let somebody else run the ferry." I pounded the beanbag chair, denting the velvet. "They can deal with all the headaches and disrespect."

He waved his hand a couple of inches in front of my face, making me rear back. "I told you," he said in an abnormally high voice. "There is nobody else."

"Well, I did hear the board bantering around the possibility of giving the job to your brother again," I lied, wanting to see his reaction.

Charon sobered and narrowed his gaze on me. "Thanatos?"

"Who cares?" For emphasis, I smacked the hump between us. "You're not going to take this disrespect anymore."

All the joy of being retired seemed to evaporate. Charon glowered at a spot across the room, and I could almost hear the wheels of his plan screeching to a stop. I glanced at Nate and gave him the let's get out of here head flick.

"Time to go." Nate crawled off the cushion and stood, holding his hands out to me. "Come on. You, too."

"Now?" I groaned, dragging it out for effect. "But I was having fun."

"We've got early classes in the morning."

"All right." Slapping my hands into his, I let Nate haul me to my feet. "Great party, Char. Thanks for inviting us." He squinted up, but I could see he wasn't paying attention, or maybe he was more out of it than I thought.

With a shrug, I strode away, fairly certain Charon hadn't noticed or didn't care. Falling in behind us, Mara and Cam followed to the elevator.

Once sealed inside, Nate pushed the lobby button and turned to us. "Well, that was interesting?"

"Did you get anything from Charon?" Mara asked.

"I don't think he actually meant to stay retired. He hasn't signed the retirement contract, doesn't seem to be in a hurry, and sure wasn't happy when I said Hal's name had been bantered around as a possibility for a ferryman."

Cam's brows lifted. "Did they?"

"No." I grinned. "But Charon doesn't know that. Even if he's determined to follow through with his decision now, we might be able to manipulate him into going back to work by making him jealous." I scrunched up my face. "I'm just saying, he seems a tad shallow."

"It's a long shot," Mara said, "but I'm willing to try anything at this point."

The door opened onto the lobby and the three of us got out, needing to catch different elevators for their floors. "I think I'll head to bed." I gave Mara a pointed stare. "I'm in room twenty-six-nineteen, so this is my elevator."

"We could all meet for breakfast in the morning." The stress she put on "meet" let me know she understood to come to my room. "What time do classes start?"

"Nine," said Nate, the convention nerd.

"How about eight o'clock in the lobby? We can decide where we want to eat then," she said.

"Sounds good." Cam punched the button of the elevator directly across from mine. "Coming, Mara?"

"Yep." She climbed in the elevator and as the door shut, gave me a single nod.

Stepping back into the car, I gave a quick wave. "See you in the morning."

"Night." Nate continued to watch me as the door closed.

Did he know something was up? Suspicious, maybe, but he had no idea Mara, and I were about to take command of the U.S.S. Styx, and several thousand souls. Boy, I sure hoped we weren't going to screw this up

# CHAPTER TEN

Where was Mara? Twenty minutes had passed since we'd parted in the lobby. Maybe I'd misread the signals, and she hadn't agreed to come to my room after all. I picked up my phone, getting ready to text her when a knock sounded on my door.

Not checking the peephole, I yanked the door open. Relief washed over me. "I didn't think you were coming."

"I couldn't get away from Cam." Mara pushed past me into the room. "Suddenly he was Mr. Get-in-touch-with-his-feelings and wanted to talk." She spun to face me. "Whatever Charon was smoking messed Cam up."

"I think it might have affected Nate, too, but I feel fine." I closed the door, bolting it and swinging the bar across. "Either that or he's suspicious. He just stood there, staring at me until the elevator closed."

"Well, we can't worry about them now." She glanced at the clock. "Midnight, we'd better get moving."

"Yeah, we have a long night ahead of us." The twenty minutes I'd spent sitting on the comfortable bed, waiting for Mara, allowed my exhaustion to catch hold. But now that she was here, my energy rallied. "Hal, we're ready."

In a rare show of punctuality, the thin beam of light appeared a second later, elongating into a door. The tension between my shoulders eased a bit. Knowing Hal was cooperating relieved some of the stress from our overwhelming task.

When the door slid open, he stood, clad in head-to-toe black. "Ladies, your chariot awaits."

Mara looked at me and smirked. "You've got to admit, he's got style."

"Yeah." I strode forward into the elevator. "Among other things." She followed me in, and within seconds we were winging our way to the river. "Any words of advice, Hal?"

He folded his arms over his chest. "Don't pick up hitchhikers."

"I didn't know that was an option," I said. "Anything else?"

"Don't forget to look up every once in a while."

"Okay, good advice." Despite the odd nature of his suggestions, I took them to heart. "Another question—how many souls can we ferry at one time?"

"The ferry will know."

"What does that mean exactly?" At this point in the game I needed more than cryptic answers.

"It means what I said." He tipped his chin down and gazed at me over his pair of square black sunglasses. "Let the ferry do its job and you'll be fine."

The urge to argue crept up my throat and stuck. Of course he didn't give me a straight answer. As a whole, I think paranormal beings liked speaking in riddles or vague references. "So, don't pick up hitchhikers, look up every so often, and let the ferry do its job." I made a check mark in the air. "Got it."

My stomach did a loopy-loop, and the elevator slowed to a stop. "We're here." Hal glided forward, and the door slid open. "Watch your step." We exited the car and started down the steep stone steps. "Ladies," Hal called. When we turned back, he propped his shoulder against the doorframe and gave us his most wicked grin. "Have fun."

With that, he eased backward into the car and the door shut, the elevator compressing into a thin pink line before vanishing. I shook my head and continued down the steps. At the arch we both slowed. I really didn't want to be blown off my feet again. Trusting that we'd already been vetted, I took a breath and walked under.

When nothing happened Mara followed, also without incident. She sauntered toward me way more confidently than earlier, when she'd practically tiptoed under the arch. "No problem."

"Chicken."

"Cautious," she countered.

The riverbank looked the same, millions of spirits wedged tightly together, only this time their grumbling was a lot louder and terser. They shouted questions at us as we made our way to the ferry. Instead of answering all of them, I figured I'd address everybody at once when we were about to board.

Thankful to be away from the mob, we climbed up the ladder and onto the deck. "Let's do a quick check that everything is ready."

Mara arched a brow. "And how do we know what we're looking for?"

"I don't know." I waved my hand absently. "Frayed lines, holes in the hull, stowaways. Anything that looks off."

"Alrighty." She slowly spun and walked in the opposite direction, scanning the deck, and then walked to the side and looked over. "All good here, Captain."

Okay, so maybe I had no idea what I was doing. It wasn't like anybody had handed me The Complete Guide to Ferrying the Dead. This was all gut instinct. I walked around of the front of the ferry, taking extra time to examine the two giant masts on either side. Besides having no idea how or when I was going to get the sails unfurled, everything seemed in order.

"All good up front." I edged my way along the thin walkway next to the hull and stopped at the back of the ferry. "How about you?"

Mara joined me. "All good here from what I can tell, and cabin space seems good too."

"Then—" I hesitated, "I guess it's time to address the passengers." I climbed onto the back of the pontoon and held up my hand. "Can I have your attention please?" All eyes focused on me and the crowd fell deathly silent. "First, I want to apologize for the wait. We had an unforeseen emergency but have found a temporary solution." I pointed to Mara. "For now, my associate and I will be captaining the ferry." A deafening cheer erupted from the mob. Appreciation, gratitude, that's what I was talking about. I

could get used to this. No wonder Charon loved his
admirers. He had a new group every time he ferried.
Holding up my hands, I shushed the souls. "If you could
enter in an orderly fashion, no pushing please, we'll get you
loaded and be on our way. For those of you who don't get
on this time, we will be making multiple trips, so please be
patient."

The excited din of the crowd escalated again. I
jumped down from the pontoon and joined Mara on the
opposite side.

"Now what?" she asked. "The barrier keeping the
souls out is still up."

"Hal said the ferry would know. I just figured that
also meant letting the people in when it was time to leave."
Suspicion that he'd been feeding me a line of malarkey
crept through me. I patted the top of the glass dome. "So,
let's do this."

Nothing happened.

"We're locked and loaded, so anchors away."

The barrier between the ferry and souls remained
solid.

I glowered at the boat. "Come on, ferry. Ready and
willing. Time to hit the road." My voice grew louder with
each phrase. "Giddy up! Move 'em out!" Frustration gripped

me. I clenched and unclenched my jaw. This was Charon's boat, and he'd probably programmed his preferences into it somehow. I gave Mara a knowing smile and said, "Let's get this party started."

Instantly the barrier disappeared, and the souls surged forward. Both of us stepped back, the instinct to get out of the way kicking in before we remembered that the souls passed through us.

The spirits poured into the belly of the ferry, leaving me with no clue, or even a close estimation, of how many souls it held. I guess that wasn't my problem. All I needed to do was get them safely to wherever we were going. Yet another mystery to be solved tonight.

"Excuse me." The spirit of the woman wearing the sequined cruise-wear running suit stepped to the side, pulling her short, round, silent husband with her. "Can we upgrade to first class? We always travel first class."

"I'm sorry, ma'am, there's only one class," I said.

"Of course there's a first class." She puffed up like an angry ostrich. "There's always a first class. You just don't want us to have it." She pulled out a spectral pen and notebook. "Who is your superior? I'm going to file a complaint about this."

I slid a glance to Mara and back to the woman. "That would be God."

"Well, he's certainly going to hear about this when I get to Heaven."

"Who says you're going to Heaven?" Mara took a step forward, flames flickering in her eyes. "I suggest you sit down and shut up before we take a detour and drop you off in a much—" She paused for effect. "—hotter location."

The notebook fell from the woman's hands, disappearing when it hit the deck. She stumbled backward, her eyes rounding to the size of gold coins. Grabbing her husband's hand, she shuffled back into line, but before the flow swallowed them, I caught the faintest smile turn up the corners of her husband's mouth.

When they were gone, I said, "Nicely done."

She gave a haughty toss of her head. "I still got it."

"And then some." I shuddered. "Remind me never to piss you off."

"Don't be silly. I'm a pussycat." The way she stated that told me she was anything but.

The stream of souls slowed. Several had made it to the edge of the ferry, but were pushed back onto the bank when the barrier sprung upward again. It was a handy tool that made doing a headcount unnecessary. The doors to the cabin slowly closed and locked, sealing the souls inside. Pressing our faces to the glass, we surveyed our passengers.

"They're fine." The scene reminded me of a cattle call but at this point, with so many souls to ferry, that's exactly what this was. "Don't you think?"

"Yeah." Mara's reply didn't instill confidence. She stepped back. "They'll be all right."

"To the bridge, then."

Skirting the dome, I watched the black watcher lap against the carved pontoons. From everything I'd read or had been told about the River Styx, dangerous things lurked under the surface. Even the shallows were treacherous. We climbed the stairs to the helm, and I stopped at the giant wheel positioned at the front. Everything looked the same. Couch, chairs, kegorator, just as we'd left it.

I was prepared to shout "Let's get this party started" again, but when I took hold of the wheel, the ferry came to life. The stings of party lights overhead winked on the stereo flashed a few times before roaring to life.

Mara slapped her hands over her ears and then yanked open the glass door of the entertainment center and cranked the volume knob to low. She leaned in, reading the cassette tape. "Party Tunes from the 60s, 70s and 80s."

Craning her neck, she looked over her shoulder at me. "On or off?"

"Off for now. I need to figure out how to drive this thing first."

She silenced the music and shut the door, joining me at the wheel. "Now what?"

"I'm not sure." I inhaled, held my breath for a second, and then whispered, "Forward."

Loud creaks emanated behinds us. While I remained rooted at the wheel, Mara investigated the noise. The sound of ropes sliding through rings hissed and thunked to the deck.

"It's the sails." Her breath caught, and she jumped back. "They're unfurling."

I twisted to see but didn't let go of the wooden spokes. More ropes slithered down the masts, losing their hold. The creaking increased. From the sound, I would have sworn the masts were about to snap.

Slowly, three, thick, wooden poles lifted away from the main mast. At the bottom was the longest pole; the next one was half the length, the top pole being the shortest. As each rose, the sails opened into huge ribbed fans. They reminded me of dragon wings or the sails on a Chinese junk.

Aged by time, the yellowed fabric expanded and stretched tight when the poles locked into place.

The sight rendered us both speechless. I'd never seen anything like this ferry, nor did I think any manmade vessel could come close to its magnificence. Toss in the whole supernatural higher purpose aspect, and the situation became awe-inspiring.

I lurched backward when the ferry began to move. My grip on the wheel tightened, and the sound of rocks scraping against wood quickly faded as we moved into deeper water. Afraid I'd screw something up, I stood wide-eyed and white-knuckled, my gaze riveted on the widening river in front of us. I was afraid to breathe, or move, or look away.

"You all right?" Mara asked, coming to stand next to me.

"Uh-huh." I didn't, well, couldn't look at her, certain if I turned my head we'd run aground or sink. "I got this."

"You're doing great." She covered my hand with one of hers and rubbed. "But I think you can relax a little."

"I am relaxed. Don't I look relaxed?"

"No, you look like one of Medusa's stone statues." Moving behind me, she gripped my wrists. "Let go of the wheel for a second."

"No." If possible, my hold tightened. "We'll crash."

"No we won't." She wedged her fingernails under my palms. "I promise."

"You don't know any more about this than I do." Thrusting my hip sideways, I tried to bump her away from me. "Those souls in there are counting on us."

"Well, that was their first mistake," she said. I gasped, my head whipping toward her. "I'm kidding, but seriously." She released me and leaned her hip against the front half-wall. "Do you think Charon stands here the entire trip, glued to the wheel?"

That did seem pretty unlikely, but he'd been running the river for millennia. "No but let me get used to steering this thing before I start slacking."

"Fair enough." She turned and pointed down river. "Styx stays like this for quite a while. It's wide and deep, so a good place to get your bearings and figure out how the ferry works." Then she straightened. "I'm going to sit over here. Yell if you need me."

"Okay." I nodded. "Good idea. I'll practice."

I spent the next half an hour or so, who knew because there was no time in this dimension, trying different steering techniques. Right off the bat it became clear that the wheel was strictly for show. No matter which way I turned it, the ferry continued on course. At one point something along the far shore caught my attention. As I concentrated on the spot, the ferry began to turn in that direction.

"Thought-controlled." I refocused on the river, and again the boat slowly veered back on course. "Brilliant."

There went the nap I'd been planning on taking, and I'd have to limit my beer consumption, or we'd end up parked on the left bank having a beach party. Feeling more confident, I focused down river and kept that course fixed in my mind. Then I slowly backed away and sat on the leather chair. Mara watched me with a querying expression, but didn't say anything. I counted to twenty and then stood to check our course.

"We're still headed in the right direction."

"I take it you figured out how this thing runs?" She stood and followed my gaze.

"Thought. If I keep focused on our course, then the ferry stays on course." I sat down again. "Once I know the river better and with a little practice, I should be able to relax more."

"What about the wheel?" Mara took her seat again. "Is it important?"

"Only to Charon's ego." I propped my feet up on the coffee table, resting my elbows on the wide rolled arms of the chair. "It's for show—doesn't guide anything."

"I wonder if he's overcompensating for something."

"No doubt." Still not completely comfortable putting the ferry on autopilot, I stood and took my place at the helm again. "Considering how many reapers there are in the world, I think he overcompensates in a lot of areas of his life."

"I don't even want to think about that." Mara rested her hand on the front wall and pointed down river. "Around that next bend the waters become more turbulent."

"Are there rapids or rocks I need to watch for?"

"No, nothing like that, but…" She shifted from one foot to the other, her gaze darting downstream and back to me. "Don't slow down. Actually—" She hesitated a second. "—if you can speed up some after we turn that would be best."

"Why?" My heartbeat quickened. The small amount of calm confidence I'd gained evaporated. "What's there?"

"It's nothing, really. I mean…I'm not a hundred percent certain. It's been a long time since I've been in this area of Styx, but I think—" She swallowed hard. "I think that's where an abyss of lost souls is."

"An abyss of lost souls?" Panic raced through me. "Is it dangerous?"

"Ehhhh." Her face scrunched into an *I don't want to lie, but I don't want to tell you the horrifying truth, either* grimace, and her shoulders shrugged, holding near her ears. "Maybe."

"You mean yes, don't you? When has an abyss not been dangerous?" I gripped the wheel, my breath coming in short pants. "You can't say the word abyss without it not being scary. Abyss of Lost Souls—terrifying. Abyss of Magic—nope, not going to mess around in there. Abyss of Kittens." My voice grew uncontrollably loud. "Still scary!" I glared at Mara. "How did those souls get lost, anyway?"

"I don't think we should get all caught up in how those souls got sucked into the abyss." She patted my hand and her voice took on a soothing lilt. "Let's just maintain a positive attitude and keep this ferry moving." Her petting stopped, and she squeezed my fingers. "As fast as you can, because I'll be honest, there is no coming back from that." She pointed toward the water. "Once lost, always lost."

My grip tightened on the wheel. "Like…forever?"

"Forever and ever."

"Right." Even though the gigantic wheel did nothing as far as steering the ferry, holding onto it helped me focus on our course. "I can do this."

"Maybe I should warn the passengers and ask them to stay calm."

I nodded, but didn't take my eyes off the river. "Good idea."

Mara opened a small door near the stairs and extracted a microphone. "Attention passengers." Her voice reverberated from speakers placed around the ferry. "In a few minutes the water might become a tad rough. We ask that you remain calm and seated until we're through this turbulent stretch of river." She sounded like a flight attendant. Her smooth announcement even calmed me slightly. "When we're safely through, I'll let you know and you'll be able to move around the cabin again. Thank you for your cooperation." She replaced the mic and smirked. "Like a pro."

"Warning the passengers was the easy part." I flicked my head toward the bend. "Now it gets tricky."

She joined me at the wheel. We each gripped a spindle and leaned forward, stretching to get a glimpse of the river ahead. When the ferry began its slow turn, I expected to see roiling water. Instead, Styx was glassy calm. I gave Mara a questioning glance, but she shook her head.

"They'll come," she whispered. "Wait for it."

"Okay, that was super creepy and not helpful at all." Refocusing on the stretch of river, I slowly blew out the breath I'd been holding and urged the ferry faster. "Go baby, go."

The pontoons split the water, gliding almost as if on top. Neither of us spoke, each waiting for the slightest hint of turbulence. Mara hadn't expounded on what connected rough water and the abyss, but I'd seen enough movies to figure it out.

A muffled thump sounded from the underside of the right pontoon, but the ferry didn't so much as rock. The breath froze in my throat, and both of us inched forward to peer down at the water slushing between the floats. Thankfully, unlike a catamaran, the ferry had a two-foot wall around the deck. Anything trying to get on the boat would have to climb over the sides.

Another thump resonated from under the pontoon, and then another. My hand shot out, and I gripped Mara's arm, but I couldn't take my eyes off the river. The water began to roil, both around the ferry and up ahead. In the overcast light, I thought I saw an arm reach out of the water and then disappear into the inky depths.

"Holy crap." I released Mara and latched onto the front wall. "Was that a person?"

"If you can call them that." Mara pointed to the left pontoon. "And there's another one."

Before I could utter a curse, two more arms shot out of the water and grabbed onto the ferry. Though subtle, I felt us slow down. "No—no—no." I leaned over the edge. "They're trying to get on board. We need to get them off."

"I'll do it." Mara grabbed my shoulders and gave me a solid shake. "You need to make us go faster."

I nodded and moved back to the wall. Instead of using the stairs, Mara vaulted over the front wall and landed on her feet. She broke into a run, snagging a spiked pole from its holder against the left mast, and jogged to the front of the ferry.

"Man, that was so cool," I muttered.

I couldn't take my eyes off her as she spun and jabbed at the ghostly white and blue mottled limbs. The heavy thuds hammered the underside of the ferry, making it rock. Cries from the passengers erupted every time we were knocked to the side.

"Lisa!" I focused on Mara, but was having a hard time breathing—or thinking. Nearly paralyzed with fear, I couldn't move, let alone focus. "We need to go faster!" Without looking, she swung the pole, catching one of the invaders across the throat as it rose above the wall. "Snap out of it!"

Right, I needed to shake it off, and we needed more speed. My breath huffed out of me but at least I was starting to think clearly again. I picked a calm spot on the horizon, and leaning forward over the wall's edge, willed the ferry faster. The pull on my body was instantaneous, and the boat surged forward. I could do this. We were going to be okay.

Mara's scream wrenched the air. My gaze snapped to her an instant before the white hand that was wrapped around her wrist yank and pulled her over the side.

# CHAPTER ELEVEN

"Mara!" Desperation and panic propelled me down the stairs and to the spot where she'd disappeared. I leaned over the side, not considering that I could meet the same fate. Among the chalky wet limbs, fighting to keep her grip on the edge of the ferry, glinted blood red fingernails. "My God, Mara!"

Scooting forward, I grappled for her wrist, but the lost souls blocked my attempts, clawing at me. Sharp nails gouged deep furrows in my arms and blood trickled down my wrist. Pain shot through my arms, but I ignored it, bending lower. "Hold on! Don't let go!"

Tears burned and filled my eyes. I blinked them away, not wanting to give into the fear and desperation. The long spear rolled toward me and knocked against my boot. I wiggled back enough to grab it, and then swung it over my head, bringing it down hard on the white arms. The sickening crunch of bone meeting metal ricocheted through me. My stomach heaved and vomit rose up my throat, but I didn't stop. Again, I jabbed, sending one of the lost souls melting into the blackness.

Enough space cleared for me to reach Mara. Not waiting, I tossed the pole aside and clamped my hand around her wrist, bracing my knees against the wall. I threw myself backward. She lifted from the water, but grotesque white hands clawed at her, wrapping around her neck and threatening to drag her down again. My legs burned with the effort of holding steady.

"Don't let go, Lisa!" Mara's face crested the edge of the ferry, real fear mirrored in her eyes. "Come on. Pull!"

The fact that she was a demon and scared shook me to my core. My footing slipped and we both scream as she dropped into the water. Adrenaline surged through me. I would not lose her. With every ounce of strength I had I heaved back and dragged her chest level. Her arm released the edge of the boat and clamped on to the low wall.

I dropped to my knees, first wrapping one arm around her torso, and then released her wrist to grab her with both hands. She was soaked and my fingers slipped, loosening my hold. I jerked her against my body and locked my hands around my wrists. Dragging her out of the water was like trying to land a halibut. Unseen hands below the water yanked at her legs and it was all I could do to hold on.

Inch by inch, I worked her over the ledge. Her waist had just cleared the wall when two pale bodies burst from the water and latched onto Mara's thighs. I fell forward, my hips smashing against the edge of the wall. A jolt of fire spread across my hipbones and down my legs. If we got through this, I'd have some war wounds to show for my efforts.

Lower and lower, they dragged her. My cheek pressed against her as I struggled to hold on to Mara. When my grip slipped, a panicked cry whimpered from her. I wouldn't lose her. Determination, fear, and anger swelled inside me. My vision narrowed on my friend. A surge of power I'd only felt once before sparked through me, setting my skin on fire.

I. Would. Not. Lose. Her.

Ribbons of black vapor swirled around me. They extended and thickened, arching to the front of my body. Fear and desperation drained away. My only thought was saving Mara. When the sooty veil brushed across one of the arms holding tightly to her, blue-black fire burned across the marbled skin. Screams erupted from the creature and it released her, sinking back into Styx.

I slowly rose, bringing Mara with me, burning away the remaining lost souls that held on to her legs. We stood, gazes locked, the black cloak inching around us. Ageless and dark, her soul called to me for release and I needed to reap her, because that's what I was meant to do. She opened her mouth as if to speak but the words strangled in her throat. No more loneliness. Sweet oblivion.

"Don't." The single word, spoken so quietly by Mara, snapped me out of my trance.

Though I couldn't look away from her, my mind screamed at me to let go. I would not reap her soul. Inch by inch, I forced my hands to loosen, and finally fall to my sides. The black garlands of vapor thinned and evaporated, releasing me from its hold. I took a step back, my breathing still shallow, but my thoughts a lot clearer.

"Sorry." I filled my lungs and slowly exhaled. "That happens sometimes with paranormal beings." Actually, it had only occurred one other time when I was reaping the soul of a rather nasty vampire. She, however, did not get away. I propped my fists against my hips. "Whew." A weak chuckled warbled out. "That was close."

"Yeah, it was." She shook her head. "I don't know what scared me more, thinking I was going to be dragged into an abyss by a horde of groping spirit zombies, or getting reaped by you." Wariness lingered in her gaze even though she didn't move away from me. "You were seriously spooky with that black cloak stuff and eerie silver glowing eyes."

"My eyes were glowing?" Obviously, I'd never had a mirror handy when this paranormal phenomenon happened, so I had no idea that I transformed. "I thought it was just the black, vapory thing."

"No, they were shining like—" She hesitated, her eyes staring into the distance.

"Like what?"

"Sometimes Cam's eyes do that." When she looked at me, it was with an expression so filled with sadness a lump formed in my throat. "It's a thing angels do with demons, showing us what being fallen has cost." Her voice dropped to a whisper and broke when she added, "What we lost."

Fallen? I'd learned stories of fallen angels when I was a kid, especially Lucifer, but I'd never lumped Mara into that group. She didn't fit the stereotypical evil I'd believed demons to be. Then again, a widowed mother of three bore no resemblance to Hollywood's Angel of Death. Despite her demon label, Mara was my friend and I could see the regret she was battling. I'd also felt the desolation of her soul. So what could I say in the face of such an epic loss?

"We all have stuff, Mara. Things we did or should have done but didn't. Things done to us that we had no control over. Regrets. Loss. Shame. I don't know your story, but what I do know is that you do have a soul."

"No, I don't, Lisa." Her eyes bore into me. "I lost it the day I fell."

"No, you didn't." Seeing the conviction in her eyes, I stepped toward her and took hold of her hands. "That's why I had that crazy reaper reaction. If you were an empty shell that wouldn't have happened." I inhaled, shaking my head. "I'll admit, your soul is rather dark and desolate, but I think that's because you have no hope."

Her fingers tightened on mine. "Hope about what?"

"Hope that you'll be forgiven. Hope that you deserve a second chance. But don't you see, you've already got a second chance. You're doing good work with GRS. They need you and your unique talents, and…" I gave her hands a shake. "You need them."

"I've always believed when I fell, I lost my soul." Her grasp loosened, and I let go of her hands. She turned and walked to the edge of the ferry, staring down river. "I can't believe it."

"Well, believe it. I wouldn't lie." I leaned forward and grabbed a handful of wet shirt, tugging her backward. "And don't make me save your life again just to prove it."

"Good point." Holding out her arms, Mara looked down at her dripping clothes. "Damn it, those bastards tore my pants."

The seriousness of the moment passed, and I was glad. The whole regrets, lost soul, realization thing was exhausting. "At least they didn't get your boots."

"I would have dived back in for those." She shook out her arms, flipping water everywhere. "You don't mess with my shoes."

"The universal law." I glanced behind us. The river had settled back to a glassy calm, the only ripples stirred up from the ferry. Facing forward, I scanned the river ahead. Somehow, during the watery attack, I'd managed to keep the ferry moving forward. Not very fast, but enough to get us out of the danger zone. Maybe I did have a knack for this job. "How far until we get there?" It seemed like we'd been on the river for hours and I still didn't know where there was. "And, are there any other hot spots I should be aware of?"

"Not far, maybe another mile, and not that I can remember." Water splattered against the deck when Mara twisted the bottom of her shirt. "Still, that doesn't mean there aren't other obstacles."

"All right, I'm going to the bridge to get a better view. I don't want any more surprises."

"Good idea." Mara circled her finger over her head. "I'm going to do a walk-around to make sure nothing got damaged."

"Don't get too close to the edge," I said, heading to the stairs.

While she made the rounds, I took my place at the wheel and urged the ferry faster. A light breeze brushed across me, bringing with it the fresh scent of rain mixed with the sharp tang of sulfur. The only trees I'd seen reminded me of tortured souls, pleading for mercy, their dark barren branches twisting upward from gnarled trunks. No birds circled in the sky. This was the land of the dead, gray, and lifeless.

Thankfully, the rest of the trip was uneventful. Nobody tried to kill us or destroy the ferry—not even an odd ripple broke the surface of Styx. At the final bend I guided the boat around the curve and sighed with relief when I saw the long dock jutting from the point where the river split in two.

About a hundred yards from the docking bay my mental control of the ferry faded. We glided forward, slowing until the upward curves of the pontoons bumped against a row of floating wooden barrels attached to the scaffolding of the dock, stopping us.

The clanking of chains and creaking wood sounded behind the ferry, drawing us toward the noise. A plank walkway extended along the back, in essence blocking in the ferry. Unsure what to do next, I stopped beside the glass dome and waited for something else to happen.

When nothing did, I glanced at Mara. "What are we supposed to do?"

She crossed her arms and leaned against the bulkhead. "I have no idea."

"Halt!" The word echoed through the air, making me jump. I snapped to attention. Footsteps thundered against the creaking dock and a few seconds later a beefy-gladiator looking guy stomped along the walkway and stopped behind the ferry. A leather harness crisscrossed over his hulking shoulders, and what I could only describe as leather briefs, hugged his square hips. His head was bald, except for a top-knot ponytail, and he glared at us from black, deep-set eyes. "Who are you?"

"Hey," I plastered on a friendly smile, giving him a little wave. "I'm Lisa and this is Mara. We're filling in for Charon."

If possible, his scowl deepened. He crossed his arms over his chest, causing his biceps to bulge, and settled into a wide-legged stance. "Where is he?"

"In Vegas." I made air quotes. "On vacation."

He harrumphed, stared for a few more seconds, and then straightened. "Get those souls off the boat."

"Uh-huh." I nodded, as if I knew what I was talking about. "How?"

"Normally, I do it for Charon." I think he smiled, but it looked like he was baring his fangs at me. "For a price."

"How much?" I'd left my purse in the hotel room but doubted I had enough, even with the extra six hundred dollars still remaining. Did they even use dollars in the netherworld?

"A bag of gold."

"What are we talking here?" I held my hands a few inches apart. "Sandwich-bag size?"

His smile turned upward on one side to a sneer. "Fifty pieces."

The saying you can't take it with you didn't seem to apply to afterlife employees. When I reaped vampire souls

in northern Alaska, I had to give Hal gold to transport them.
I think now I was seeing the trickle-down effect.

"We don't have any gold," I said. Nor did I know
where I was going to get some. There was the big bowl of
coins at the arch entrance but doubted I could take what I
needed. That seemed too easy—and things were never easy.
Still, I had no idea how to unseal the cabin doors and release
the passengers. He started to turn away, and I panicked.
"But we'll bring double on our next trip."

I could feel Mara's gaze burning into me, but I
didn't look at her. If he agreed and opened the doors at least
I'd know how. Getting the souls ferried was our first
concern. I'd worry about paying him back later.

"One hundred pieces of gold?" He asked. "On your
next trip?"

"Actually, it would be one hundred-and-fifty pieces,
since we'd be bringing another load." At this point, I didn't
want to screw things up by lying. I was already vulnerable
enough in the netherworld and adding a strike against me by
cheating this behemoth wouldn't help our situation. "One
hundred for this trip and fifty for the next."

His expression dulled a little, as if doing the math in
his head—or trying to. After several seconds he jabbed a

meaty finger at me. "One hundred and fifty, not a single coin less."

"I promise."

A grunt vibrated from him before he tromped down the walkway and climbed a rickety ladder. Groans emanated from the scaffolding when he hauled himself onto the narrow ledge. He turned sideways and scooted along the foot-wide rise, rounded the corner, and stopped at an opening in the framework, directly in the front of the ferry between the angel and demon. Mara and I followed his progress. He knelt and picked up an iron pole resting at his feet and then stood again. Holding on to the scaffolding rail with one hand, he leaned forward, balancing the iron pole in the other, and fit it across the palms of the statues. I waited for the doors to open but nothing happened.

Hulk—that's what I'd mentally named him—reared back on the platform and then leaped, grabbing the pole with both hands.

"What the—" My jaw went slack, and I was, unable to finish my sentence.

Like an agile gymnast, he lifted his knees and flipped upside down, locking his legs over the top of the bar. Every muscled across his back rippled. The harness pulled so tight against his skin I expected the straps to break. With sheer arm and abdominal strength, he pulled himself into a sitting position on top of the bar. He braced his hands on either side of his body and lifted his butt six inches off the bar before dropping onto it again.

The sound of wood creaking groaned from the statues. He lifted and dropped again. Metal scraping against metal screeched and then stopped. One last time Hulk fell on to the bar. The arms of the angel and demon slowly descended. When the bar reached waist-level it locked into place. He jumped onto the pontoon, taking the iron pole with him, and followed it all the way to the far end. From there he jumped back onto the dock and strode away. Like clockwork, the doors of the cabin slid open, and the souls filed out in an orderly fashion.

I spun toward Mara. "What kind of a crazy-ass process is that?"

"Now we know why Charon pays him."

"Who the hell do they think I am, Nadia Comaneci? Even if I wanted to open the doors I couldn't even lift the bar." I lowered my voice. "Where are we going to get a hundred and fifty pieces of gold?"

"From the toll dish at the arch?" She drummed her fingers against the glass. "Or Tabris. He'll have to give us the gold if he wants us to ferry."

"Yeah, it's a job expense." That made the idea of commandeering the gold from the arch more palatable. "It's not stealing."

"Right. We can't do the job without it," she said, backing me up like a good partner in crime should.

When the last soul had disembarked, the arms of the statues cranked upward to their lifted position and the gangway slid back. As if by magic, the ferry drifted out of the slip and slowly spun in preparation for our return trip. At a hundred yards out, I took control of the ferry again and propelled us forward.

"Come on." I headed for the bridge. "I need a drink."

"Great idea," Mara said.

The return trip seemed to take a fraction of the time and was smooth sailing. Even over the abyss the river remained silent and still—not a single bump. Probably because we didn't have any souls to steal. We poured a couple of beers and sprawled on the deck, leaning against the bridge wall.

"Cheers." I held up my cup. "To our first delivery."

Mara lifted her beer. "May the next cruise be as boring as hell."

We clicked the plastic rims and drank deeply to our success. Not only had we triumphed in the battle of the abyss, we hadn't lost a single soul, including our own, and delivered them safely to their destination. We were awesome—truly amazing.

I heaved a sigh. "Only several million souls to go."

# CHAPTER TWELVE

Climbing the stone steps to the elevator made my legs burn worse than any Zumba class I'd ever taken. I latched onto the waistband of Mara's pants, hoping she'd pull me up the stairs. We'd done two more trips with nothing worse than complaining passengers to deal with. Whatever can of reaper-demon-whoop-ass we opened on those white bastards of the abyss must have made an impression.

And thankfully, we hadn't been set upon by the hounds of Hell when we pilfered two hundred gold coins from the toll bowl. Next time I was bringing my wheelie carry-on. My plan was to fill it up and leave it on the ferry. When we got low, I'd just roll the suitcase to the arch and replenish our supply. Preparation and organization were the keys to our success.

"You two look tired." Hal leaned against the frame of the elevator, arms crossed, decked out in gauzy light yellow pants and shirt, looking very fresh and rested. "But alive."

"That we are," Mara said, stopping at the top and pulling me up. "Barely."

I shuffled past him and into the elevator. At the corner I turned and slid down the wall, drawing my knees to my chest to sit in a fetal position. This wasn't a normal tired. My soul felt drained and my spirit depleted. Though I didn't voice my worry, I wondered if a little of my life had been drained from me tonight—just like Katrina's. "Home, Hal, before I pass out from exhaustion."

Mara joined me, squatting in the opposite corner. "I know I'm a badass demon and all, but dealing with thousands of chatty dead people nearly sucked the life right out of me." Her head dropped onto her knee. "I'm not even joking."

"Then let's get you home." Hal stepped inside and closed the door. "So we can do this all again tomorrow night."

We both groaned, but I didn't have the energy to lift my head to glare at him. I must have dozed off. It felt like I'd shut my eyes a few seconds ago and now Mara was pulling me to my feet.

"Come on, Killer." She guided and pushed me out of the elevator. "Thanks, Hal."

"Yeah, thanks, Hal." I gave him a limp-armed wave. "See you tomorrow."

"Sleep tight, ladies." Before the door slid closed he added, "I'm glad you survived."

The elevator compressed into a thin pink line and shrank to a tiny dot before vanishing. "Wow," I said, "I think he likes us."

"That's a good thing." Mara's hand hovered on the handle of my door. "We need him." She pulled it open. "And we need to be at breakfast at eight o'clock. Don't forget."

I glanced at the clock. "That's only eight hours from now. Actually seven hours and forty-five minutes. But then I need to shower, so really seven hours."

"Then I suggest you get to bed and get your beauty sleep." She started to pull the door closed but stopped. "Hey, thanks again for saving my life." Her gaze locked with mine. "Nobody has ever done that for me before."

"You would have done the same thing for me."

She scrunched up her face as if contemplating that. "I'd like to think I would have."

"You would have." I gave her a cocky nod. "We're friends."

Though she didn't reply, she did smile and nod once before closing the door.

I took a quick, very hot shower to rinse off any traces of river water and cleaned the cuts on my arms, and then fell into bed. My party girl roommate must have still been shaking her stuff at Charon's. For that, I was eternally grateful. As it were, I'd only get seven hours of sleep after being awake for nearly twenty-four hours. I was guessing a full day, but who knew since there was no time in the netherworld.

After checking the alarm was set for seven, I shut off the light, and curled up under the covers. The steady hum of the air conditioner relaxed me, but I didn't fall asleep right away. My mind insisted on sifting through the events on the ferry. The passengers had been the easiest part, and I bet Tabris knew that when he'd sent Mara and I to check out the situation earlier this afternoon. We hadn't really known what to expect, and even if I had known what dangers waited for us, I don't think I could have refused to ferry. Tabris had made sure there was a lot of back-up authority in the room.

Having only done three runs on Styx, I already understood Charon's need to periodically take a break. I couldn't even fault him for wanting to retire—if he truly did. Maybe it was because I was human, but ferrying wasn't a job I wanted to do for very long. Maybe being a supernatural being meant the effects of the Underworld were less...soul sucking.

At some point during my recounting of the day I drifted off to sleep and woke to the annoying beep of the alarm at seven o'clock the next morning. When I rolled over to shut it off an all-over ache resonated through my body.

"Owww," I groaned. The shrill alarm pierced my skull. I swiped for the clock but missed the snooze button. Muscles I hadn't used since my physical testing to be a reaper cried out in protest. Tiny muscles under my armpits throbbed when I lifted my arm again. Unable to keep my arm raised, it dropped like a block of concrete onto the clock, silencing the alarm. "Somebody put me out of my misery."

Nobody appeared to answer my plea, which meant I'd have to get up. Using my feet, I kicked off the covers. Well, not really kicked them off, more like grabbed the blankets with my toes and worked them down my body. My toes were the only things that didn't hurt. Once free from the bonds of my sheet, I rolled to the side of the bed, and let my legs drop over the side. Pain radiated across my ribs and through my abdominal muscles. It took all my strength, but I gritted my teeth and pushed to a stand. Though I'd taken a shower last night, I shuffled into the bathroom for another. Hot water and ibuprofen were the first order of the day.

I peeled off my T-shirt and set it on the bathroom counter, not wanting to have to bend to pick it up later. I cringed at my reflection. Large purple bruises spread across my hipbones from where I'd hit the wall when trying to pull Mara out of the river, and scabbed-over gashes slashed across my forearms. Of course, saving her life had been worth the injury—of course it had.

Some of my grumpy mood lessened with the pulsing massage of the hot jets. I rubbed the raven pendant hanging at my neck, hoping for some of its healing magic. The familiar tingle skittered across my skin, followed by what felt like the gentle brush of wings. The aches eased a bit more, but certainly didn't vanish. I'd learned this little trick by accident after my physical testing. The pendant took injuries to a tolerable level.

Feeling fifty percent better than when I woke, I dressed in comfortable clothes and opted for minimal makeup and hairstyling. At a quarter to eight my phone dinged with a text from Nate, saying we were meeting for breakfast in the same restaurant as yesterday. I spent a few minutes gathering things I thought I'd need for the day: my phone, my conference badge—pain reliever.

At eight on the dot, I strode into the restaurant. Nate, Cam, and Mara were already there. She watched me with a cross between sympathy and exhaustion.

"Morning." My purse slid from my grasp to the floor and I slowly lowered to the chair, trying my best to ignore my protesting abs and thighs. I looked at Mara. "Sleep well?"

"Meh." She held out a hand rocking it side to side. "How about you?"

"The same." I pulled the carafe of coffee to me and poured. "I must have slept wrong. I'm a little achy today."

"I slept like a baby," Nate said.

"Me, too." Cam's smile was all bright and cheery. I wanted to smack him. "Usually I don't sleep well in hotels, but for some reason I'm having no problem here."

"I didn't think angels needed to sleep." I swirled my spoon around my cup, mixing in the creamer. "Don't you have unlimited energy?"

"Not when we take a physical form," he said.

And what a physical form it was.

"Same for us," Mara added. "Demons have all the same weaknesses as a human: hunger, injuries, libido."

"Wow, I'd never thought about that." I took a sip of coffee and set the cup on the table. "You learn something new every day."

"Sometimes you learn a lot of new things." Mara grinned at me.

"Indeed."

Conversation flowed easily through breakfast. We discussed our plans for the day. Nate was hot for a couple of seminars on guerilla tactics for reaping violent souls. Cam said he had a few non-Charon cases to follow up on. At some point I figured Mara and I would be summoned to Tabris to give a report, but until then we decided to do more shopping. Today the vendors serving GRS opened their booths in the Expo Center. I couldn't wait to check out the latest technology for grim reapers.

We flashed our badges at the security guard stationed at the door, but he stopped us, giving our pictures a closer look. The man towered over both of us, his massive shoulders rolling forward like a gorilla's. Our badges looked tiny in his wide hand, and I couldn't help shifting under his dark, scrutinizing gaze. After giving us a thorough once or twice over, he let us pass into grim reaper heaven.

I'd assumed there were gadgets and baubles for those of us dealing with the afterlife, but I'd completely underestimated the elaborate array of products. Everything from clothing to spirit-tracking devices was available for purchase.

The first booth we stopped at displayed clothing. I picked up a pair of black mittens. Thick fleece lined the inside, and the outer shell felt like a cross between neoprene and rubber.

"Aren't those nice?" asked a woman dressed in a camo tank top and army green cargo pants. Her frizzy mass of dishwater brown curls sat piled on top of her head and secured by a green scarf. "They've got a thin layer of ectoplating between the lining and outer shell."

"Ectoplating?" I assumed that had something to do with ghosts.

"It's the newest thing." She slipped the mittens on and held her hands in front of her. "You can wear these when it's cold out and not have to worry about taking off your gloves to hold on to a spirit. You just—" She lunged forward, as if catching a spirit. "Grab the ghost and the ectoplating magnetizes to the soul. No holding on or gripping required." She gave a violent shake. "No matter how hard they fight, they can't break free."

"What if you've only got them by one hand?"
Though spirits naturally stuck to me, there were times when
I'd had trouble holding onto them. If they were stronger, the
soul could break free. "For instance, if I was driving a
scooter?"

"Because our ectoplating is ten times stronger than
the old brand, you could easily hold two full-size spirits."
The woman's eyes rounded with excitement. She really
believed in her product. "Or three smaller ones with one
hand."

"What if the spirit is wet or has fallen in a vat of
oil?"

Mara cocked her head, her brow pinching together.
"Seriously?"

I shrugged. "You never know. Remember who I
reap."

Her expression relaxed. "You've got a point."

"Oil, water, snow—" The saleswoman waved her
hand. "None of that lessens the magnetizing effect."

These mittens were something I could use. Over the
last few months I'd traveled to remote villages to reap souls.
The planes were small and cold. The villages rustic. I
needed versatile clothing "How much?"

"Forty-five dollars." When I started to set the pair back on the table, she added, "But the conference price is thirty dollars, fifty for two pairs."

I pursed my lips and narrowed my gaze on the mittens. Of course I was going to buy two pairs. I would have shelled out forty-five for one. Routinely I paid upwards of twenty-five dollars for the gloves I buy my kids, which they lose within a week. After a few seconds I nodded. "I'll take two pairs."

"Excellent." She dropped the mittens into a plain white bag. "Be sure to tell your friends about them."

"I will." I handed her a fifty and took the bag. "Thanks."

"Sucker," Mara mumbled as we walked away.

"Even if they don't work, at least my hands will stay warm."

The booths stretched endlessly down the center and spread in a maze of tempting treats. Mara bought a silver Wingblade and demonstrated it for me. The tips of two serrated blades curled in opposite directions, forming an S, and could catch an attack from behind or front. When closed, four finger holes allowed her to wear it on her hand like brass knuckles. The Wingblade was intimidating, the efficiency with which Mara wielded it—terrifying.

We tried out the latest spirit tracker software and GPS systems, checked out mirrors designed to trap demons, and contemplated a Tibetan protection amulet. But after an hour of browsing, neither of us had purchased anything else. We worked our way down the last aisle near the exit and were about to leave when my gaze fell upon the most beautiful sight. The iconic weapon of a grim reaper and the missing piece of my soul.

"I want." Like a tractor beam, the gleaming scythe drew me in. We stopped at the display rack of hand carved handles and blades of varying size. "They're beautiful."

"Custom made," the vendor said. He touched a pole with skulls carved along the handle. "You can pair this handle with any blade. If you want something a bit more feminine, we have carved lilies, or maybe something simple like this black polished handle." He picked up a cylinder that was slightly larger than a beer bottle. "We even have our compact model."

He held the cylinder in front of him and pressed the silver button at the side. From either end a wooden pole extended, and from there, another length at the bottom shot out. A thin curved metal blade snapped out from the upper section and locked in place, creating a scythe a little shorter than me.

"Whoa." I took the weapon from him. It was surprisingly light and my hand fit around it perfectly. "That is so cool."

"What do you do with it?" Mara asked.

"What do you mean what do you do with it? It's a scythe." I swung it in a shallow arc, not wanting to damage anything or anybody. "It's a reaper's signature tool."

"Well…" The vendor gave me a sheepish grin. "Mainly they're for show or decorative purposes." A nervous laugh escaped him, and he gestured at me. "I'm sure you already know how reapers obtain their scythes."

I did not. Until I saw the gleaming weapons, I'd basically thought most folklore about grim reapers was untrue and hadn't given the scythe a second thought. "Refresh our memories."

"It's bestowed on them, either inherited from a family member or after performing an act of epic proportions at great cost to themselves." His head bobbed up and down. "From what I hear there's only a few hundred true scythes in existence."

"Oh, right, I remember reading about that," I lied, handing the scythe back to the guy, the gleaming weapon losing its appeal. I didn't want a fake, something to hang on my wall, which undoubtedly would raise questions. I wanted a real, working, personally-bestowed-upon-me scythe. "Thanks for showing this to us. It's amazing."

"You bet." He twisted the base, and the weapon contracted. "I'll be here until Sunday if you change your mind."

"Sounds good," I said. That was my stock answer, which meant I wouldn't be back but didn't want to be rude. We headed toward the exit. "I wonder if Charon has a scythe."

"You would think so if he's the ferryman," Mara said. "He's always holding one in all the artwork I've seen."

"I think I'll ask Nate when I see him."

"Ms. Carron? Ms. Mara?" a voice said from behind us. We turned to see Tabris's tall assistant standing a few feet away. "Mr. Tabris would like to speak with you if it's convenient."

I glanced at Mara and she nodded. "Okay, we'll head there now."

"Very good." He bent in a shallow bow. "I'll let him know you're on your way."

We strolled across the open area and when I glanced back, the guy was gone. The fact that he suddenly disappeared didn't faze me was a testament to how numb I was becoming to the paranormal world. Things that would have made my jaw drop a year ago now barely made a blip on my radar.

"I wonder what Tabris wants," I said.

"Probably wants to know if we ran into any problems." She glanced at me. "What should we tell him?"

"The truth." We turned down the hall, passing several convention attendees headed to the Expo Center. "He probably knows everything already."

"And we should mention the gold. Make sure it's okay that we used the toll money." We stopped in front of the golden doors. Mara lowered her voice. "I'm also going to ask him to reimburse us for the clothes."

I knocked. "Especially since your pants got ruined."

A growl rumbled from her. "I freakin' loved those pants."

The door opened before I could agree, not surprisingly by Tabris's assistant.

"You sure do get around," I said, entering the room.

He smiled. Unlike his usual placating expression, mischief laced this grin. It was the first time I noticed the intelligence in his eyes. Normally he drifted in and out, only noticed for a second. No doubt he'd overheard more confidential conversations and knew more secrets simply by being a fly on the wall.

"Ladies." Tabris skirted the gold desk, a white smile gleaming against his coppery skin. "I'm anxious to hear how your first adventure went. Smoothly, I hope."

Mara and I glanced at each other. "Not too bad," I said, looking back at Tabris. "We had a few bumps in the road, but nothing we couldn't handle."

"Excellent." He turned to Mara. "And you had no problem following the river?"

"Nope." She shook her head. "It hasn't changed much. A few more branches off the main stream, but everything seems basically the same. We did run into a situation when we docked at the juncture."

"But we handled it," I said, jumping in to reassure him. "It seems Charon pays the guy fifty gold pieces to open the cabin once they dock."

"We didn't have any gold on the first trip," Mara said, picking up the story. "So we took it from the toll plate at the arch."

"I hope that's okay." I tensed, unsure what his reaction would be.

"You may spend your money however you wish," he said.

Relief washed through me. "Okay, great, I didn't want to break—" His statement suddenly sunk in. "Don't you mean the money, or Charon's money?" An unsure giggle slipped from me. "You said 'your', sounding like you meant it's my money."

"That's right." He slipped his hands into his front pockets, pinning me with a coppery stare. "When you passed through the arch and were vetted, you officially became the new ferryman, or in this case, ferrywoman. At that moment, all rights and benefits of the job reverted to you—including the gold."

The breath stopped in my throat and I choked out, "You're joking?"

"I'm dead serious," he said, smiling.

My gaze cut to Mara, and she appeared to be equally surprised. "I guess that whole clothing reimbursement issue is solved."

"Wait." I followed Tabris to his desk. "If I'm the one now getting paid, what about Charon?"

"Unless he signs a new contract and returns to the ferry, his wages are cut off."

"Okay, but isn't he going to be a tad pissed off about that?" The thrill of being a hell of a lot richer warred with the fear of facing Charon when he found out.

"It doesn't matter," Tabris said. "What's done is done." He scooted the white leather chair up to the desk.

"The gold is exchanged and will be transferred into your account." He slid an index card toward me. "You authorized direct deposit when you were hired. I hope it's all right that we used that same account."

"Way all right." I looked at Tabris. "What about Mara?"

"The position is only authorized for one person. Any arrangements for compensation for her will have to come out of your pay."

"Of course, we'll split the money." It didn't matter that I was the designated driver. Without Mara by my side, I would have died at the abyss, not to mention lost all the souls. Hell, I probably wouldn't have even managed getting into the elevator with Hal. I grabbed her arms. "And we are so buying you some new pants."

"Sweet," Mara said, nodding.

"Also," Tabris said, interrupting the list of ways I was going to pamper Mara and myself. "Nate updated me about last night and Charon. As I'm sure you've already figured out, finding him was the easy part."

"Yeah, he's being very stubborn." I didn't mention the chat I'd had with him, or that I'd planted the seed they'd gotten somebody else to ferry. Most certainly the board of directors hadn't told us everything, either. "Any suggestions on how we get him to agree to go back?"

"Not yet. We're batting around some ideas." He smiled at me, but it didn't radiate through his eyes. "Some possible changes for the future."

"Well, as long as we can get this done by Sunday." I laughed and Tabris's smile tightened. "I've got a third grade choir concert to go to."

"A concert." His body remained perfectly still and his face blank—except for his eyes. If someone could stare sarcastically, then that's what Tabris's eyes were doing. OMG, she's got to be kidding practically emanated from his amber orbs, but I wasn't fazed. I would be back for that concert. He slowly stood. "Thanks again for the update, and great job with the ferry."

Though polite, we'd definitely been dismissed.

"You're welcome." I backed up a few steps. "And thank you for the pot of cash."

"You earned it."

With that, Mara took my arm and discreetly, yet forcefully, guided me out the door. We didn't speak until we rounded the first corner.

"I'm sorry, but did you get the impression he wasn't telling us everything?" Mara asked.

"Yes, I definitely got that impression." I glanced over my shoulder. "And now I'm officially the new ferryman and officially getting paid for it. How did I officially get a job I never applied for?"

"This all seems very sketchy on their part." She nodded. "And he never did tell us how we're supposed to convince Charon to return."

I stopped and spun toward her. "What if they don't want him back?"

"He has to go back. Who else would they get?"

We stared at each other, neither of us wanting to answer that question. Me. I was the only option, but that was crazy. I had a family and laundry. No way could I be the next ferryman. Then again, hadn't I said the same thing about being a grim reaper?

# CHAPTER THIRTEEN

A text alert dinged in Mara's pocket. She pulled out her phone. "Cam needs me in one of the banquet rooms." Slipping the phone back in her jacket, she sighed. "I wonder what's going on now."

"Nothing bad, I hope." Events and responsibilities seemed to be piling up on all of us. "I'm going to go take a nap. I'll catch up with you later."

"Okay." As she started down the hall, she said over her shoulder, "I'll call you later."

"Roger that."

The possibility of a nap pulled me to the elevator. I prayed Tandy wasn't in the room, but it wouldn't matter. At this point, I could sleep through a train crash. It wasn't just the physical strain of ferrying and attending the conference. It was also the emotional burdens heaped on me.

Not telling Nate about our extracurricular activity was starting to feel more and more wrong. As much as I hated to admit it, he was much better at taking a situation and viewing it from all sides. I worked from emotions, where he worked from logic. Though I was only going on gut instinct, it felt as if a lot more was going on than Tabris cared to share.

Only the hum of the air conditioner greeted me when I opened the door to my room. It was blissfully empty. I tossed my purse on the chair, kicked off my shoes, and crawled into my already-made bed. Snuggling under, I found a comfortable position and closed my eyes.

The seconds ticked by but my body refused to relax. I turned to lie on my other side and blew out a breath, trying to quiet the thoughts bopping around in my head. After another few minutes I rolled to my back and let out an exasperated growl. No matter how much I wanted or needed a nap, I wasn't going to get it.

I threw off the covers and sat on the side of the bed. Attending classes seemed like unnecessary torture right now. At this time of day, the kids were in school and my mom was at her yoga class, so I couldn't even call home. Still, I needed a little down time.

I dug in the dresser and pulled out my black one-piece swimsuit. If I could find a lounge chair in the shade by the pool, I might be able to relax enough to read the book I brought. The sunscreen I'd brought was thick enough to not let me burn during a solar flare. I tossed the bottle, a towel, water bottle, my book, and sunglasses into my bag. Over my swimsuit, I put my black sweatpants and T-shirt back on. Not traipsing through the hotel in a sheer cover-up was a favor to all hotel guests. I shoved my feet into black flip flops, grabbed the room key, and headed to the pool.

The place was packed and none of the women there looked like they'd never let the juicy goodness of a hamburger pass their lips. Normally, I would have been intimidated but my view of what was and wasn't important had changed over the last twenty-four hours. I'd captained a ferry on the river Styx. I'd met angels, demons, and a primordial deity, and I'd saved Mara from a freakin' horde of water zombies. A little more junk in my trunk didn't even ping my self-confidence radar.

Already it was getting hot. The sun reflected with blinding strength off the rippling surface of the pool. I fished my polarized sunglasses out of my bag and put them on. Instantly, the glare cut to a tolerable level and I realized my first assessment of the pool had been wrong. It was packed, but the majority of the lounging people were spirits. My stress level amped up. We must have ferried over two-hundred-thousand souls last night. Why were they still popping in?

Ignoring everybody, dead or alive, I worked my way around the gigantic pool to a row of orange cabanas. A few had been taken by living people and another claimed by the ghost of a fat guy, wearing thick gold chains. Wanting to stay as far from him as possible, I chose the cabana on the end and spread my towel over the beige cushioned lounge chair. I had no idea if these cost extra or if I was supposed to reserve it first, but I figured I'd play dumb until they kicked me out.

The heat felt good and the sound of splashing water soothed me. Little by little, the tension eased from my shoulders and neck. It was nice out here, away from the convention hubbub and pressing matters. I felt safe inside the cabana, almost like the paranormal world couldn't touch me out here—almost.

A shadow fell across my chair and I opened my eyes, shielding them with my hand.

"What a coincidence." Charon stood above me, smiling. "Do you mind if I join you?"

Yes! I should have been excited about getting one-on-one time to try to convince him to return to Styx, but at that point I just wanted to be alone—to not have to talk, lie, or connive. I forced a smile. "Of course I don't mind."

He pushed a lounge chair over until it was a mere foot from me. This guy needed a lesson on personal space. Once he was settled, he folded his hands in his lap and looked at me. "Did you have a good time last night?"

"Yeah, it was quite a party." I sat forward and grasped the back of my chair, pulling it up a few notches so I wasn't lying down. "Did you ever find your elephant?"

"Not my elephant." Charon stroked his goatee. "A beloved pet of one of my guests."

"A pet?" I shook my head. "Gee, I won't even let my kids get a cat." I settled against the chair and let my gaze roam over the pool area. "Lots of spirits." I looked back at him. "More today than yesterday."

He stared at the frolicking ghosts, a smirk quirking up the corner of his mouth. "There sure are." His gaze skated to me. "Guess they haven't replaced me yet."

"Guess not."

"You said last night they'd mentioned something about giving the ferry run back to my brother." Though he didn't look at me, his tone was definitely digging to see what else I knew about the situation. "Perhaps you misunderstood them."

You wish I misunderstood them. "Maybe." I smiled and shrugged. "I'm just a reaper—low man on the totem pole."

"I highly doubt that, Lisa." Now he did look at me. "Lowly reapers don't meet Nyx."

"That's only because your brother is my porter." I screwed up my face, working up my best lie. "It has nothing to do with me personally."

He harrumphed and shifted to face forward in his chair. Stretching out his legs, he unbuttoned the sheer black shirt he wore to expose his chest. There was no arguing—he was a good-looking man. I glanced away, feeling pervy about finding my grandfather good-looking, even if he was a thousand times removed.

This was probably a great opportunity to work Charon toward returning, but there were things that weren't adding up for me. Tabris had said only a few could ferry and none of them were available at the time. He must have meant to permanently ferry the boat because the living couldn't survive. That had been the reason behind Charon replacing Hal. But there were still things that didn't add up, like why did Tabris choose me to ferry? Was it simply a coincidence of Hal being my porter and Mara my friend? Or, was there some other reason I was chosen? "I'm curious. If you're the ferryman, why can't any of your offspring take your place and run the ferry?"

"You can thank my mother for that." He scooped his fingers through his hair and closed his eyes. "It was one of the conditions for me taking the helm. I can create a legion of grim reapers but none of them can ferry." Shifting again and settling against the lounge chair, he gave an indignant sniff. "It seems a little short-sighted on her part if you ask me."

"Yeah, it does." A dull ache throbbed behind my eyes. I didn't know if it was from the heat and reflecting sun, or trying to fit all the pieces of the puzzle together. My phone erupted in my bag. I jumped and fumbled inside, pulling it out. "Hello?"

"Hi, Lisa," Mara said. "Sorry if I woke you up."

"You didn't. I'm at the pool, talking to Charon." I thought that would make her happy, but it seemed to have the opposite effect.

"I was wondering—" She grunted. Then came the sound of shattering glass. "If you're not too busy, could you text Nate, and both of you come give Cam and I a hand?"

Cam's distant shout and then what sounded like toppling chairs interrupted Mara. A series of scuffles erupted, as if she'd pressed the phone to her chest and then she barked something at Cam. I held the phone away, looking at it, and then pressed it to my ear again. "What's going on?" When she didn't answer I raised my voice. "Mara?"

"Yeah, sorry," she panted. "Hall D. Hurry!"

The phone call ended. Not wasting any time, I texted Nate and then stood. "I've got to go."

"Anything wrong?" Charon cracked open one eye to gaze curiously at me.

"Nothing you need to worry about." I tossed all my stuff into my bag and hastily dressed. Mara asking Nate and I for help, mixed with the angry shouts, meant something was definitely wrong. "Catch ya later."

"You can count on it," he said, closing his eye again.

I jogged through the hotel to the convention center, which in itself was amazing. I don't run, not even walk-jog, unless my life or the lives of my children depends on it—or if the liquor store is about to close. Though I knew where a couple of the rooms for our events were located, I had to stop for directions. Rounding the corner, I saw Nate hauling butt from the opposite direction. We arrived at the doors at the same time.

"What's going on?" he asked.

I shook my head, breathing a little heavier than I was proud of. "I don't know. Mara didn't explain."

The hulking security guard who had been stationed at the door of the Expo Center now stood in front of the double doors, hands folded in front of him, legs spread wide. When he saw us he stepped aside and flicked his head toward the room, not speaking. My nerves were strung tight and the fact that Mara and Cam needed a guard outside the door didn't help calm me at all.

We reached for the door handles at the same time and yanked the doors open. The chaos and destruction inside stopped us in our tracks. Dozens of tables had been upended, their tablecloths tossed about the room. Glittering glass shards sprinkled the dark carpet and an empty gold frame rested against the wall near the door.

"Don't let them escape!" Mara shouted.

I didn't know what them was, but Nate and I tugged the doors closed and turned back to the mayhem. Cam and Mara stood in different areas of the room, looking up. My gaze tracked to the ceiling.

"Sweet Jesus," Nate whispered.

"What—?" I grabbed his arm and pointed. "—the hell is that?"

Attached to the ceiling, directly above Cam, its yellow eyes blazing, was a skeletal creature straight out of my nightmares. An identical monster skittered up the back wall. It slithered like a lizard, its arms and legs moving independent of each other. Chills raced up my neck and I couldn't help shuddering against this thing's unholy movements. Mara tracked its path up the wall, never taking her eyes off it.

"Demons," Mara said, pointing to her right. "We need you guys to hold that mirror up."

My eyes snapped to where she directed. A rectangular mirror set in a silver frame rested flat on the floor. It stretched about three feet across and was a lot nicer than the ones in the Expo Center.

"We're going to drive them toward it," Cam said. "But make sure the demons don't touch you. These guys are nearly impossible to get out once they've possessed you."

"Possessed me?" Even though I knew I'd heard him correctly, the question had to be asked. "As in invading my body?"

"Yeah." Mara leaped for the demon but missed, landing squarely on her feet again. The thing continued to creep along the top of the wall toward us. "Remember The Exorcist and those demons locked in the bowels of Hell?"

"Yes?" Nate and I scooted toward the mirror lying on the ground, never taking our eyes off the creatures.

"Well, these are their slightly less dangerous cousins."

"Shit, shit, shit." That seemed to be the only word I could form.

The mirror was heavier than it looked. The metal prickled unusually cold against my palms and I could have sworn the mirrored glass churned like liquid mercury. I pulled my fingers back, making sure to keep them on the frame. No way did I want to find out if these mirrors worked on reapers, too.

"Ready," Nate said.

"Speak for yourself," I mumbled.

Never again would I complain about being a reaper. Spirits, even those of violent criminals, were a walk in the park compared to these horrifying monsters. One of the demons leveled its piercing yellow gaze on me. Jagged, black fangs flashed when its thin lips pulled into a jack-o'-lantern grin. My grip loosened and the mirror slipped toward the ground. The demon hissed its threat. The urge to run swamped me, and my breath caught in my throat. I knew that thing would run me down in a matter of seconds and nothing the others could do would stop it.

I tightened my fingers and adjusted my footing, fortifying my determination. Whatever Cam and Mara had planned, I was ready.

"You okay?" Worry tinged Nate's question.

"Yeah." I inhaled, keeping my eyes locked on the demon. "We got this."

The creature hanging from the ceiling didn't seem to have any intentions of coming down. Propping his hands on his hips, Cam stared at it. "If you don't come down, I'm coming up."

Could he do that? He was an angel, after all. My gaze darted from the demon to Cam several times. I won't lie, I was seriously hoping to see some angelic awesomeness. Bolts of fire or quaking earth. Maybe trumpets preceding his supernatural smiting.

What I got was even better. Blue-white light emanated from Cam, surrounding his entire body. The demon hanging from the ceiling cringed and screeched, as if Cam's brilliance burned. Giant white wings rose from either side of Cam's spine and unfolded. When completely expanded, he gave several shallow flaps, as if shaking out his wings.

At the sight, the demon shot with surprising speed across the ceiling, but Cam was quicker. He launched into the air and with a single flap, skimmed a foot below the ceiling. The demon dodged around the wide, round light fixtures, but failed to elude the angel.

I couldn't take my eyes from Cam. Imagining what seeing an angel would be like was nothing compared to the full visual. Power thrummed through the room. The demon's fear was tangible and to be honest, I couldn't blame the thing. The expression on Cam's face wasn't anger or even concentration. Righteous determination, as if this were his true calling, the one thing that completed him. I don't think I've ever felt that way about anything. Reaping—Zumba—even motherhood—never garnered this kind of reaction from me.

When Cam tucked in his wings, his body spun like a missile. At that point the demon had no chance. His speed increased, and Cam shot toward it, grabbed its leg, and peeled it off the ceiling. Its talons dug into the plaster but lost its grip. The creature dangled from Cam's hand, flailing and screeching, but couldn't get free.

They circled the room and when Cam headed toward us, I braced my feet and leaned into the weight of the mirror. A few yards away his wings extended, pulling him to a full stop in midair. With what looked like not more than a flick of his wrist, he chucked the demon toward us. The creature spun head over feet, its arms thrashing, trying to stop its inevitable imprisonment.

When the demon hit the mirror, the front wavered as if the creature had jumped on a waterbed. Nate and I grunted against the force. A dull pain ricocheted across my shoulder where the metal frame dug in, no doubt adding another bruise to my already vast collection. No matter how much it tried to get away, the surface held tight. Inch by inch the creature sunk and disappeared under the glass until the mirror again appeared solid.

I hadn't fully recovered from capturing the first demon when the second sprung from the wall. Like a dog, it ran on all fours across the carpet. Its talons ripped at the fibers with each lopping gate, heading directly for me. Chaos erupted. Mara spun and took off after it, jumping onto a chair and literally ran across the tables. Cam dove, coming at it from the opposite direction. Nate and I held fast with the mirror, but to be honest, I was frozen with fear and couldn't move when I should have.

The demon took a final leap. At first, I thought it would hit the mirror, but at the last second it veered left, slamming into me. We toppled backward and landed on the floor, the creature on top of me. For a split second it leered down, its claws digging into my flesh. A scream lodged in my throat but I couldn't expel it. In the next second the demon disappeared—inside me

# CHAPTER FOURTEEN

My body convulsed several times as the demon pushed its way inside me. No way was there enough room for a full-sized demon and all my personalities. When it tried to elbow me aside, I got pissed. Though I had no idea what I looked like from the outside, I bet it was disturbing to say the least. I had no control over my muscles but could feel my arms and legs twitching as we fought for control.

Our wrestling match reminded me of my twin boys. Lots of pushing, shoving, and kicking, but nobody really getting the leg up.

"Get out!" I don't know if I actually shouted or if I only thought the command.

I mentally reared back and slammed my fist into the creature's jaw. It hissed at me and braced its legs against the inside wall of my body and shoved. It felt like being pushed down a drain hole, my soul compacting to fit. I grabbed a taloned foot and used my imaginary legs to push upward until I was face to face with the demon. It hissed at me again, its yellow eyes growing wide with shock.

I don't think it usually had this much trouble possessing somebody, but I was getting really tired of people, spirits, and now demons encroaching on my personal space. This thing needed to go back to Hell—now.

I felt the familiar stirrings of what I referred to as my reaper superpower. Though the attempt to possess me was happening inside my body, it helped to treat it as if everything was going on outside me. Black ribbons streamed, and when the first tendril touched the demon, it howled and released its hold. It threw itself backward, ripping free of my body's constraints.

My limbs when limp and I flopped onto the floor, the battle over. Or so I thought. I opened my eyes just in time to see the demon leap from me to Nate and disappear.

"No!" Without thinking, I jumped to my feet and grabbed Nate around the waist.

For a second, he didn't move, staring at the far wall. Then slowly, he tilted his chin and grinned at me. The blood in my veins turned to ice. Though I was staring at Nate's face, it was the demon leering back at me. A second later, Cam stopped behind him, putting Nate in a wrestler's hold, locking his fingers at the back of Nate's neck. Mara hauled the mirror off the floor and slid it directly behind me.

"Do whatever it was that expelled the demon," Mara said. "That thing you did to me."

Cam's gaze cut from her back to me, but he didn't say anything. Nate started laughing, the voice nothing like his, instead deep and grating. My arms twitched, wanting to let go and back away, but this was my partner. That thought strengthened my determination. I focused on Nate's eyes.

"Get out." That phrase had been so effective in The Amityville Horror, I thought I'd give it a try. Instead of the demon fleeing, it laughed louder. Anger surged through me. Heat burned along my spine and again I felt the flutter stir around me. "Get out."

The laughing stopped and Nate's now-yellow eyes narrowed on me. "I will not leave. This body is mine."

Rage blanked my mind, and I slipped into the reaper zone. Usually the black vapor extended in tendrils and ribbons, but this time it shot from me like a blanket of darkness. No gentle winding or testing the soul. It folded over us, wrapping Nate, the demon, and I in a cloak of swirling blackness.

Instantly I felt Nate's soul struggling to break free of the demon's confines. The only fear I felt from him was from not being in control. The other presence was the demon, but there was no soul to reap. It was like touching ash and smoke, sifting through the tiniest crack in Nate's will. The black vapors tugged against me and I released whatever hold I had on it. Swooping forward, it plunged into Nate's chest. His body went rigid in my arms, but I held tight.

The demon condensed, shrinking away from my touch, confused by the new invader. It was long enough for vaporous blanket to wrap around the demon, capturing it. My arms fell from Nate's waist and I stepped away as the blackness spiraled back around me, holding the demon to the side. Though the creature kicked and clawed at the black tethers, it couldn't break free. It shrieked and my hold tightened, cutting off the piercing noise.

Cam lowered Nate to sit on the ground and then ran around me to grab the other side of the frame. I slowly pivoted and focused on the silver mirror. With a single thought, the black vapors unfurled, piercing the glass, and depositing the monster inside. The demon flung itself against the mirror, beating against the glass with a dull thud, before disappearing.

The blackness evaporated, and I shook my head, clearing the muddiness doing in my head.

While they carried the mirror to the door, I spun and dropped to the floor next to Nate. "Are you all right?"

His eyes were wide with either fear or shock. Then his gaze focused on me, and before I knew what was happening, he clutched the back of my head and pulled my mouth to his. I fell against him, bracing one hand on his shoulder and one on the floor. His lips slanted over mine and though he didn't slip me the tongue, he kissed me like a starving man, and I was a juicy steak. I didn't pull away. I'm just going to say it's because he took me by surprise.

When he broke the kiss, he didn't let me go, but instead rested his forehead against mine. "Thank you."

I'm fairly certain he was thanking me for getting rid of the demon and not the kiss.

"You're welcome." I sat back on my heels, pulling out of his hold. "Are you all right?"

"Yeah." He rubbed his hands over his face and then looked at me. "How did you do that?"

I shrugged. "It's kind of my thing. Only works on paranormal beings."

"Why haven't you told me about that before?" He shook his head. "Does Constantine know?"

"I don't know." It was my answer for both of his questions. "The subject never came up."

Cam and Mara squatted beside us, cutting off our conversation. "Thanks, you two," Cam said.

"Yeah, we could have handled one demon, but two of them split our attention." She patted Nate on the shoulder. "Sorry about the possession."

"It's all right." He shifted and pushed to his feet. The three of us followed him up. "But I never want to experience that again."

"And you?" Cam laid his hand on my shoulder. "I've never seen anything like that before." He rubbed my shoulder a couple of times. "Are you okay?"

To be honest, my head was still spinning from the kiss Nate had given me more than kicking that demon's ass. "I'm fine." I ran my hands up and down my arms. "Just a little shaken up is all." I held out my arms. "So, demons—in the Venetian? What's up with that?"

"Nothing good." Cam crossed his arms over his chest. "The spirits who have been reaped but are popping back to the physical plane are free game."

"Wait, what?" I shook my head. "That can't be."

"It's the loophole Tabris told us about," Mara said. "They've been reaped, and normally would have been delivered by now. But if the soul isn't claimed within a certain amount of time, it's up for grabs."

The weight of getting the souls ferried pressed down on me with crushing importance. Hearing about the threat was one thing. Being possessed by it was quite another. Even though we'd done three ferry trips, reapers were still reaping, filling the shores. So, not only were souls flooding the physical world, now we had demons sniffing after them.

"It's like open season on souls," Nate said.

"What about the ones that aren't reaped?" My thought went to Tandy. "Can they be taken by demons?"

"No, only the ones who have been reaped and unclaimed," Cam said.

Mara and I glanced at each other. We seemed to be thinking the same thing. We needed to get as many souls ferried as possible. I brushed my hands down the front of my shirt and pants, as if ridding myself of the last bit of indecisiveness. Everybody needed to pull their heads out and face the problem. "Somebody should tell Tabris about this."

Cam nodded. "I'll do it."

Nate still didn't appear to be one hundred percent.

"Maybe you should go lay down for a while." I smiled at him. "Until you feel normal again."

"I have a splitting headache so I think I will go to my room." His eyes tracked over the three of us. "Thanks, guys."

With that, he left. Nate can be annoying sometimes with his know-it-all attitude, but I actually felt sorry for him. The poor guy had been so out of it he'd kissed me—really kissed me. Heat spread up my neck and I tried to silence the flutter of butterflies that had erupted at the thought of how that kiss had made me feel, and was still making me feel, which was stupid, because it meant nothing.

"I'll catch up with you two later." Cam stood. "Let me know if you run into any more problems."

I nodded my head and Mara gave him a half salute. When he was gone, she turned to me. "We've got to go ferry."

"My thoughts exactly." I inhaled. "Unfortunately, I think we need to do a lot of runs."

"Yeah." She scowled, her eyes scanning the overturned tables. "This Charon thing is getting out of control. Why does it seem like we're the only ones trying to solve this?"

"I know, right? The last time we talked to Tabris I got the distinct impression we'd reached our—" I made air quotes by my head. "Need-to-know-limit." A sigh eased from me. "I'm going to run my bag to my room and change out of my swimsuit."

"Okay, I'll meet you there in thirty minutes. I want to check on Cam and find out what Tabris said."

We exited the hall. Neither the security guard nor the mirror were anywhere in sight. I imagine GRS had some kind of paranormal warehouse where they stored that kind of stuff. God knows I wouldn't want to chance breaking a mirror that imprisoned a couple of nasty demons.

I stepped into the elevator and the doors slid along the track. A second before they closed, Charon slipped in. Irritation rippled through me. Because of this guy, Nate and I had just been possessed by a demon. The supernatural world was seeping into the physical, and not only was all my free time spent trying to fix it, I was actually spending my trans-dimensional free time dealing with the aftereffects of his hissy fit.

He spun toward me, looking equally aggravated. "Where's the money?"

My brow pinched, having no idea what he was ranting about. "What money?"

"My money." He waved his electronic tablet in the air. "I just checked my accounts. No deposit has been made in the last twenty-four hours."

Oh, that money. I screwed up my face. "How should I know? I'm not a banker."

"But you have been working with Tabris." He took a step toward me. "You also said something about them getting another ferryman."

I backed up, my heels hitting the wall. "At which point you replied that there wasn't anybody else."

"It's Thanatos." His eyes narrowed on me and his lips pinched together. "Isn't it?"

For the first time since I'd met him his power became evident. It filled the elevator and thrummed against my body. It took all my effort not to shrink back. I squared my shoulders and leveled a bored stare at him. "I think you're being a little paranoid."

"If I'm paranoid—" He took a step toward me, pointing the silver end of his walking stick at my chest. "—then explain where my money is."

If I let him get the upper hand, he'd definitely know somebody was ferrying—because I'd spill my guts. I needed to flip the situation and get control. It was a technique I used on my kids when they tried to pin me down for an answer. "Let me get this straight." I propped my fists against my hips and channeled my southern church lady. "You're pissed because you're no longer receiving the gold for ferrying souls?"

"That's right." He straightened his shoulders but some of the certainty in his expression melted. "It's part of the compensation for being the ferryman."

"Right, which you are no longer." I crossed my arms over my chest and shook my head as if any idiot could figure it out. "And you think they should continue to pay you when not only are you not doing the job, but are creating a lot of freakin' headaches for the rest of us?" The elevator hiccupped, and the doors opened onto my floor. I let my arms fall to my sides and shook my head as I strode to the exit. I slapped my hand against the metal slabs to keep it from shutting and craned my neck to look at him, as if he were an afterthought. "Stop acting like a spoiled brat and either get back to work or shut the hell up." I stepped out and turned. "Because everybody is really getting tired of your crap."

Stunned, that's how I'd describe Charon's expression as the doors glided closed. His eyes had rounded and his mouth curved into a pouty frown. He may have awesome supernatural powers, but he was acting like a thirteen-year-old drama queen—and that might have been insulting the teenager a bit.

I hadn't given him time to reply, or maybe I'd knocked the wind out of his sails, but at this point I didn't care. I could only deal with so much victimized attitude and Charon had reached his limit. He'd officially climbed to the number one spot on my shit list and would stay there until this situation was solved.

Most of my time as a mother was spent cleaning up other people's messes—laundry, dishes, school shenanigans—but those were my kids. Being responsible for the ethereal world was really twerking my gourd, and I couldn't be held responsible for my actions if one more afterlife asshat dumped another job on me.

Halfway down the hallway a scream wrenched the air. In an ectoplasmic burst, Tandy exploded out of our room. When she saw me, she pointed at the door, her hand wavering. "In there." A sob broke from her. "It's horrible."

My stomach twisted. "Please tell me it's not another demon."

"Demon?" She stiffened and scrunched up her face. "Where did you see a demon?"

"Long story." I stopped next to her. "So what's inside?"

She crumbled again with a dramatic wail. "A poltergeist."

My shoulders slumped with relief, a testament of how bad things were getting. "Is that all?"

"He called me a fat cow." Her lip quivered. "And said I couldn't dance."

"Tandy, it's a poltergeist. They love to insult people, especially when it's not true." Okay, I'd never encountered a poltergeist in my life, and besides what Nate had told me, almost all my information came from the Ghostbuster movies and Peeves from Harry Potter, but she didn't need to know that.

She nodded but her pout remained. I blew out a long, soul-weary breath, and opened the door. Unlike regular spirits, poltergeists were a conglomeration of energy caused by events and people's states of being. Teenagers most commonly attracted them, but with the chaotic state of the hotel, it was no wonder poltergeists were now showing up. I just wondered why it was in my room.

My eyes tracked the energy as it shot along the ceiling and then back to the other side, as if swimming underwater laps. White sparks snapped, winking among the swirling pink, purple, and gray energy that made up its body. It was about the size of a sled, its head was round and blunt with no definable arms or legs.

After watching it for several seconds, I yelled, "Hey!"

The poltergeist stopped midway across the room and floated into what I'd describe as a vertical position. It hovered there, I assume watching me, though I didn't see any eyes. Tandy had said it called her names, but it seemed to be all talked out.

"You need to leave." I pointed toward the door even though I knew poltergeist could traverse through solid objects.

It didn't move.

"Now. This is my room and I'm already sharing it with one too many people."

"I thought you like being my roommate," Tandy said from behind me.

I shushed her with a wave of my hand. Still, the energy didn't move. Time to pull out the big guns. Mara would be here in a little while and we had important ferrying to do. "Either leave or I'll reap you."

Chatter that sounded vaguely like laughing echoed around the room. The poltergeist started flying in circles. The lamp on my bedside table flashed and the clock's alarm erupted with loud beeping.

"I don't think it's leaving," Tandy shouted.

"Me, either." If I could get a hold of it, maybe Hal could dispose of the thing. Though I'd never reaped a poltergeist, I did know it wasn't easy, and usually they came back unless the situation where they were haunting changed. Since ectoplasmic energy was off the charts with all the lingering spirits, I suspected my attempt to expel the poltergeist was futile, but Tandy's wide-eyed fear propelled me forward on my fool's mission. "All right, then." I climbed on the bed. "Don't say I didn't warn you."

The circles it was flying got wider, which in turn brought it within reach. On its first pass over my head I jumped but missed. More of that creepy laughing filled the room. I began jumping, trying to sync my bounce with the poltergeist passing above me. I leaped and missed again. The thing was teasing me, which only made me more determined. Again, I bounced, and again I missed.

On its fourth pass, I anticipated where the thing would be and launched off the bed, latching on to the blob's widest part. I assumed we'd fall to the floor, my weight enough to drag us down, but that's not what happened. My toes scraped along the comforter and a second later I was hanging in the air.

"Lisa, what are you doing?" Tandy stood near the door, ringing her hands.

"Well, I'm not actually sure, Tandy." We made a wide circle around the room. My arms strained from holding on, but I didn't want to let go. My ankle beat against the desk when we turned. "Ouch."

When we were over the bed, I tried to hook my foot on the headboard but missed. I also attempted the move on the chair, and again as we passed the entertainment center. At one point, I considered having Tandy grab me, but since she was weightless, I figured that wouldn't do anything but made this situation more ridiculous.

As we rounded the corner again, I hooked my foot under the desk. If I could just get a little leverage, I could probably pull the poltergeist down enough to lie over the top of it and force it to the ground. No way would it be able to get out once all my lusciousness pinned it to the floor.

It yanked to a stop. My ankle burned from where the edge of the desk scraped against my skin, but I held on. What sounded like a high-pitched growl vibrated from the blob of energy. It jerked against my hold again. When we rebounded, I shoved my other foot under the desk, locking it in place. With all my effort, I dragged the poltergeist toward me, eliciting an especially unlady-like grunt in the process. The muscles under my armpits screamed against the movement.

For a second, I contemplated how badly I wanted to get rid of this thing. Would it really matter? How much damage could it do, anyway? Suddenly, the blob dove toward the floor. I dropped, my feet hitting the ground, and releasing their grip from under the desk. My knees shoved into the joints, adding more pain to my already aching body. Before I could recover, the poltergeist shot to the ceiling again, and dragged me in a big circle.

I considered letting go and having Mara help when she got there, but the blob spun and shot toward the wall-wide expanse of window. I shrieked and released my grip, hitting the floor in a crouch. I stumbled, trying to catch myself, but the momentum carried me forward and I smashed into the glass. My hands barely stopped my face from colliding with the window, but my hips rammed the ledge, no doubt giving me bruises on top of my bruises.

The poltergeist hovered on the other side of the window. The top part of its body morphed into a vague semblance of a head and mouth and effectively blew a raspberry at me. What I assumed was its tongue flapped exaggeratedly, cartoon style. I slowly stood, glaring at it, and then stuck my tongue out. A muffled laugh penetrated the window. Then the blob made several loop-de-loops and sped away.

"Son-of-a…" I grabbed the curtain rod and yanked the heavy drapes across the window. Not that it would keep the poltergeist out, but no peeping toms allowed. "Bastard."

I turned and blew out a breath. First spirits, then demons, and now poltergeists, I didn't even want to think what other paranormal surprises were getting ready to pop into our world.

# CHAPTER FIFTEEN

When I yanked the door open, Mara immediately took in Tandy cowering against the wall and my sour expression. "What's wrong?"

"Just an obnoxious poltergeist and a few more bruises." When she slanted a questioning look at me, I said, "More supernatural chaos we can't do anything about right now." I shut the door and followed her into the room. "What did Cam say?"

"Nothing much. Only that Tabris had a fit about the demons. Said he needed to call an emergency meeting of the board of directors." In a rare show of exhaustion, Mara rubbed her hands over her face and then lowered her arms. "I have no idea how they're going to fix this."

"What's going on?" Tandy crept into the room. "What do you mean...?" She chewed on her bottom lip. "Demon?"

"Demons, spawns from Hell, Satan's minions, however you want to spin it, they're alive and well in Vegas." Risking the icy burn, I gently grabbed Tandy's arms. "You need to stay here, Tandy. It's not safe running around the hotel." Cold cut to the bones of my fingers and a few seconds was all I could stand before I released her. "And stay away from Charon."

Her brow pinched together. "Who?"

"Big C." I shook my head. "He's bad news and I don't want you getting caught up in his mess."

Tandy was a good spirit, but was a bit too trusting and a little dingy. I didn't want to see anything bad happen to her—something we couldn't fix.

"I'll just stay with you then." Her head bobbed, and she gave us a bright, clueless smile. "You can protect me."

"When I'm here, that's fine." I pointed to Mara. "But we're leaving for a while."

"Then I'll go with you," Tandy said.

"You can't."

Her smiled turned to a hurt frown. "Why not?"

"Because—" At this point not telling her what was going on could cause more trouble than telling her would. I didn't know if taking her to Styx meant she was officially reaped, which would put her in danger from the demons. I also didn't want her telling Charon I was the one who'd usurped his job. "Where we're going is really dangerous and I won't be able to protect you and still do what I have to do." I patted her shoulder. "I don't want anything to happen to you, Tandy, so please, stay here until I get back. You'll be safe, I promise."

She chewed on her lip again but nodded.

Good, that was one less thing I had to worry about. Before calling Hal, I grabbed my carry-on from the closet and dumped my dirty clothes and a bundle of plastic quarts-size bags onto the bed. Normally, I used the Ziplocs for wet swimsuits or leaky shampoo, things like that. Their job today would be as moneybags. I tossed the bundle back into the suitcase, zipped it up, and looked at Mara. "Ready?"

"Let's do this."

We moved to one end of the room before I said, "Hal."

The thin pink light instantly appeared. Tandy's jaw went slack and when the elevator door slid open to reveal Hal in all his purple satin wonder, her eyes rounded and her mouth dropped open. "Whoa." The word hissed from her. "Who is that?"

"Tandy, this is Hal Lee Lewya, my porter. Hal, Tandy."

He bent at the waist and touched his fingers to his chest. "A pleasure."

"No, the pleasure is mine," she replied. A girlish giggle escaped her. "You're very handsome."

Mara and I did a double take at her words. From Tandy's breathy sigh I wondered if we were looking at the same Hal. Sure, he wasn't hideous, but handsome—not so much.

"Thank you." He straightened. "That's quite a compliment coming from such a beautiful woman."

Tandy giggled again, and I made a gagging noise reminiscent of my daughter. "Okay, Romeo." I marched into the elevator. "Can we please go?"

Mara followed me in, smirking. Tandy wiggled her fingers, waving goodbye to Hal, and he smiled back as the door closed. Music, the kind my mom listened to, piped in from the speakers. Nobody spoke. I stared at the ceiling and after a few seconds, Mara started whistling. The seconds ticked by, all of us refusing to acknowledge the sparks that had flashed between Hal and Tandy.

"So," I said, gripping the handle of the bag a little tighter. "I ran into your brother today."

"How unfortunate for you." Hal rested his hands on the bar running along the wall.

"Yeah, and he knows somebody is running the ferry." I tipped my head toward him. "And he was rather miffed."

"He's always—" Hal puckered his lips for a second and then dragged out the word, "Miffed."

"Yeah, well, I suggest you stay on your toes." I straightened. "He's probably coming after you."

His mouth tightened. "I've been warned."

When the elevator slowed to a stop, I moved to the front of the car. The door glided open, and I looked at my porter. "See you later, Hal."

He gave a single nod but didn't reply.

Mara followed me out, giving him a quick glance, tipping her head. "Stay on your toes."

"You, too."

Behind us the elevator compressed and disappeared. I didn't look back or comment. Hal could take care of himself, both from Charon and Tandy. Right now, I couldn't think about either situation.

Determination pounded through me and I stomped down the steps. With Mara by my side, we loaded up the carry-on with gold and barreled our way through the massive crowd of spirits, dragging the bag behind us. I just hoped the seams held until we made it onto the ferry. It took the two of us to lift it, but once on the smooth deck, I rolled it to the steps of the bridge, leaving it there. No way was I going to exhaust myself manhandling it up the stairs. I was reserving my energy for the numerous trips that lay ahead.

When I rejoined Mara, I said, "Ready?"

"Let's do it."

"Can I have your attention?" I held out my arms, shushing the crowd. "We will be doing a number of runs today, so if you don't get on the first time, there will be more chances." I lowered my hands. "What I ask of you is to file quickly into the ferry. As soon as the border closes, we'll launch. All right." I pointed toward the spirits. "Let's get this party started."

The shield keeping the spirits at bay opened, and the souls flooded in. Mara and I walked to the front of the ferry.

"We've got a few minutes before the boat is full," Mara said. "I think we should do a quick search and see if we can find anything that might help us have a smooth trip."

"Good idea. Unless Charon has super powers, he must do something to keep the lost souls off the ferry." At least I hoped so. "I'll take the right side."

We separated. Starting at the front, I walked out on the pontoon, examining it. When nothing caught my attention, I made my way along the carved float and onto the deck. Another spear stood against a pole at the front corner, and when I got to the mast, I noticed a spotlight imbedded at the side near the bottom sail. I circled the mast. Four more lights were fixed at different heights, all angled toward the water. Now I had to find the switch.

I jogged up the steps to the bridge. At first, no switches were apparent, but then remembered the intercom secreted behind the small door. Running my hands along the paneling, I searched for another door and found it to the right of the wheel. I pulled it open. Inside reminded me of my fuse box at home. I knelt and tried to read the labels beside each switch, but time had nearly worn the words off. I was able to make out the right and left spotlight tabs, one for music, and another for lifeboats, which was very off-putting considering these people were already dead. At the bottom was a red switch with no label.

I flipped the right spotlight lever. I'd never experienced lights that bright. They made my eyes ache. I shielded them with my hands and leaned over the side. Mara had her arm across her forehead, but was also looking at the water. Even though the spotlights were crazy bright, it only penetrated a couple feet down. Then the river faded to inky blackness again. I flipped the switch off. The spotlights darkened, still glowing slightly for a minute. Without the lights, the day seemed excessively gray.

"That should help with the lost souls," Mara turned toward the bridge. "I bet that's how Charon does it."

"I hope so." The thought of battling those creatures again made my stomach tighten. "Did you find anything?"

"No. A couple of spears, but that's about it."

Behind me, a groan hummed through the crowd. I pivoted to see the shield appear, blocking the souls from boarding. I sighed and tried not to dwell on the fact that all those souls waiting to be transported were sitting ducks for demons. Hopefully, we'd be able to make a dent in the crowd.

As the cabin door squeezed shut, the sails began their slow, creaking rise. Focusing on the river, I willed the ferry out. Rocks tumbled beneath the pontoons and fell away when we moved into deeper water. A minute later Mara joined me on the bridge. We both leaned our arms on the wall and stared out at the river.

"Is it my imagination or do things look different?" I scanned the shore. "Those hills weren't there last time, were they?"

"Things definitely changed. Since there's no time here, this dimension can sift through time periods that have passed in the physical plains." She pointed to the horizon. "I wouldn't be surprised to see pyramids out there on our way back."

"I guess that's cool, but I don't like the uncertainty of things." I sighed. "Maybe I'm a stick in the mud."

"Nothing wrong with that." She drummed her fingers on the wood. "There's a lot to be said for no surprises and routine."

"So true. I can't believe I'd much rather be doing laundry than ferrying souls. This whole saving-the-world thing is not for me."

"Me, either. Too much responsibility," Mara said.

No truer words were ever spoken. If I had it to do all over again, I probably would have never stepped foot in the Holiday convenience store on the fated day I became a reaper. Instead of ferrying souls to their final destination, I probably would be getting groceries or contemplating a new diet. Or, maybe I'd still be in a slump, just getting through each day. No doubt I would have had to get a job by now. My husband's life insurance policy sure didn't hold us over very long. Strictly speaking, working for GRS wasn't the worst job in the world. Yes, there were long hours and currently, dangerous work conditions, but normally it was all right and paid the bills.

The straight stretch of river hadn't changed much, only the landscape beyond, so it was easy to maneuver. I'd gotten the hang of mentally guiding the ship and was getting pretty good at it, I might add. During the first part of the trip, we bagged up gold and chatted. Our conversation steered clear of anything too heavy, mainly touching on things we had in common. I was surprised that Mara was a huge do-it-yourselfer, too. For some reason I'd never connected minion from Hell and DIY. Go figure.

"The bend." I flicked my head toward the telltale landmark and stood. Just beyond was the Abyss of Lost Souls. Though we hadn't had much trouble after the first ruckus the last time we ferried, I was betting those watery bastards weren't going to let us pass so easily. "There are two spears. What do you think about patrolling along the sides?"

She shuddered. "I think I hate the idea, but it's probably for the best."

"And this time we have a little help." I jogged up the steps and, opened the panel, and flipped the spotlight switches for both sides. Styx lit up. As an afterthought, I snapped on the music tab and Hispanic party music filled the air. Bobbing my head, I descended the steps and smiled at Mara. "It's party time."

I performed one of my lame conga line moves, making Mara laugh, which probably meant it was even lamer than I'd originally thought. She shimmied her shoulders and grooved across the deck, plucking the spear from the pole. With a coordinated spin, she tossed the pole to me, and then retrieved the other one for herself. We were a couple of badass—salsa dancing—transportation specialists. I only wish we'd had a bright orange safety vests to wear. That's right, minion, don't mess with the reaper in the reflector vest.

Taking up our posts at the sides of the ferry near the middle, we scanned the water for any sign of white limbs. I mentally pushed for more speed and felt a slight increase. As I stared at the water, I could have sworn I caught sight of a very large fin. My heart jumped to my throat.

Please stay in the river. Please stay in the river.

Though the spotlights gave us much better visuals, I'm not certain that was one hundred percent good. The first bump hit the pontoon about a quarter of the way across the abyss. Mara and I glanced at each other, confirming that we'd both heard it. I leveled my gaze on the water. A flash of white dipped below the ship. There was no need to tell Mara. From the way she leaned out, trying to get a better glimpse, and then stepped back, I was sure she saw them too.

More thuds reverberated from underneath the pontoons, becoming more frequent. Cries from the souls in the cabin rose and fell with each hammer against the side, and I had to wonder how strong the hull was. If the lost souls punched a hole through the side they'd drag everyone into the dark depths and we wouldn't know until it was too late.

A white arm shot out of the water and grabbed onto the float, but a second later it released the wood and sunk into the depths. I took tiny breaths, trying to calm my racing heart, and braced myself. Three feet from where I stood, a body shot out of the water and grabbed hold of the wall. Its deafening screech pierced the air. I wanted to drop the spear and slap my hands over my ears, but resisted. With measured shuffles, I sidestepped along the deck, coming level with the screaming body. Its white-blue mottled skin glimmered under the blazing lights like a rotting fish on the beach, and its white-silver eyes stared up at me. I think it was a male, but couldn't be sure. It reached for me and I raised the spear. Before I could jab at it, the lost soul released the boat and threw itself back into the water, disappearing under the black waves.

I waited but no more arms grabbed hold, no bodies shot out of the water. However, the thumping under the boat increased in frequency and strength. I backed up toward Mara. "They're under the ferry. What are we going to do?"

"I don't know. With enough of them they could punch a hole through the side."

"Surely Charon has dealt with this before." I ran up the steps and yanked open the panel. "I can't make these three switches out." I pressed my finger against the red switch and glanced up at Mara. "What do you think? For an emergency?"

She grimaced. "Try the one above it first."

I snapped the switch. Creaking wood sounded from above. From the middle sail another length of pole extended and a second sail unfurled. Instantly we picked up speed. "These—" I pointed to the other unlabeled switches. "— must be for the other sails." My finger slid back to the red switch. "Here goes nothing."

I pushed lever to the right. The River Styx lit up. We jumped to our feet and peered over the side. Lights burned under the water, illuminating the underside of the ferry and twenty feet beyond.

"Oh my God!" I gripped her arm. "That is horrifying."

Hordes of white bodies swarmed under the boat in a roiling mass, each one trying to escape the lights.

"But effective." Mara gave me a satisfied smile. "Wish we would have known about these lights on our first trip."

"Yeah, your red pants wouldn't have been ruined," I said, making light of the fact that I'd saved and almost reaped her. "Okay." I released her and took a step back. "I don't think I want to see what else lurks in Styx, so I'm going to stand here."

"Good idea."

Her good idea must have been meant for me, because she remained in place, watching the water. Every so often, she'd flinch or make an icky face, driving home the fact that only a thin layer of wood separated us from certain torment. We kept the lights on even past the abyss. She seemed to be having such a good time surveilling the water I didn't have the heart to shut it off. Finally, she gave up her watch and flipped the switch. I inched forward. Thankfully, Styx was once again dark, its secrets and terrors hidden.

With only a little time left until we reached the junction, we relaxed on the couch and chair. Every few minutes I'd stand and make sure we were going in the right direction, but for the most part, I had this steering thing down and just needed to make sure nothing new had cropped up in the middle of the river.

"I'm going to bring a magazine next time," I said, propping my feet up on the coffee table. "And maybe some snacks."

"We didn't have a whole lot of warning this time." She mirrored my actions and flopped her arms over the sides of the chair. "I wonder if my tablet would work down here. I could crush some candy, jam some cookies, and pop some pandas."

"You know, once you get past the possible loss of life and soul, this is kind of the perfect job."

She arched a brow at me. "Seriously?"

"Yeah." I held up my fingers. "Great pay, basically you're your own boss, vacation time." I lowered my hand. "And think about it. I could do this job any time because we return at almost the same moment we left."

"True, but I think it would get lonely here if you were doing it by yourself."

A snort murmured from me. "What I wouldn't give for some alone time. Just think, if the kids were driving me nuts I could lock myself in the bathroom, pop down here, do a few runs, and dash back, calm and rejuvenated." Now that I thought about it, maybe I should suggest it to Tabris. We'd figured out the spotlight thing, eliminating any major threats from the lost souls and I had Hulk to help get the passengers out. Sure, there was some danger, but a lot of benefits. "I always say I wish there were more hours in the day, and well I'd actually have more hours, since this job literally takes no time."

"It sounds good in theory." Mara lowered her feet to the ground and sat forward. "But remember what happened to Katrina. Styx is for the dead and to my knowledge; you don't fall into that category—yet."

"Yeah, you're probably right." I'd definitely been exhausted in a soul-weary way after our first venture into the netherworld, and already I could feel the river's pull, draining me. "It's probably better to get Charon—"

"Hello," said a female voice, cutting off my reply to Mara. "Are you there?"

"Tell me I'm hearing things," I said.

Mara shook her head. "Then we're both hearing things."

"You-hoo," the voice called again.

Simultaneously groaning, we both stood.

# CHAPTER SIXTEEN

A hundred feet off the left side of the ferry stretched a thin sandbar. I was fairly certain that hadn't been there last time we ferried. Standing on the sandbar was a young woman. She had long dark hair, and wore an orange and white short set, but her feet were bare. When she spotted us, she waved and smiled. "Hi."

We both returned a weak wave and gave an even weaker, "Hi."

"I was wondering if you could give me a ride." She shuffled along the stretch of sand, keeping up with us as we glided past. "I'm not sure how I got here. One minute I was talking to a cute guy on the river bank and the next thing I knew I was here."

"You were waiting for the ferry?" I mentally slowed the boat.

"Yes." She smiled and held up her hands. "And then pop. Now here I am."

"Just a second." I glanced at Mara. "What do you think? Is it a trick?"

"Oh, I definitely think it's a trick." She scowled at the young woman, and I could see the conflict in Mara's expression. "But I'm not sure what kind of trick."

"Do you think since the banks are full the souls are now popping all over the netherworld?" Talk about adding pressure to the job. Not only were souls materializing on the physical plane, and were free for demons to snatch up, now they were scattering throughout the Underworld. "Why didn't she return to the human world? There's still a lot of room. I think."

"It doesn't make sense." Her gaze narrowed, and she lowered her voice. "Remember what Hal said?"

I racked my brain, trying to recall his pearls of wisdom. "Don't pick up hitchhikers."

She nodded. "Exactly."

"But this is coming from Hal." Propping my fist on my hip, I copped a bit of attitude. "He also said to look up."

My smile faded, and we both tilted our chins upward a second before something large and pointy dove at us. I shrieked and hit the deck. Mara ducked too, without the wussy cry.

"What the hell was that?" I shouted.

"Oh, no, you didn't." Mara jumped to her feet and glared upward. "That was a demon, straight out of Hell."

My blood turned to ice, and I struggled to a half-standing-half-hunched position. Another scream filled the air, and we spun to see the woman on the sandbar transform. Leathery black wings sprouted from her back and her orange and white short set changed to reddish brown scales. Even from a hundred feet away I could see her yellow eyes glowing in the dim light.

"Oh, crap." I could barely speak. Every time I tried my words, breath, and spit lodged in my throat. "Oh, crap," I said again, rounding out my eloquent summation of our situation.

The demon shot into the sky, joining its partner. They circled overhead once before dive-bombing us. I flattened my body against the deck but Mara didn't move. Her head swayed, watching the creatures' course.

"What are we going to do?" I climbed to a crouch. "We need one of those mirrors you and Cam used against the demons in Hall D." I swallowed hard, keeping my gaze locked on the demons. "Or a really—really—big cross bow." Not that I knew how to use one, but if they got close enough, at least I could stab them with the arrows. I pointed to the white poles we used on the lost souls. "How about the spears?"

"I've got this." Like the first time I'd met her, Mara's voice poured over me. But now the tone sent a shiver down my spine. Very slowly, she faced me. Her green eyes glowed, pale and icy, but yellow flames flickered in their depths. "You should probably step back."

Even if I'd wanted to stay, my mind forced me away. With each step I took, she changed. Her clothes seemed to melt from her body, replaced by a ginormous set of black wings, and small black horns. Instead of scales like the other demons, her skin looked like red leather. A thin tail, resembling a braided whip, curled from her lower back and wrapped around her leg. As demons went, she was the prettiest and least terrifying I'd seen. Her eyes settled on me.

I gave her a strained smile. "No wonder you liked those red pants so much."

The corner of her lip pulled up, revealing a white fang. "I'll be right back."

"Take your time." I slid to a squat, sitting on my heels, with my back pressed to the bridge wall. "I'll just—I'll just wait here."

She crouched and launched into the air. My heartbeat so hard I could feel it in my throat. I cupped my hands over my mouth and stared at the sky. But I'll be honest, at that point I couldn't really focus on what Mara was doing. Panic raced through me, attacking my thoughts and dredging up the worst possible scenarios. What if they killed her, or whatever demons did to each other? Not only would I lose my friend, but probably my soul. Those creatures would be on me and my shipment of tasty souls like a fat chick on a cupcake.

Fire exploded above me, pulling me out of my what-if frenzy and drawing my gaze back to Mara. The two demons circled like sharks. She hovered in the center, her wings lazily flapping. Her arms were held out to her side and in each hand she held a ball of fire. It was difficult to get a clear view of her face, but I think she was enjoying herself, and was maybe even goading them to attack.

Though I'm not Catholic, I made the sign of the cross. Forehead—chest—shoulder—shoulder. Out of habit, I muttered, "Spectacles, testicles, wallet, watch. Amen."

My dad used to perform that every day before he left for work to make sure he hadn't forgotten anything. It might not have been a straight up prayer, but I think God understood that I wanted him to keep me safe.

One of the demons dove at Mara. I screamed, and she spun, nailing them with one of the fireballs, making its body light up like a torch. The demon screeched, tucked its wings, and spiraled into the river. No way did I think that thing had given up. It probably needed to cool off and would be back in a second.

I rose and scanned the river. If I saw it take flight again, I'd warn her. I might not be able to do much more, but I didn't have to cower in the corner. More fire burst above me, but this time she missed her target. The demon attacked. Mara easily avoided the exposed talons by dropping several feet before flaring her wings again. With another push, she took off after her prey. The demon screeched, spinning in an effort to escape the fiery volley.

They swooped through the sky, progressively putting more distance between them and the ferry. I continued to scout the river but kept glancing toward Mara. Pretty soon they were pinpricks on the horizon and every so often the sky lit with a small explosion.

I gripped the top of the half-wall, willing her to put an end to the demon and get back to the ferry—and to me. All right, so being the ferryman was not the perfect job for me. If I couldn't handle a couple of demons, which I couldn't, then somebody more capable needed to man this vessel, and be responsible for getting those souls safely to where they needed to be. I'm a big enough person to admit that person wasn't me.

Splashing water sounded to my right. My head whipped in that direction in time to see the black talons claw at the pontoon. The first demon dragged his scaly body out of the river and crouched on the float. It extended its wings and shook them. The edges were frayed from being set on fire but as I watched, the membrane repaired itself. I didn't think the demon knew I was there—had prayed it didn't, but then it stood and glared at me. Cracked lips drew back exposing its black fangs, and it hissed at me. That single noise said a whole lot of things I didn't want to hear. I'm going to eat your soul. There's no escape. Hope you enjoyed your life because it's over. And I'm fairly certain there was something about my ample thighs too.

My mind raced but my body wouldn't move. Why hadn't I grabbed one of the spear poles when Mara had them both in the air? Its gaze locked onto mine and I suddenly felt like I was being pulled into a black void. I managed to close my eyes, and the sensation faded some. I grabbed my pendant and rubbed, freeing me completely from the demon's hold.

I opened my eyes, scanning the bridge for something to fight with. I could rip the handle off the kegorator but even in my panicked state I didn't want to do anything rash. If we survived, I'd need a cold one. Eight-track tapes or cassettes weren't going to help unless I wanted to sing the demon into submission. If I were Jason Bourne, I'd be able to disembowel the beast with one of Charon's girly magazines and a Ziploc bag. But I wasn't.

Instead, I held the wheel and kicked at one of the spindles sticking from it. My hand slipped and instead of breaking off a viable weapon I received another punishing bruise, this time on my anklebone.

"Mutha!" I grabbed my leg and hopped around, unable to care if there was a demon ten feet away. "Fargen—fricken—fracker."

I'm renowned for my creative and colorful use of F-words that weren't actually swearing, and at that moment, the netherworld was getting an earful. I grabbed the wheel, intent on giving the kick another try despite the high odds that I'd be injured again, but my knee halted mid-lift.

The demon landed with a heavy thud on the wall. With its wings fully extended, its talons curled over the side and dug into the dark wood. At that point, any pretense of cool and collected evaporated. A blood-curling cry I didn't know I could produce exploded from me. In turn, the demon screeched. As I backed away, the thing hissed at me again. Time seemed to slow, even though time didn't exist there, and my life passed before my eyes. In the next second everyone I loved, and who loved me, would be ripped away. The demon crouched, preparing to lunge. I wanted to scream again, but nothing could get past the block of fear clogging my throat.

I think it smiled at me, if it could be called a smile, and then launched from the wall. I did scream then, crossing my arms over my head and dropping to the deck. However, no collision came. Only a loud thud, the rush of wings, and a demon's scream.

Keeping my arms over my head, I lifted my chin and peeked up. The demon was gone. Slowly, I lowered my arms but remained crouched. Was it some kind of cruel trick? Was it toying with me? If I stood, would it attack me from behind?

After another minute and still no demon, I braced my hands on the floor and began to stand. Out of nowhere,

Mara dropped onto the bridge, still decked out in her demon persona. I screamed again and fell onto my rear end.

She grinned at me. "That's right, bitches, you've just been Jimmied!"

Though I loved her enthusiasm, for which she used our new favorite word, her fanged smile and the whole demon persona was more than a little intimidating.

"Holy crap, you scared me." I stood, unsure if transforming to a demon also changed her attitude, or if she was still the same Mara I knew. "So, they're gone?"

"For now." She sashayed toward me, stopped, and propped her hands on her hips. "I'll admit..." She inhaled. "That felt good." Her wings expanded behind her. "It's nice to stretch my wings sometimes."

"That was quite a stretch." My eyes tracked up and down her body, lingering on her horns. I nodded. "Cute."

"Thanks." She smirked. "Want to touch them?"

I snorted. "Duh." I took a step but stopped. "You're not going to set me on fire or possess me, or something demon-spawnish are you?"

"No, but thanks for thinking I could." She tipped her head. "Go on, I won't bite."

The horns were about eight inches long and twisted once in the center and again at the tip. Though the ends weren't sharp like needles, they certainly could do some damage. Small striations ribbed the horns but other than that, they were smooth. I lowered my hand. "Those are so badass."

She turned and flared her wings. "Check these out."

I ran my hands over the leathery ridges along the top. They were thick, and I could feel the strength in them when they flexed. "Don't you miss these?"

She folded them against her back and turned to me. "Yes and no. They've been a part of me for six-thousand years." The reddish hue of her skin faded to pale pink, then to her tan skin tone. The horns, tail, and wings shrunk until they'd disappeared, and Mara's clothes reformed. She was human again. "But having wings also means I'm part of something I don't like."

"You mean demons?"

"Yeah, and evil." She held her arms out. "When I'm like this, things are easier."

It was difficult for me to understand how she felt. No doubt there was a constant pull between her demon self and working for GRS. "What do you mean, easier?"

Her shoulders lifted in a single shrug. "Easier to know the right thing to do. That's why I like being in human form on the physical plane. For Cam, it's difficult to connect to the heavenly realm when he's human. The sensations and temptation block his angelic radar so to speak." She gave me a sad smile. "But for me it lessens the pull of the Underworld. Decisions are easier to make and paths are more clearly defined."

"Wow." I shook my head. "I never realized how hard it was for you."

"Meh." She waved away my empathy. "It is what it is."

"Which is a lot. I have a hard enough time staying out of the fast food drive-thru. I'd be a maniac if I were a demon. Make every wrong choice. Choose the easiest path. Only consider my needs. Actually, that doesn't sound so bad." I smiled. "Maybe just once a month or so."

"You wouldn't be a maniac." Kneeling, she picked up one of the speared poles. "You're too good by nature." She rose and shoved it into the holder on the mast. "Too perky."

"Perky?" Never had that been a word used to describe me. "I think I take offense to that." I walked to the other pole and picked it up. "I'm dark and complex." That was the description my daughter used about herself. From Mara's snort, it was obvious she didn't agree. I shoved the spear in its holder. "Can I ask a personal question?"

"Of course."

I turned to her. "How did you become a demon?"

"Kidnapped." Her lips pressed into a thin line and her gaze skated to me. Clearing her throat, she folded her arms over her chest. "Ironically, by a demon named Mara." As if remembering that awful time in her life, her features pinched and then relaxed again. "He's the one who tempted Buddha—a really bad guy. He kidnapped five females, locked us in the bowels of Hell, and turned us into demons."

"That's horrible." I wasn't sure how to reply to her startling revelation. "So sorry" sounded lame and didn't scratch the surface of how I was feeling. "How long did he keep you there?"

She lowered her arms and absently shook her head. "I don't know. A thousand years. Two-thousand. Long enough to change our way of thinking and believe Mara knew best." She sneered. "Long enough not to rebel against him."

The very idea of what she'd gone through made my heart clench. Silence stretched between us while I struggled to wrap my head around everything she'd told me. Now that I'd had the great displeasure of encountering true demons, the idea of being locked in the worst part of Hell for a thousand years was comprehensible.

Finally, breaking the silence, I asked, "What were you before?"

Her emerald gaze lingered on me a few seconds, the saddest smile I'd ever seen hovering on her lips. "An angel."

"Wait." It was my turn to cross my arms over my chest, a surge of indignation coursing through me. "You were an angel, were kidnapped, and nobody did anything about it?"

The sad smile turned into an amused grin. "It's a long, convoluted story, and maybe someday I'll tell you all the gory details. Let me just say that Cam tried." She shook her head. "Though I didn't know it at the time and pretty much hated his guts for an eon, I later learned he had tried. Now we're partners." She gave me a mock expression of excitement. "Who could believe my luck?"

"I thought you were only six-thousand years old." The irony of that statement wasn't lost on me.

"As a demon. As an angel a lot longer."

"I will never complain about anything ever again." I harrumphed and walked to the steps leading to the bridge. "Seriously, I've got no problems." Before climbing, I pinned her with a stare. "And yes, some night we are going to buy several bottles of wine and you are going to tell me all about it. We'll get drunk. We'll laugh. We'll cry." I waved my hand at her. "You can transform and set something on fire. Whatever we want, but I need to hear the rest of this story."

She saluted me. "Aye, aye, Captain."

Knowing Mara had once been an angel, though tragic, did give me a measure of reassurance. Sure, she was a demon, but she'd been an angel first, and now worked for GRS as a good guy. Not only did I believe she was more good than bad, I was certain I'd made a friend for life. She was like a beautiful secret weapon. If we ever got in trouble, she had a mad demon lurking under the surface that could kick everybody's ass, not to mention keep me safe.

# CHAPTER SEVENTEEN

The front of the pontoons tapped the floating barrels, and the walkway slid across the back when we pulled into the junction. I grabbed a baggie full of gold and held it over my head. "Okay, Hulk, do your thing."

He strode to the side of the ferry and glared up at me. "The name is Franklin, not Hulk."

A laugh slipped from me before I could catch it. "Franklin?"

"Yeah, you got a problem with that?"

Indeed, I did not have a problem with that if I wanted him to open the cabin doors. "Can I call you Frank?"

His scowl deepened. "No."

"Frankie?"

"No."

I cocked my head. "How about Frankenstein, Frankfurter, or the Frankinator?"

"No."

"Okay." I tossed the bag of gold to him and he caught it in one hand. "Franklin it is."

He examined the plastic bag, turning it over in his hand. "What is this?"

"It's called a Ziploc. Just slide the white tab across the top to open it."

He tried it a couple of times, smiling.

"They're handy for storing things but be sure to keep them away from the river." I leaned on my elbows and gave him a sarcastic smile. "I'd hate for any of those river monsters or soul-sucking water demons to get tangled up in it."

"You got any more of these?" he asked.

"Loads, Franklin, and if you can get us in and out of here uber fast, I'll give you one every time I pay you."

"You got yourself a deal." He shoved the baggie into a leather pouch tied around his waist and got to work.

Mara and I moved to the lower deck. When the cabin doors opened, the souls spilled onto the gangway. They seemed no worse for wear, not at all phased by the attack from the lost souls or demons, which kind of irritated me. I had to remind myself that they were dead and I wasn't, so suck it up.

The souls of two couples loitered off to the side, out of the flow of traffic, but still on the ferry. Their conversation was animated, and I caught snippets of having an acquaintance in common.

I clapped my hands. "Okay, people, you don't have to go home, but you can't stay here." When they didn't budge, continuing to chat obliviously, I walked briskly to the other side of the ferry and waved my hands at them. "Move along. Make a hole."

One of the women huffed at me, her lips pursing, reminding me of a dog's butt.

"Hey, lady, unless you want a ride back to the river bank and go to the end of the line—a very long line I might add, I suggest you disembark…now."

A guy who must have been her husband, wrapped his arm around the woman and herded her off the ferry, managing to give me a withering glare in the process. When I was certain they had fully disembarked, I rejoined Mara.

"I've noticed a lot of couples die together. I wonder why."

"Car accidents, house fires." She gave me a serious nod. "You'd be surprised how many sex-related deaths there are, especially in the geriatric community."

"Oh, don't tell me that." I covered my ears with my hands. "Because those are the people I'll have to reap." She laughed but didn't disagree. The cabin door sealed again, and the gangway pulled back. "We're doing a lot of runs today, Franklin, so be ready."

He braced his legs against the floating dock. "I'm always ready."

"No doubt," I muttered.

Now that we'd discovered the tricks of the trade, we were able to do four more, incident free runs before stopping for the day. I had to hand it to Franklin, he was ready for us each time the gangway slammed across the back, getting the passengers unloaded in minutes. By our third delivery, he'd even taken to yelling and clapping at the passengers, using my lingo. I think the plastic baggies were a big motivation for him.

By the time Hal dropped us off at my room, we'd put a small dent in the waiting crowd and were exhausted. I glanced at the clock and groaned. "It's not even noon."

"I don't care," Mara said. "I'm going to take a nap."

"I need a shower." Lifting my arm, I sniffed. "I smell like a coconut from my suntan lotion."

"Oh, that was you? I thought I smelled coconut on the ferry. And lime." She smiled. "Now I want a Pina colada."

"Go take a nap." I pushed her toward the door. "We need to stay sober." When I released her, I blew out a breath. "No doubt we have a lot more ferrying to do today."

"Party pooper." She pulled the door open. "I'll text you later."

"Sounds like a plan. Get some sleep."

I closed the door behind her and pressed my back against the wood. The room was empty, and I wondered where Tandy was—hopefully far from Charon. I'd warned her and at the moment, that's all I could do.

No doubt Nate would be calling me in the near future. Then I remembered his brush with the demon this morning, actually, not too long ago now that we were back on the physical plane. He hadn't looked so good when he'd left the hall—and he'd kissed me. I reminded myself it had been a stress kiss, or a glad-to-be-alive kiss. Nothing more.

Still, I needed to make sure he was all right. I dug my phone out of my purse and dialed. The phone rang once and then went to voice mail. Maybe he was lying down.

When the beeper sounded I said, "Hey Nate, I wanted to check on you and make sure you're okay. I'm going to jump in the shower, but call if you need anything. Otherwise we can meet up later."

Nothing else came to mind, so I ended the call. Despite our constant bickering and his obvious lack of confidence in my skills, I cared about Nate. Having a demon inside me had been awful, but not as invasive as it had been for Nate. Where I'd been able to resist the demon and push it out, he'd been consumed by it in a matter of seconds. He fancied himself one of the best reapers and had the awards to prove it. Being helpless must have come as quite a blow to his ego, but he was a survivor, and he'd deal just like the rest of us did.

My shower was quick, and sleep was impossible. After putting on fresh clothes, I decided to go downstairs and maybe grab a quick bite to eat. I now viewed the breakfast restaurant as my place, having eaten there three times. I slid into the booth in the corner, trying to hide from the world, and ordered a cheeseburger, fries, and a diet soda.

When the waitress was gone, I pulled out my phone. Bronte would be in computer lab and from what she'd told me, the students worked independently. I dialed her number.

If she couldn't talk she'd let me know, probably by not answering or hanging up on me.

"Yo." Her voice sounded on the other end of the phone, and I suddenly had to blink back tears. It was so good hearing someone from my normal, boring life. More than anything I wanted to be home, waiting for my monsters to run through the door, dropping coats and backpacks on their way to raid the refrigerator.

"Yo yourself." I fought to keep my voice steady and light. "What are you doing?"

"Broadening my mind. Planning for my future. You know, the usu."

Usu was short for usual. I know this because I'm a cool mom and am well versed in all the current slang. Also because Bronte corrected me in her annoying mocking tone when I thought it was a German term, like uber, which I also know how to use now.

"Sounds like fun."

She snorted. "What are you doing?"

"Getting ready to eat a giant cheeseburger. You know, the usu." That actually got a chuckle from her. "But before hogfacing my lunch I wanted to check on you, see how you're doing."

"You mean am I surviving Grandma's house?"

"That's part of it." Bronte's behavior had been sporadic at best over the past few months, talking to herself, starting easily if I surprised her, cloistering herself in her room. All of it could be normal teenage behavior, but I wanted to make sure. "So, how is Grandma?"

"Crazy as ever. She spoils the boys." She paused for a second. "When are you coming home?"

There seemed to be a little more to the question. "Sunday, but sooner if I can finish up here."

"Good. I miss my bed."

"I miss my bed, too, and you kids." The waitress set my soda and straw on the table. I pulled it toward me. "Well, I just wanted to check in and make sure there were no problems."

"Everything is cool here." I could hear a man's voice in the background, probably her teacher. "I've got to go." She lowered her voice to just above a whisper. "We've got a substitute today, and he's being over-the-top vigilant."

"All right, well, I love you."

"Love you, too," she rushed out. "Bye."

"Bye."

The line went dead before I got the entire short word out. I sighed and dropped my phone back into my purse. Suddenly I was tired, not physically, but mentally and spiritually. I wanted to go home. I wanted the spiritual world to be right again. But most of all, I didn't want to be the one responsible for getting it back on track.

I ate my burger in relative peace, and the only interruptions were the waitress refilling my soda and my own invasive thoughts. Neither Mara nor Nate had called or texted, so I wandered into the casino after lunch and took up residence at a penny slot machine.

I fed a twenty into a machine and for the next half hour mindlessly hit the max bet button, winning and then losing. In the end, I cashed out with six dollars left. My heart wasn't into gambling. Those were words I'd never thought I'd hear myself think.

As I wandered through the casino, I noticed a lot fewer spirits than the previous night. Maybe ferrying had made enough room for the backflow. Which meant the riverbank would probably be full again. I wasn't sure how we'd ever catch up. At this rate Mara and I would have to ferry around the clock. Five trips had been exhausting and kind of boring. Besides always having to be on alert and the subtle landscape changes, we were basically running the same course. Knock on wood, no new creature had attacked the ferry, but it made for a boring ride.

It was nearly two o'clock and still no word from anybody. Taking the opportunity to shop for the kids, I wandered along the Grande Canal, window-shopping. I realized I hadn't checked my account to see exactly how much money I actually had. Though I wanted to get the kids something nice, I didn't want to go overboard and spend money I didn't have.

When I pulled up the bank app and logged onto my account, I nearly dropped my phone. In savings, I had over three-hundred-thousand dollars. I stared at the amount, not believing what I was seeing. Sure, Tabris had explained I would be getting paid for ferrying, but I'd figured with it being so crowded, no new souls had been reaped—or at least hadn't gotten past the arch.

No wonder Charon had been pissed. I scowled at the long-board displayed in the shop window. Greedy bastard. He'd been collecting gold for centuries and he was throwing a hissy fit because now he wasn't getting paid?

"Well tough titty," I said, before marching into the store.

By the end of my shopping spree, I'd bought each of the boys a skateboard and three new video games, my mother and father some fancy chocolates and a blinking Vegas refrigerator magnet, and Bronte the coolest pair of women's motorcycle boots I'd ever seen. They had skulls embossed on the sides and a chain around the ankle with a skull charm dangling from it. Even though this smacked of my reaper job, my daughter was every bit a quasi-Goth girl, and would appreciate these boots. Besides, if she didn't, I'd wear them. I also got her a black leather jacket that had a steampunk feel with its double-breasted buttons at the waist, but wasn't too theatrical.

I'd definitely splurged, but figured my kids deserved to have something nice for once. Wanting to dump my purchases in the room, I climbed into the elevator. Before the door could close, Charon slipped in—again.

I grunted with irritation. "What is it with you and this elevator?"

The doors glided shut, and he spun on me. His glare pushed me back into the corner. "Who is it?"

"Who is who?"

"Who's ferrying? I know somebody has taken over." He took a step toward me. "Who is it?"

Geez, the guy had a real personal space issue. I tugged my bags up to my chest like a shield. "I don't know." His eyes narrowed on me and I scowled back. "Why do you care? I thought you were retired."

"That's not the point," he said, as if I were completely dense.

"Exactly. You being retired isn't the point, because you had no intention of staying retired." I dropped my arms to my side, the bags crinkling against my legs. "What did you think was going to happen, Charon? They'd plead and beg you to come back?" I pursed my lips and gave him an assessing stare. "Let me guess, this isn't the first time you've pulled this."

He sputtered a few indignant grunts, bristling at my accusation, but didn't deny it.

"Well, guess what?" I reached around him and punched the twenty-sixth floor. "They didn't fall for your crap this time."

"So there is someone." He stamped his walking stick against the floor. "Tell me who it is."

"There's no way in hell I'd tell you." I inched toward him, backing him to the door. "Do you want to know why? Because this morning I had to help capture two demons, one of which thought it would be a lot of fun to first take a turn inside me, and then my partner's body."

His heels hit the door, and he pressed his back against the metal. "So?"

"So." I leaned in, bringing my nose a couple of inches from his. "If you want your job back, I suggest you tuck your tail and go beg Tabris for it." The elevator hiccupped to a stop and dinged. "I just hope it's not too late."

The doors slid open, causing Charon to jump aside. Without another word or glance, I marched out of the elevator. On the outside I might have looked tough, but inside I was praying he'd take my advice. I wasn't sure how much more ferrying I could take—or GRS at that point.

# CHAPTER EIGHTEEN

I'd barely dropped the bags on the floor when a knock rapped against my door. Opening it, I found Mara waiting on the other side. "I couldn't sleep." She strode into my room. "I texted Cam, but all he said was he was in a meeting with Tabris."

"I haven't talked to Nate, either," I said, closing the door.

She paced along the side of the bed. "I don't like it. Something is up."

"Well, Charon just cornered me in the elevator and he is big time pissed." I plopped onto the bed and leaned back, bracing myself with my arms. "You know, he had no intention of staying retired."

"Figures." Mara perched on the chair next to the bed. "What a douche."

"Seriously." Neither of us spoke for a few seconds. Then I said, "What should we do?"

"I hate to say it, but I think we should ferry. The more souls we deliver the quicker things can get back to normal."

"Yeah, and I'm worried about more demons showing up." I sat forward, ignoring the pang of dread weighing in my gut. "All those souls are like sitting ducks."

"Agreed."

We both stood and for the second time that day I called Hal. When the light expanded, and the door slid opened, his look of surprise was genuine. "Again? So soon?"

"Gotta get it done and right now nobody seems to need us," I said.

"You're going to burn out." He closed the doors and peered at me over his silver sunglasses. "Like a two-wicked candle."

"I'll be all right." I wasn't so sure that was true. Each time I stepped onto the physical plane after being at Styx was like taking a deep cleansing breath, almost as if being in the netherworld stole a tiny bit of my life each time I was there. I nodded, more to reassure myself than Hal. "Really, I'm fine."

He didn't argue, but I could see he didn't agree. I guess his concern should have made me happy, but all it did was confuse the situation more. A lot of souls depended on me—for the greater good and all, but deep down I knew I couldn't continue much longer. And, I had to wonder about Mara. She liked the physical world—it dampened her demon urges. As I looked at her now, I could see the signs of strain around her eyes. Of course her strain made her look exotic and sensual, where mine just made me look tired.

We managed three more runs before calling it quits. They were quick, with no disruptions. Franklin had the souls off the ferry in record time, receiving his Ziploc of gold in return. Mara and I didn't speak much during our runs. She prowled around the perimeter of the ferry, watching for anything nefarious, and I stayed on the bridge, keeping us moving as quickly as possible.

I think both of us had a lot on our minds. Concern that the board of directors were tired of Charon's antics and wouldn't give him his job back plagued me. If that's what they decided there was only one solution that I could see— keeping me on as a ferryman. My stomach clenched at the thought. Well, I wouldn't do it. It was as simple as that. I squared my shoulders, my internal dialogue running through my head. They couldn't make me—could they?

Not one for small talk, Hal didn't say much on our ride back. I knew what he was thinking, his disapproval evident on his face.

"You're a worse worrier than my mother," I said. He smirked but didn't reply. When the doors opened, I strode out. "Thanks."

"Don't call me again for at least six hours," he said.

I spun, but the elevator was already compressing into a thin line. A growl vibrated from me.

"He's right." Mara plopped into the chair. She pointed at the clock. "It's only three o'clock. Even though I'm pretty sure the whole convince Charon thing is done, I'm certain they'll find something else for us to do."

"Probably." My phone dinged in my purse. I dug into its depths and retrieved it. "It's Nate." I frowned at the screen and then looked at Mara. "We're supposed to go to Tabris's office."

"See, I knew it." First giving the base of my bed a solid kick, she stood. "Let's get this over with."

That's exactly how I felt. Let's get this over with—all of it. Ferrying, demons, angels, Nyx, and this stupid convention, which I hadn't really gotten to enjoy. All of it done so I could go home.

The silent security guard stood outside Tabris's door. When he saw us, he opened it and stepped aside, closing it behind us. Mara and I pulled to a stop.

"The gangs all here, I see," Mara said.

"That's an understatement." I looked at Nate. Though he didn't seem a hundred percent, he also didn't appear to have had a psychotic episode. "You okay?"

"Fine." He drew up beside me and faced the rest of the room. "There's a lot of debate about a lot of different things that have been going on."

"I can imagine." My gaze tracked over the room's occupants. Tabris, the board, Nyx, Cam, Nate, and a very angry Charon.

"So, what is going on?" I asked no one in particular.

"Please, if everybody could have a seat, we'll get started." Tabris gestured to the chairs.

Nate slipped his hand around my arm and guided me to the seating section and then pulled me down beside him on a loveseat. Even though he released me, my hip and thigh was smashed against his. He made no move to scoot over, which then made it awkward for me to shift away from him. Cam and Mara chose the seats next to Nate, and Charon dropped into the chair opposite me and crossed his arms and legs, obviously still miffed.

"Now," Tabris began, "as all of you know we've been fighting an uphill battle lately, trying to keep the souls contained. And—" He nodded, his gaze tracking around the group. "—had been doing a pretty good job I thought." Holding out his hand in Charon's direction, but not looking at him, Tabris's voice took on an edge. "However, Charon has taken issue with our efforts."

"When you say efforts, you mean you've replaced me, right?" Charon sat forward and jabbed a finger in my direction. "I asked Lisa, but she refused to tell me who it is."

"Why does it matter?" I asked. "You said you were retired."

"Yes, but…" He waved his hand in the air but didn't have a comeback.

"But what?" He was flustered, and I had the upper hand. I wasn't sure what I had the upper hand in, but I was feeling cornered. "You're retired but you want them to keep paying you or beg for you to come back?"

From the look on his face, we could all see that's exactly what he'd expected.

"It doesn't matter what Charon does or doesn't want." Nyx floated forward, her black dress swirling around her legs in ribbons of smoke, and then settled again into the lower half of her gown. "We've decided to take a different approach."

"What approach?" Charon asked.

"Yes, what approach?" I echoed. They sure as hell better have hired somebody else to ferry.

She waved her hand in the air. "We'll get to that in a minute. First, why don't you tell Charon what he wants to know?"

All eyes snapped in my direction, but the ones I was most aware of were Nate's. "What's she talking about?" His voice pitched low.

"Crap." I licked my lips, trying to moisten them, but all the spit seemed to have dried up with her one announcement. "I, uhhh." I looked at Nate. "Mara and I have been ferrying the dead, trying to keep the spirits from sifting back to the physical plane."

He screwed up his face. "When were you doing this?"

"Just about every chance we got." I sighed. "We're exhausted."

I saw Cam flash Mara a questioning glance. She nodded and said, "Later."

"I knew it!" Charon stood, pointing an accusing finger at me again. "No wonder you didn't want to tell me who had taken my place." He glared at me. "My own flesh and blood, a traitor."

"Well, to be fair," I said, "who isn't your flesh and blood? You bang everything that holds still long enough."

"Actually, that's not entirely true," Nyx said.

"Okay, well, maybe not everything," I corrected, "but he does sleep with a lot of people."

"I mean…" Her jaw clenched and unclenched. "He is not your flesh and blood. At least not like everyone thinks."

"You've lost me." I held up both hands. "Which is not all that difficult to do right now."

"Call Hal, Lisa." Tabris said.

"What?" My eyes darted to him. I'd heard Tabris, but didn't understand why he wanted me to bring Hal here. He gave me a single nod. "Okay." In a weak voice I called, "Hal."

Instantly his pink light glowed, elongated, expanded to form the elevator. The door slid open and Hal moved forward. At the first sight of the crowd, he stopped. His chin tipped down and his gaze scanned the room over the rim of his sunglasses. "What's going on?"

"You're part of this discussion too," Nyx said. "You deserve to hear it."

Charon skirted the chair, stopping beside his mother. "What does he have to do with all of this?"

"Hush." She held out her hand and waved me to her. "Come, Lisa."

My first instinct was to look at Nate. Whether for permission, help, or out of fear, I didn't know. Maybe all three. Being the center of attention, especially in this group, was almost as bad as the dreams I had where I was in the middle of the airport, sitting on the toilet. At least from that nightmare I could wake up. I stood and walked to Nyx.

"Do you know the story of Thanatos, Lisa?" she asked.

My eyes cut to Hal. His spine stiffened but his gaze remained on me. "You mean about Thanatos falling in love with Katrina and Charon taking his place as the ferryman?"

"Basically, yes." She faced me. "The part of the story nobody else knows, including Thanatos, is that when I took Katrina from him, she was with child."

Murmurs echoed around the room, but I couldn't speak or take my eyes off Hal. Though he didn't move, not even to bat an eyelash, I could see the pain in his eyes, as if he'd lost her all over again.

"What happened?" I finally asked, still not looking away from him. But I already knew what her answer would be.

"I kept Katrina with me until the baby was born and then did what needed to be done." A sigh heaved from Nyx, as if she was finally releasing a heavy burden. "I gave the baby to Charon and told him to find a good family to raise her."

"Which I did," he said smugly.

"Yes, you found her a good home, and you've been holding it over my head ever since," Nyx snapped.

"Her." Though Hal spoke the single word quietly, it cut through the room.

"Yes." His mother looked at him. For the first time, compassion for her son ghosted across her face. My heart tightened. Even if she was a supernatural being, she was still a mother, and that I understood. "A baby girl. Healthy, despite her mother's condition."

"You never knew?" I directed my question at Hal. "Never saw her?"

He sniffed and squared his shoulders. "No."

"It had to be done, Thanatos." His mother's voice was almost pleading. "You were not fit to raise a child. Don't you remember?"

"I remember I didn't have a choice when you took Katrina from me." His voice cracked slightly, and he cleared his throat. "And now I learn you took more than just her." His gaze narrowed on her. "You had no right."

"I had every right." The powerful deity was back and all traces of the guilty parent gone. "Someone had to release her and it wasn't going to be you."

His lips thinned into a straight line and his gaze leveled on me. It was as if a wall had come down over his emotions. Not a trace of what he was thinking showed on Hal's face. "Am I to understand that Lisa is from my line?"

"Yes." Nyx's hand was warm on my shoulder. "That's why she has the powers she has and is able to ferry the souls."

"Oh, thank God." My shoulders sagged with relieve. "No offense, Charon."

He glared at me.

Nyx smiled, but the warmth didn't reach her eyes. "Which brings us to the next issue. The board of directors have decided to keep you on as the ferryman. Or, should I say, ferry person?"

"Wait, what?" I looked from her to Charon.

"It's been working out so far." She pointed to the elevator. "Hal will continue to transport and you will continue to ferry."

Nate stood and marched toward me, his mouth pulled into a thin line. "She's already got a job as my partner."

Nyx waved away his argument. "It's a lot easier for you to get a new partner than for us to find a new ferryman."

"You can't do this," Charon said, his voice raising an octave. "That's my job."

"Not anymore." His mother faced him. "How many times did you think you could pull this, Charon? You've gotten your way for too long. Whenever anything didn't go your way you threatened to tell your brother about his child. Well, now he knows, and you have nothing left to bargain with." She indicated the board of directors. "We are all tired of your antics and tantrums. Lisa has done a wonderful job. It's the perfect solution."

Okay, I could play this one of two ways. Either freak out and refuse to do it, or do this right. "Sounds good." I nodded, smiling at Charon. "But I have a few demands first."

"Such as?" Tabris stepped forward and Nyx slowly turned to face me. "You've already been vetted and have received pay."

"Lisa." Nate stepped toward me, his gaze questioning. "What are you doing?"

"Nobody else can ferry, right? Are there any other relatives from Hal's line who are qualified?"

Tabris's gaze darted to the board of directors and then back to me. "No. There are a few but they are not—" He hesitated. "—qualified either due to age or physical condition."

"Wow, I'm it then." I held out my arms and performed a slow spin, letting my gaze fall on every board member. "Lucky you."

"This is ridiculous," Charon said, stamping his walking stick on the floor. "She can't handle the rigors of the job."

"What rigors are those?" I folded my arms over my chest. "Demons? Did that. Lost souls? Check. And Franklin and I are really good friends now. Oh, by the way, I gave him a raise," I lied. "So, I think I got this under control."

"Maybe I could pop in and keep you company sometimes," Mara said. "I mean, now that I'm vetted, too."

"Great idea." I gave Tabris my widest smile. "So, here's what I would like. A written contract, to include full health benefits, a generous retirement package, and two months of paid vacation, which will be broken up into two-week increments," I cringed. "We wouldn't want another mess like this."

"Anything else?" Tabris asked.

"Yes. Two option clauses. The first one is the option to retire from the ferry when I turn sixty-five. Then I can spend my final years enjoying my money. And the second is the option to be rehired after I die." I held up my hand. "And I want it all spelled out in a binding contract."

The entire room was silent, all eyes resting on me. I waited for their reaction—any reaction, but still the silence stretched.

Charon was the first to break. "That only gives you thirty years before she'd retire."

"That's just the option to retire," I corrected. "I might stay on longer."

He turned to the board. "I'll sign a five-hundred-year contract, no health benefits, and only my usual vacation time of three weeks every hundred years." He waved his hand absently in the air. "To be broken up however I want but not to exceed that time limit."

"No way." I jabbed my finger at him. "This is my gig. Besides, you'll just end up throwing a hissy and screw things up again."

"You can put that in my contract." His finger waved wildly at Tabris, as if the guy was holding an actual contract. "No strikes or boycotts. Five hundred years. You can't beat that."

Nyx eyed me, a hint of a smile tugging at her lips. "It seems we have a decision to make." She spun toward Charon. "Lisa presents an enticing offer. It might only be for thirty years but she's already proven herself to be a valuable leader." She cocked a black brow. "You, on the other hand, are a pain in the ass."

"I won't be anymore." He folded his hands together. "I promise, Mother."

She turned to the bronze angel. "What do you think Tabris?"

"I think we should let Lisa decide."

Relief washed through me. It had been a long shot, but it had worked. High-five for reverse psychology. "I'll step aside on two conditions. First…" I looked at Charon. "Every hundred years you throw a party to honor Charon and everything he does. I know he's a jackass sometimes, but the job isn't as easy as it seems. He deserves a little recognition."

"That's all I want, a few atta-boys." Charon said. "And she is right. The job isn't easy."

"I think that can be arranged." Tabris gave me a patient smile. "And second?"

My grin stretched as wide as it could go. "I get to keep the money."

Charon's nod switched directions, turning into a violent shake. "No way, that's my gold."

"You may keep it," Nyx said, cutting off his tirade.

Though he puckered his lips and glared at me, he didn't argue further. A thrill raced through me. "Okay then, we got ourselves a deal."

Out of the corner of my eye, I saw Hal step back into the elevator and disappear. Who could blame him? Whether I was or wasn't the new ferryman didn't matter to him. He'd just found out he'd had a child he'd never known and my heart broke for him.

The board of directors joined the group, everybody congratulating each other on the satisfactory outcome.

Nate grabbed a handful of my shirt and tugged me away from the crowd to where Cam and Mara were standing. "Why didn't you two tell me you were ferrying?" Nate asked.

"Tabris told us not to, and then Nyx showed up with her vapor dress and scare tactics." I dragged my eyes to his face. "I mean, come on, they're supernatural beings and I'm a mere mortal. We were trying not to get smited."

"That's not a thing," Nate said.

"Yes it is." I look to Mara for help. "Right, smited?"

"How about struck down, burned to cinders?" she asked.

"What she said. And..." I pointed to Mara again. "We didn't want anything to happen to her new GRS status." I reached over and punched her in the shoulder. "She's worked hard to get where she is."

"So have you." Nate half-groaned and half-sighed. "You weren't serious about wanting to be the ferryman, were you?"

"I actually considered it at first. I mean, the pay is great, and time stops so I'd still have my whole day free on the physical plane. It seemed like the perfect option."

"But?" Nate asked.

"But, then there was the demon attack and the abyss of the lost souls." I cringed. "Plus, I think that place literally sucks the life out of you."

"You, too?" Mara asked. "I didn't want to say anything but man Styx is depressing."

"It was not your imagination." I lowered my voice. "I don't think Tabris and Nyx had any intention of letting me be the ferryman. They just wanted to get Charon over the barrel and into a binding contract so he'd stop his shenanigans."

"Well, it worked, thanks to you," Nate said. He patted me on the shoulder. "Nicely done."

"Thanks."

Charon's voice rose above the muddle. "Write up the contract and I'll sign it right now."

"Man, that guy is an asshat," Nate said.

I laughed. "I am so glad he isn't my grandfather a kagillion times removed."

The crowd dispersed and each board member stopped to thank the four of us for helping solve the problem. Charon gave me a solid glare before stomping out of the room and I dearly hoped I wouldn't be running into him ever again.

Nyx glided to us. "Lisa, may I have a word with you?"

"Of course." I stepped around Nate and followed her. She led me away from the group. "Thank you for giving Charon his job back."

"Yes, you played that well." I shrugged. "Despite all his faults, he is the perfect man for the job."

Stopping behind one of the giant pillars, she turned to me. "You look a lot like Katrina. I knew you were from her line the second I saw you."

"Really?" Knowing I resembled one of my ancestors gave me a sense of connection to my line. "I've never taken the time to research my family, but I will when I get home."

"I think you'll find some extraordinary people in your ancestral history. Some reapers and some not." She hesitated and I could see there was something she wanted to say. "I know Thanatos is angry with me, but I want you to know I didn't keep the child from him out of spite."

"Why did you keep her from him?"

"When Katrina died, he was devastated. I reaped her because he asked me to—because he couldn't. When I realized she was pregnant, I took care of her until the child was born. But there was no hope for Katrina. She'd spent too much time with the dead." She folded her hands in front of her. "It was the second hardest thing I'd ever done. Keeping the child from my son the first."

"Why didn't you ever tell him about his daughter? Surely, at some point he was well enough to know."

"Time moves differently for us. Many think I punished Thanatos for keeping Katrina with him, but that's not the case. We kept him in Purgatory for centuries, making sure he was ready to join the living again without fear of hurting anybody. By the time he had healed, she'd already passed."

"That's so sad."

"That is life and Thanatos is death. With a single touch, he can take a life, even today." Nyx nodded. "Luckily, he has more common sense and respect for life than all of my other children combined. That's why he couldn't reap Katrina."

"It's ironic that death respects life," I said.

"That's how it should be. In order to wield so much power, you must first understand and respect it." She placed her hand on mine. "You have some of that power too. Where Charon has little regard for where he spreads his seed, Thanatos's line is pure, a single branch in our family tree."

"Wow, that's amazing." I smiled at her. "Can I call you Grandma?"

Her hand slipped from mine, and a single black eyebrow arched. "You can try."

I cringed. "I'll take that as a no."

"Wise." Her eyes searched my face for a second and then she said, "When you see Thanatos, can you try to explain to him what I've told you?" She licked her lips and then slowly swallowed. "And tell him I'm sorry—for everything."

"Yes, I can do that." I wanted to hug her, but even though she was kin, the fact that she was a powerful deity kept my feet riveted. "It might take some time, but I will put in a good word whenever I can."

She sighed and gave me a genuine smile. "Thank you." Turning, she started to walk away but stopped. "Maybe I'll come and visit you some time."

"Oh, great." Again my head bobbed up and down as if I had no control. "That would be wonderful."

With that she pivoted and evaporated in a cloud of smoke and ash. I stared at the spot for a few seconds. Seriously, my great-whatever grandmother may or may not pop in—to my house—the same house my kids lived in.

I could see it now. "Oh, hey, this is your great grandmother, thirty-six-thousand times removed, who also happens to be the primordial deity of darkness, and oh by the way, did I mention I'm a grim reaper? Mac and cheese, anyone?"

I shuffled back to Nate, Mara, and Cam, honestly the only three I considered normal at this point.

"Everything okay?" Mara asked.

"Couldn't be better." Glancing around, I noticed most everybody but Tabris had gone. "What now?"

"Before you make plans," he said, walking toward us, "I want to let you know that your next three days are on GRS. Food, shows, the spa, whatever you like."

"That's very generous," Mara said.

"It's the least we can do to show our appreciation." He gave me a sheepish grin. "And to apologize for everything."

I held up my hand. "I'm just glad it all worked out for the best."

"Well then," Cam said, "It seems dinner and drinks are on GRS tonight. Lobster anyone?"

"Would you like to join us?" Nate asked Tabris.

"I'd love to, but as you can imagine, I've got a lot of follow-up work to do and a contract to write up." He sighed. "But thanks."

We said our goodbyes and headed for dinner.

"The first thing I plan on having is the biggest gin and tonic they make." I locked arms with Mara. "And another with my meal, and probably another for dessert."

"Me, too. If we drink at that rate we'll be Jimmied by six o'clock," she said.

"Well," Nate interrupted. "Before you get too…jimmied, I want to hear about your adventure ferrying."

"Yeah," Cam added. "You know, the demon attack. The water zombies. What else?"

"Sea monsters," Nate said. "All of it. We want to know everything."

"Okay, but it's pretty horrifying stuff." I shook my head. "I hope you can handle it."

"I had a demon inside me this morning." Nate shuddered. "I can handle anything."

# CHAPTER NINETEEN

The three days I'd spent in Vegas after the big throw-down with Charon were heaven. I'd taken full advantage of the spa, pool, and money I'd earned as a ferryman. Even after transferring Mara's share, the amount left over would give us a real boost. I even contemplated buying a new washer and dryer.

Sitting on top of my suitcase, I zipped the sides and pulled it upright onto its wheels. I had to buy more luggage at one of the souvenir shops in order to pack all the gifts I'd bought everybody, but the extra baggage fee would be worth seeing the kids' expressions.

"Well, that's it." I turned to Tandy and smiled. "All ready to go."

"When does your flight leave?" She looked like a teenager, hovering a couple of inches off the bed, knees bent, and ankles locked.

I glanced at the clock. "Three hours, but I like to get there early. You never know how long it takes to get to the airport or how long the security line will be."

A pout curled her lips. "I'm going to miss you." She floated to a stand. "It's going to be lonely here now that everybody is gone."

"It doesn't have to be." I held out my arms. "I am a grim reaper. You could pass on to the next big party."

"Cross over?" She grimaced. "That's a little scary."

"The unknown always is." I smiled. "You'll get to ride with Hal."

Instantly she perked up. "Really?"

"Yep. And I'm certain he knows where the best parties are." If he answers me. I hadn't seen him since he'd ducked out of the powwow in Tabris's office—since he'd found out he'd had a daughter.

She chewed on her bottom lip and then smiled. "Okay, I'll go." Clapping her hands, she did her signature perky bounce. "This is so exciting."

"I know, right?" As I dragged my suitcase toward the door I called, "Hal."

From the way he'd blown out of Tabris's office I wasn't sure he'd show up. This would be my first attempt. Before I'd made it to the door, Hal appeared, surprising me.

"Hello, Lisa." He tipped his head toward Tandy. "Pretty lady."

She tittered and stepped toward him. "So, Lisa said you know where the best parties are."

"Indeed, I do." His white smile glinted at her and I had to admit, he seemed in good spirits. Stepping aside, he ushered her in. "After you."

Once Tandy was inside the elevator, she faced me. "Will I ever see you again?"

"I hope not for a very long time." I wiggled my fingers in a wave. "Have a good time."

She clapped and bounced again. No doubt, wherever she was going she'd be an endless supply of fun and energy.

"Don't leave yet," Hal said.

His statement caught me by surprise. "I've got to catch my plane."

"You have plenty of time." He backed into the elevator. "I'll be right back. I have a gift for you."

"Okay, but hurry." When the elevator started to close, I remembered Estelle. She was probably still waiting in the bathroom. "Hey, can you swing by the fifth floor bathroom and pick up Estelle and the girls? They love a good party."

He gave me a wave of acknowledgment and disappeared.

A second later, someone knocked on my door. When I opened it, I found Mara leaning against my doorframe. "I thought you'd left."

"Well, I actually live in Las Vegas so leaving is sort of a relative term."

"You live in Vegas?" I shook my head. "Why didn't I know that?"

"Oh, I don't know. Maybe because we were busy fighting demons and shuttling dead people?"

"True." I nodded. "Come in."

"I can't." She rolled her eyes. "Cam already has us on another case and I need to meet him in a little bit." Lifting her hand, she held up a business card. "My private number."

I squinted at her. "But I already have your phone number."

"This is my private-private phone number." She shoved the card in my hand. "Cam doesn't even know it. The number is for my close friends." She shrugged. "People I want to keep in touch with."

"Wow, I'm honored." The white rectangle of paper had a ten-digit phone number and nothing else. "Thank you. I will definitely call."

"You'd better, and I have your number too, so it goes both ways." She exhaled. "Okay, one more hug and then I have to go."

I stepped into her outstretched arms and wrapped mine around her. We stood like that for several seconds—longer than a simple goodbye, but short enough that it didn't get weird.

When she released me, she stepped back. "Have a great trip home."

"I will." I almost said "you too" but lucky her, she was already home. Instead I said, "Drive safely," not even knowing if she drove.

The urge to watch her walk away pushed at me, but again, that would probably be weird, so I stepped into the room and shut the door.

"Lisa."

I started and pivoted to see that Hal was back already. "That was fast."

"I'm good at my job. The ladies invited me to meet them later." He cocked an eyebrow at me, looking a lot like his mother, but I didn't tell him that. "I trust you won't be reaping anybody between here and Alaska?"

"I have no plans to, so go have a good time." I gave him a knowing smile. "And, even though you don't want or need it, I give you and Tandy my blessing."

He let out a bark of laughter. "You are correct. I don't need it. Tandy is beautiful and fun, but the girl has too much energy for me. I might be a supernatural being but even I have my limitations."

"You could show her around at least. Let down your hair for a while."

"Thank you, but I don't need my granddaughter giving me advice on how to pick up women." He cleared his throat and I think it was the first time I'd seem him look uncomfortable. I wasn't sure if it was from the topic of conversation, or because he'd called me his granddaughter. I didn't ask, not wanting to spoil the moment.

"All right then, if you don't want my pearls of wisdom on dating, what did you want?"

"To give you this." He unhooked a slender cylinder from his belt and held it out for me to see.

It was black and had an intricate silver pattern embossed on it. I'd noticed it before and had seen him fiddle with it when he was irritated. "What is it?"

"Something you deserve to have." He wrapped his hand around the cylinder and whispered his name, "Thanatos."

At the same time, the ends extended, and I instantly knew what it was. "A scythe?"

Unlike the expanding scythe the vendor was selling, this one slid silently from its confines to form a long black handle. What looked like a cloud of gray vapor clung to the top and then formed into a gleaming blade. Power hummed from it, the smallest movement making the air vibrate.

My hand shook when I extended my arm to take it from him. "It's beautiful." The weapon purred against my skin. "But this is yours. I can't take it."

"Was mine," he corrected. "Now it's yours."

Words escaped me. This gift was beyond anything I could have wished for or imagined. "Hal, I don't know what to say."

"When you want to use it you say Thanatos. It means death." He took it from me again, held the scythe upright, and tapped the end on the ground twice. The ends compressed, the blade fading to vapor, disappearing into the cylinder again. "Then it is ready for next time."

"When would I use this?" I took the cylinder from him. "Usually I can grab onto the souls and they stick."

He nodded. "The scythe is used in dangerous situations or with paranormal beings you reap. It erases the need for gold or a porter. One swipe and they are instantly sent to their destination."

"I sure could have used it this week." I envisioned myself hacking my way down the riverbank, sending souls on without having to ferry them.

"Nyx forbad me to give it to you." He pursed his lips. "Said she needed you to ferry until the last possible moment so Charon would come crawling back for his job."

"So you knew?" I pursed my lips. "I don't know if I should be pissed that Nyx totally manipulated me or touched that you asked your mom if you could give me your scythe."

He leveled his yellow stare at me and growled, holding out his hand. "Maybe I made a mistake."

"No you didn't." I clutched the cylinder to my chest. "I'll keep my pie hole shut and not tease you." Grinning, I chanced another peek. "This is so cool. Thank you." I looked at him. "Hey, can I call you Grandpa?"

"Not if you want me to transport you home."

My brow pinched together. "What do you mean?"

"You'd be home in a few minutes." He indicated the elevator. "Unless you have an unhealthy preference for crowded airports, tiny packets of food, and uncomfortable seats."

"No." I shook my head vigorously. "I don't. Oh my God, that would be so amazing." I grabbed the closest suitcase and shoved it at him. "Here, I've got one more, just a second." Getting home to see my family was better than all the massages and facials I'd gotten in the last three days, plus the pasta dinner and wine I'd had last night. But not the scythe. I'd suffer through a twenty-four-hour layover to keep that scythe. I wrestled my ancient suitcase into the elevator, gave one last look around, and got in. "Ready, Freddy."

He looked at the ceiling and took a long-suffering breath, which was so like me, and then closed the doors.

This had been a hell of a week. Even after three days of resting I was still soul weary. But now that the events were over and the crisis passed, I was glad I'd gone through most of it. So much had happened. Not only had I discovered who Hal was and why he was my porter, I'd met Mara. She'd turned out to be a good friend and somebody I'd keep in my life. Nate, well, that was still a mystery to unravel. For now, I'd be happy with him being a supportive partner and a team player. Secretly, I hoped there was another kiss in our future. One that had nothing to do with demon possession.

The verdict was still out on whether ferrying had been worth it. Yes, we'd delivered a lot of souls and made a fair amount of money in the process. We'd stopped the shit from hitting the ethereal fan, blah, blah, blah, but I'd also seen a lot of things that I wouldn't be able to unsee—ever. Stuff nightmares were made of.

When the elevator opened onto my empty, semi-clean living room, a wave of happiness washed through me. "That was so much better than taking a plane." I pushed the suitcases out of the elevator and turned back to Hal. "Thanks for the ride. I'd invite you in but you and the whole grim reaper thing would be a little tough to explain to my kids."

Hal smirked. "Not as difficult as you might think." He touched his fingers to his forehead. "No matter, I have somewhere else to be."

"Say hi to Tandy for me."

Though he didn't reply, he did nod. Then the elevator compressed and winked out of sight. Silence filled the room. I closed my eyes, drinking it in.

Boy, it was so good to be home.

Want more Grim Reality. Don't miss Fireweed and Brimstone.

## FIREWEED AND BRIMSTONE

It seems rather fitting that I'm a grim reaper who happens to be a widow. In fact, my husband's death ignited a chain of events that shook my life and landed me as GRS's newest grim reaper. He's been dead for over a year, but I can't shake the feeling that the circumstances surrounding his car accident aren't what they appear.

My suspicions are confirmed when I find a receipt for a storage locker rented in his name. Of course, I have to investigate, but what will I find? Was he leading a double life, cheating on me? If only. What I find makes me wish another family in Ohio was all he'd been mixed up in.

As pieces of the puzzle surrounding my husband's death fall into place, I discover a scheme so diabolical, it could change the face of death as we know it—and not in a good way. Using our mad reaper skills, my partner Nate and I skirt the edge of ethereal rules, call on some old friends to help, and learn there's a lot more to being a grim reaper than we ever imagined—or wanted to know.

Or for a shorter read pick up Dead Spooky and Dead Jolly, Grim Reality novellas.

# DEAD JOLLY

The holidays are here, and I'm up to my eyeballs in Christmas spirit—or should I say "spirits". Life is like that now that I'm a grim reaper.

My holidays get an extra helping of festive weirdness when the Casanova of mall Santas kicks the bucket. Instead of crossing over, he sets out to spread his own special brand of Christmas magic to a number of single ladies in town.

I'll admit, as a widow I'm hesitant to stop him from gifting his Christmas miracle, but as a reaper, it's my job to pack his yule log and jingle bells off to the netherworld.

After all, everybody knows Santa is only supposed to come once a year.

# DEAD SPOOKY

Halloween wouldn't be complete without a good haunting. Unfortunately, that means overtime for me. My name is Lisa and I'm a grim reaper. So instead of taking my kids trick-or-treating like a normal parent, I'll be spending the night locked inside an old theater with my partner Nate, waiting for the ghost of a serial killer to materialize.

Yep, that about sums up my life. The only good things I have going for me tonight is the gigantic sack of Halloween candy stuffed in my purse and the fact that Nate isn't too bad to look at. No doubt the evening will be a night to remember...if I make it out alive.

**A note from the author:**

*Thank you for choosing Styx & Stoned. I truly hope you enjoyed it.*

*Every time a reader tells me they love my books I'm humbled and thrilled. Their satisfaction means I've done my job as a writer. My readers are the reason I stumble to my office every morning with coffee in hand and create new worlds and characters. So, thank you again for being my motivation to continue doing what I love.*

*Boone*

# ABOUT THE AUTHOR

Boone is a *USA Today* Bestselling Author with dozens of titles under her belt, ranging from romantic comedy to medieval fantasy. With a particular love for all things paranormal, Boone weaves the strange and quirky into her books, and is especially drawn to stories about the afterlife.

She lives in the beautiful state of Alaska with her husband and twin daughters and truly believes with her mad survival skills she would rock a zombie apocalypse.

Follow Boone on the following sites to stay up to date with her latest release news.

*Facebook*: www.facebook.com/BooneBruxAuthor

*Pinterest*: www.pinterst.com/boonebrux

*Instagram*: www.instagram.com/boonebrux

*Twitter*: www.twitter.com/boonebrux

*Website*: www.boonebrux.com

*Bookbub:* https://www.bookbub.com/authors/boone-brux

Be sure to sign up for Boone's VIP Club on her website, or follow her on Bookbub for her latest release news.